CORSAIR

TOR BOOKS BY JAMES L. CAMBIAS

A Darkling Sea
Corsair

CORSAIR

JAMES L. CAMBIAS

A TOM DOHERTY ASSOCIATES BOOK · NEW YORK

CORSAIR

Copyright © 2015 by James L. Cambias

Edited by David G. Hartwell

A Tor Book
Published by Tom Doherty Associates, LLC
175 Fifth Avenue
New York, NY 10010

www.tor-forge.com

Tor® is a registered trademark of Tom Doherty Associates, LLC.

The Library of Congress Cataloging-in-Publication Data
is available upon request.

ISBN 978-0-7653-7910-8 (hardcover)
ISBN 978-1-4668-6612-6 (e-book)

Tor books may be purchased for educational, business, or promotional use. For information on bulk purchases, please contact the Macmillan Corporate and Premium Sales Department at 1-800-221-7945, extension 5442, or write to specialmarkets@macmillan.com.

First Edition: May 2015

Printed in the United States of America

0 9 8 7 6 5 4 3 2 1

For Diane

CORSAIR

1

Captain Black the Space Pirate sat on a king-sized hotel bed in Thailand and watched for his next prize. The name on his real passport was David Schwartz, but it was Captain Black the Space Pirate who had five fan sites on the Web and at least as many highly secure law enforcement sites devoted to tracking him. He was the absolute gold-anodized titanium pinnacle of the techno-badass pyramid. He was twenty-eight years old.

On his laptop screen he saw a tiny bright dot rising above Mare Smythii on the Moon: a booster carrying four tons of helium-3. A treasure ship worth two billion Swiss francs on the spot market. It was a Westinghouse cargo from the Japanese–Indian–American base at Babcock Crater, on course for the Palmyra Atoll drop zone. "Ship ho, me hearties!" David whooped.

His pirate ship lurked at the L_1 libration point, balanced between Earth and Moon. Officially, it was a "Lunar resource satellite," which was true in its own way, and the owner of record was a perfectly legal company incorporated in Eritrea. David uplinked to it through a commercial antenna farm in Northern Australia and set up a burn that would match speeds with the helium payload just after it finished climbing up from the Moon and began falling toward the Earth.

Having done that, Captain Black the Space Pirate went out for lunch. He was currently commanding his pirate sloop from the Shangri-La Hotel in Bangkok. It had good network connections, a nice restaurant, and an abundant supply of Western women looking for a little adventure on vacation. David ate grilled squid with his pad open on the tabletop, reading updates on the progress of his pirate ship. He had an iced coffee with condensed milk and introduced himself to a pair of leggy tanned women from Australia, but didn't get a phone number from either of them.

Thirteen hours later, the helium treasure ship had climbed to within fifty kilometers of his pirate satellite, and Captain Black was in full battle gear. He sat propped up in bed on pillows in his hotel room, wearing only shorts, a pair of VR goggles, and a pair of white gloves so his computer could see his hand gestures clearly. The system was running a really cool interface that used images from his favorite pirate shooter game. The helium payload was represented by a galleon flying the Westinghouse flag, and he was on the deck of a pirate sloop with guns, loyal crew, and a big spoked ship's wheel—all available at the touch of a gloved hand. He had told his backers the setup was essential for fast reactions in a crisis, but in fact, he mostly used it to play games.

"Testing, testing," he said over the voice mike. "You there, Barnacle Bill?"

"That got tiresome a long time ago," said Bill Benedict's voice in David's earpiece. Benedict wasn't his real last name, either. Bill was Captain Black's copilot, working from an "undisclosed location," which David had pinpointed shortly after they first teamed up.

David didn't really need a copilot, but Benedict was his connection to the people backing this venture. On his first two pirate exploits, David had been hired help, working for a flat fee that was generous but not spectacular. This time, he'd leveraged his reputation into a share of the profits. When this voyage was done, his scattered bank accounts would have enough zeros to keep David living in first-class hotel rooms for the next three or four decades.

"Ahoy!" said David. "Crowd on the canvas!"

The helium payload was practically crawling now, at the top of its long climb up from the Moon, just before going over the hump and falling to Earth. Its velocity was a miserable two meters per second, about as fast as a car in a traffic jam. His own vehicle could go from zero to sixty in twenty seconds. He used up half the sat's remaining fuel to match velocities with the helium payload.

"Barnacle Bill? Better call up the lawyers and liquidate." This was the same as running up the Jolly Roger. Until that moment, if the Americans, the Japanese, or the Indians tried to intercept his pirate vehicle, the maneuver would be a hostile act against a sovereign nation in international space. There was a sizable bloc of countries in the UN that would happily condemn that sort of behavior.

By liquidating the shell company, he was revealing himself as a Rogue Entity. Fair game. His deniable black-ops government patrons would be shocked, *shocked* to learn of this criminal activity. Anyone investigating the newly defunct Rogue Entity company would find that it owned nothing but a post office box in Djibouti and an empty bank account.

David turned the ship's wheel a notch to close with the target, and one of the animated pirates filling his vision said, "Burn complete, Cap'n."

"Um, Captain Black? There's something—," Bill began over the phone link, just as another animated figure on David's imaginary pirate ship called down from the masthead. "Sail ho! A man-o'-war coming up astern!"

. . .

Captain Elizabeth Santiago lived off-base in Fountain and bicycled to work every morning except when it was snowy. A good tough ride up the mountain in the early morning air made up for a lot of hours spent in the Pit, living on commissary pizza and Coke.

But although it was an absolutely perfect spring day, Elizabeth barely noticed. She left her apartment an hour early, nearly beat her record time getting up the mountain, and waved her ID at the gate guard as she shot through the checkpoint. Today was the day. MARIO was going to war.

Down in the bowels of Cheyenne Mountain, she changed into her duty uniform and got an extra-large double-strength latte before heading for the Pit. The Air Force had reactivated the place and spent millions refurbishing and cleaning the old Cold War bunker, but the air always felt clammy and mildewy. A hot drink helped.

The Space Control Center was a lot more crowded than usual. Elizabeth wasn't the only Gold team member to show up early, none of the White team wanted to leave, and there were even some of the Blue shift hanging around. She glanced up at the big board. There was MARIO, a bright blue circle moving along its orbit plot. Two hours until the stabilizing burn to park it at L_1. Then things would get interesting.

Elizabeth conferred with her White counterpart, Richard Lee. "Status?"

"Everything's go so far. Power's good and we did the yaw maneuver at 0300."

"Targets?"

"The Eritrean one is still on course to intercept Westinghouse 32, and the Singaporean one just did a station-keeping burn. The rest are just sitting there, acting innocent."

"Do you think they're all pirate sats?" Elizabeth looked over at the smaller display showing the half dozen or so vehicles at L_1.

"We know the French one isn't, and the Brazilian one probably isn't. But the others—who knows? Another one launched today."

"Really?"

"Yep. Called 'Lunar science observer.' A real Model UN—sea launch off Venezuela, Chinese booster, payload's flagged Liberian—"

"Always a good sign."

"And the ownership's Laotian."

"Because Laos has so many big space investors. Jesus. Why don't they just say it's a helium pirate sat?"

"Then we'd have to quit calling MARIO a 'resupply and inspection orbiter.' "

"Fine with me. I always preferred 'space superiority fighter' myself." She showed her teeth as she smiled.

A chime rang to announce the 0800 shift change. Whites gave way to Golds, and Elizabeth slipped into the command chair. It was going to be a busy day.

For the rest of the morning, the Gold team busied itself getting MARIO parked and stable at the L_1 point. Their bird was an aluminum box very much like a two-drawer filing cabinet with long photovoltaic wings stretching out on either side. Its ion motor could take it almost anywhere within the Earth–Moon system, so long as you weren't in a hurry.

The MARIO series' ostensible purpose was entirely benign—inspection and resupply of other satellites. Elizabeth's bird, MARIO 5, was a bit more aggressive. In the bay where previous MARIO orbiters had carried new components or fuel supplies to their satellite customers, MARIO 5 carried a weapon.

It was a curious sort of weapon, though. The VIGIL CORE Electromagnetic Interrogation system literally couldn't harm a fly, unless you felt like using a billion-dollar piece of electronics as a swatter. It was nothing but a very fast and sensitive wireless data handler, capable of reaching past most emission shielding to let a skilled operator read and manipulate a satellite's computer memory. A rather staggering sum had gone into developing it so that the Air Force could separate the law-abiding payloads from the pirates lurking among them, and trace the buccaneers to their lairs on Earth.

. . .

David eyed the newcomer through the crappy little camera aboard his pirate ship. He knew what it was, of course. He'd been reading about MARIO 5 and VIGIL CORE on *Jane's Defence Weekly* for nearly a year, and had even watched the launch live via webcam.

United States Orbital Command had decided to get tough, and lined up diplomatic cover and poll numbers to support the mission. Washington wanted to boost its revived "global cop" credibility going into the 2030 midterm elections, and remind pals like India just who was the senior partner in the alliance. Cracking down on space piracy was popular at home and abroad, and best of all, there'd be no wailing Third World village women or flag-draped coffins in the news feeds.

The billion-dollar question right now was, would ORBITCOM actually make a move? Or were the blue-suit boys hoping that just parking their orbiter at L_1 would be enough of a deterrent? Captain Black the Space Pirate wasn't going to give up his prey. If the Air Force wanted to fight him for it, he'd give them a real battle.

His satellite picked up a tight-beam transmission from Goldstone, and a yellowed parchment unrolled in front of him, warning him of "potentially unsafe proximity." A shot across his bow. But they didn't have any cannonballs.

"I've got tracking data from our partners," said Bill. "Forwarding it to you." A second scroll appeared. It matched what the pirate ship's own radar was telling him. One kilometer to the helium payload. When he looked through his spyglass, he could see it now—a fat gumdrop-shaped re-entry vehicle with a little booster and guidance package stuck to the round end. The treasure ship was maneuvering, trying to get away. But it just didn't have the fuel for major velocity changes after struggling up from the surface of the Moon. It was wallowing and heavy-laden while his pirate sloop was fast and deadly, with a half a kilometer per second still in the tank.

David checked the status of all his weapons and systems, each represented by a different pirate icon. When he finished, his satellite was moving toward its target again. OR-BITCOM had given up on proximity warnings.

"MARIO's making a move," said Bill. Another screen opened in David's field of view, with tracking data. The Air Force bird was closing the distance, vectoring toward his own pirate ship rather than the payload.

"Arr, Barnacle Bill!" crowed Captain Black the Space Pirate. "Battle stations!"

* * *

By noon MARIO was nearing its first target, the mysterious Eritrean bird whose owners had liquidated just a few hours ago. It was getting dangerously close to Westinghouse 32, ignoring all warnings.

"Two hundred meters and holding," said Lieutenant Cameron from the Flight console.

"Right. Keep it there. Arm, I want a visual inspection, please."

The camera on MARIO 5's manipulator arm came live, giving them a look at the suspect satellite. It was a simple aluminum can with a thruster nozzle at one end, a manipulator and a big clamp at the other, an antenna sticking out of one side, and some surface photovoltaics. Elizabeth could barely make out some logos on an exposed patch of the vehicle's skin.

"Zoom in on those, please, and let's get a record."

The camera could resolve the logo of the former owners of record, the remarkably generic Space Satellite Company. Four flags, which (with the help of Wikipedia) Captain Lee identified as Latveria, Grand Fenwick, the Klingon Empire, and (of course) the Jolly Roger. Next to the flags was a mission-patch logo of a square-rigged ship steered by a grinning peg-legged cartoon character. There was something written underneath it in grease pencil.

Elizabeth enlarged the image of the words on her screen until it was like a mosaic, filtering over and over to squeeze more resolution from the camera. The hair was standing up on the backs of her arms. "What does that look like to you?" she asked Lee.

He leaned over her shoulder and peered at the screen. "SS . . . *Scabby Whore*? Cute."

Captain Santiago didn't say anything.

. . .

JUNE 7, 2030; 02:15 GMT

Two hundred meters now. The helium carrier gave one last futile spurt of its motor; then the Westinghouse ground team decided to separate, maybe hoping to confuse him. The payload module began drifting away from the booster, just beginning the long fall to Earth.

Idiots. Now they had no way at all to evade capture. They needed their maneuvering thrusters to hit the drop zone. David reached for an Altoids tin sitting on the bedside table, took out a drug patch colored bright magenta, and slapped it to the side of his neck. In just seconds, he could feel his heart rate accelerating, and the image in his goggles suddenly looked slow and grainy.

He began tapping keys, setting up a burn to grapple the payload. "Prepare to board!"

"Air Force bird is closing," said Barnacle Bill.

On the horizon, David could see another sail approaching—a fast frigate flying the winged star emblem of the Air Force from the masthead. Its guns puffed smoke as invisible electronic fingers reached out to probe his pirate satellite. Instead of capturing the Westinghouse payload, he was in danger of losing control of his own vehicle.

"They're using electronic interrogation," said Bill. "I just got a message from Ashgabat—they want to abort."

"Strike my colors?" David yelled aloud. "Belay that! I have not yet begun to fight!" He typed a command and one of the animated pirates threw a sputtering round bomb at the Air Force frigate.

. . .

"VIGIL CORE on line," said Sobieski. "Reading target's memory—Hey!" He looked with dismay as the screen in front of him changed from orderly lines of text to a mass of gibberish.

"Tell me what's happening," said Elizabeth, clicking frantically between screen windows as she tried to figure it out for herself.

"Bastard set off some kind of high-intensity pulse. Overloaded the detectors. VIGIL CORE is off-line for the moment."

"Okay, wise guy," said Elizabeth. "Two can play at that game. Legal: I'm calling that an attack on a United States spacecraft. We're responding with appropriate means under the provisions of the 2024 Space Treaty." She looked up at the board. "Flight, we need a close rendezvous with that vehicle. Zero meters. Arm, be ready for a resisted capture." She beckoned Lee to bend close again. "Tell Command that unless I receive orders to the contrary, I'm going to catch that bird."

Two o'clock came, and early arriving Blue controllers pulled up spare chairs next to Gold ones. A few switched seats, when the Blue operator was more experienced than the Gold. John Adamski, the Blue director, took a folding chair next to Elizabeth, feeding her reports from Air Force Intelligence and NRO. Lee was still on duty, acting as her link to Command and the legal people. The back of the room had filled up with a lot of oak leaves and eagles. Even a star or two.

"Bogey has docked with Westinghouse 32," said Flight.

"Visual confirmation, hard dock," said Lieutenant Kraus at the arm control.

If the pirate followed the same script they'd used on a dozen previous payload hijackings, the bogey would start boosting soon, pointing the stolen payload at a new drop zone.

"Sobieski, I need VIGIL CORE on line again *now*."

. . .

David was in his element, multitasking smoothly, coding and calculating orbital dynamics on the fly. His manipulator arm was plugged into the payload's guidance antenna bus, and his goggles displayed a furious sword fight on deck as his hand-coded decryption software battled the data security on the helium payload. Somewhere far away, his body sat on a bed, but David himself was at the L_1 point, having the time of his life.

The Air Force bird was now just fifty meters away, demanding his surrender. "Captain Black, we've got to abort now," Barnacle Bill repeated.

"Wait for it, wait for it . . . ," David muttered. His pirate probe separated from the payload and backed off with a blast from the steering jets. He typed a message to send en clair. DONT SHOOT IM COMING OUT.

"Are you *insane?*"

"Shut up and let me work, Bill." David was controlling two spacecraft now. He backed the pirate probe away from the payload, keeping it slow and steady as a streetcar on rails.

Meanwhile he was taking control of the helium module, rapidly overwriting its command codes and guidance with his own versions. It helped that he'd politely emailed an engineer at Westinghouse six months earlier, using his old MIT address. The earnest student's questions had been complicated, so the helpful engineer had sent him copies of some of the technical documents. So much of high-tech piracy depended on being able to lie convincingly.

The galleon's deck was red with blood, and her flag fluttered down. Down in Cranberry Township, Pennsylvania, some Westinghouse engineers were probably staring in horror as their billion-franc payload stopped doing what they told it to.

"Okay, Bill, I'm putting the payload on course for the drop zone."

"We've got a problem. They want you to move the zone." A map unfurled with the new drop zone in red.

"WTF?" David said aloud, but he did the math. Two hundred kilometers north. "Okay. I can do that."

He used the last of his propellant to aim the payload at its new destination. When that was done, he told it to shut off its antennas and ignore all new instructions. That would stop the ground controllers but not the Air Force bird's fancy wireless unit. He had something else in store for that.

His orders left the payload on course until just before reentry. Then it would take a dive, falling short into the Celebes Sea. Real pirate waters, and real pirates with boats and guns would recover the cargo. The helium-3 would find its way to market through several layers of cutouts and shell companies. The whole scheme rested on the simple fact that helium atoms don't have serial numbers.

"And now for those meddling kids."

. . .

"Five meters," said Flight. Elizabeth couldn't tell if it was Adams or Thibodaux. "Four, three."

"Arm?" she said, maybe a little more nervously than usual.

Lieutenant Kraus didn't answer. Her eyes were locked on the screen showing the fuzzy black-and-white image from the arm camera, and her hands held the two control joysticks in a precise fingertip grip. "Come on come on come on come on *come on—Yes!*" She pumped both fists into the air. "Hard capture!"

Elizabeth grinned at that and made a note to send Kraus something nice when the mission was done. Maybe some flowers or a box of chocolate truffles. "Flight, vector us away from that payload before—"

She never finished, because the camera image suddenly flared bright white and then went dark. The master alarm sounded and red lights appeared on half a dozen consoles around the room. Her own screens showed sudden cata-strophic failures in backup power, gyros, radar, and cooling.

"You bastard!" she yelled aloud. Everyone knew whom she was talking to. Captain Black's pirate probe had just blown itself up. "Okay, status, everyone. What have we got?"

"Ion thruster looks good, photovoltaics are at . . . fifty percent, we've still got telemetry, VIGIL CORE's good, fuel pressure's steady. What we don't have is any sensor or attitude control."

"Fuck," said Elizabeth. With no way to steer, MARIO 5 was following the helium payload's intended course, heading for a rendezvous with the Pacific Ocean. A billion dollars down the drain.

"Tracking, what's the helium cargo's trajectory?"

"No change yet."

Elizabeth let out a breath. Maybe they'd saved it. It was expensive to trade Air Force vehicles one-to-one for pirates, but if the helium got through to the hungry fusion power plants on Earth, it was worth it.

. . .

David pulled off his goggles and whooped. "Captain Black is the awesomest!" he shouted.

"Abort confirmed," said Barnacle Bill. "Looks like the Air Force bird is a mess."

"Nobody fucks with Captain Black! Tell the suits the helium's going to drop right where they want it. And now I'm going to log off, get drunk, and get laid. Arr!"

David called room service for a pitcher of Bloody Marys and a masseuse. Maybe later he'd see if those two Australian girls were still around. While he waited, he did a little calculating. Once the money laundering was done, his share of the loot would be about ten million Swiss. He could invest it and enjoy a six-figure income indefinitely. Or he could just spend it—even pissing away a quarter-mil a year, he'd be old enough to collect a pension by the time it was gone.

He had beaten the Air Force in single combat. Life was good for Captain Black the Space Pirate.

. . .

Sixty hours later, the helium payload diverted to a drop zone off Mindanao. By the time the Philippine Navy got there, the pirates and the helium were long gone. MARIO burned up over Timor about the same time. When Elizabeth got the news, she knew what would happen next.

General McEwan called her in for a private meeting two days after that. His office was aboveground, with a view of Colorado Springs down the mountainside. The sunlight streaming in was extremely yellow and bright after three days in the Pit.

McEwan was wearing camo, which was neutral for him. Golf clothes were a good sign. A blue suit would be very very bad. He did not offer coffee.

He read from a prepared statement written on a legal pad. Bad. "Captain Santiago, your performance as mission director on the MARIO project has been entirely satisfactory, and my reports will emphasize that. Our vehicle was destroyed by enemy action, not through any fault of yours or any other Orbital Command personnel."

But . . . , thought Elizabeth.

"But I think it would be a good idea to shift you to other duties. The stress of the past few days has been hard on everyone here, you most of all. You need a break."

"I'd like to remain part of the MARIO team. You could put me back at Flight, or Systems."

McEwan looked up and his tone sharpened a bit. "You

know perfectly well that wouldn't be a good idea. You'd be breathing down the mission director's neck."

She didn't argue. McEwan was right. But . . . she wanted another shot at Captain Black the Space Pirate. She wanted *revenge*!

"Will I be part of the antipiracy initiative?"

The general looked a little uncomfortable. "No. Captain—Liz—you're a good officer, but you're too much of a fighter. This whole project is ultimately a law enforcement mission. We want evidence leading to prosecutions, not shoot-outs in space."

"But I know who Captain Black is. His name's David Schwartz. I passed that on to FBI—"

"And they can't find anything about this person. He's got no paper trail at all after elementary school."

"That *proves* it's him! If he were innocent, he wouldn't have zeroed himself so completely." Even as she said it, she knew how crazy it sounded.

McEwan waited for a couple of agonizing seconds before continuing. "As I said, that's for law enforcement to handle. Not your concern anymore. Now, here's the deal: There's a group down in Titusville working on a propulsion system that could have some good applications. They need a mission control director, and since we're putting up half their money, I want an Air Force officer in the seat. Do a good job there, and you can probably come back in a year or two."

"Seriously?"

"I don't lie to people, Captain. Think of this as a résumé-building opportunity. Spend a little time in Siberia, and you can come back fully rehabilitated, ready to wave at the tanks on May Day."

She took a deep breath. "Yes, sir," she said.

He extended a hand across his desk. "It's been a pleasure serving with you, Captain."

Somehow she made it home to her apartment without getting run over. She ate something, showered, and got into bed. It was just past sunset, and she couldn't sleep. After fifteen minutes of staring at the ceiling she got up, mixed herself a mojito and wandered out onto the balcony in her sweatpants. It was a clear evening, and the stars of the Summer Triangle were peeking through the purple sky in the east.

"Damn you, Captain Black!" she yelled into the twilight. "This isn't over yet! From hell's heart, I stab at thee!"

A family having a cookout by the pool stared up at her. She finished her mojito and went back to bed.

. . .

Anne Rogers pulled over to the side of the highway. Around her, Oklahoma farmland stretched to the horizon, interrupted here and there by a donkey rig pumping oil. She looked in the rearview mirror.

A hundred yards behind her, a pale turquoise boat sat on a trailer, just inside the corner of a fenced pasture. Anne backed up slowly until she was right next to the boat. It was a nice-looking boat—not that she knew much about boats.

The sheet of plywood attached to the fence in front of the boat had *4 SALE BEST OFR* scrawled on it in spray paint.

Below that, a phone number in reflective stick-on digits from the hardware store.

Anne looked at the big manila envelope on the passenger seat. It was stuffed with papers, but the top one was a bank check for a quarter of a million dollars.

Scott William Rogers worked hard. He spent ten-hour days broiling himself in the summer sun, installing roofs. He built new houses and fixed up old ones. He spent his vacation time and weekends picking up properties at tax auctions, bringing them up to code, and selling them. When tornadoes came roaring down Cyclone Alley, he worked sixteen-hour days repairing damage.

When his wife left him, Scott dutifully paid his alimony and child support, and let her keep the home he had built for her. After that, he lived in whatever house he was fixing up at the time.

About half of Anne's childhood memories involved the smell of sawdust and fresh paint, and sleeping in a sleeping bag on the floor of empty, echoing rooms in houses her father was working on. But one weekend when she was twelve, her father took Anne and her sister to an enormous boat show at the convention center in Fort Worth.

"Are you buying a boat, Daddy?" she asked him, trying not to be bored.

"Well, Annie, I been thinking about it. I got some money saved, and I figure when you and Sarah finish college, I might just retire. Sailing around on a boat sounds nice, don't it?"

"Where would you sail to?"

"Oh, I don't know. Around the world, maybe."

Anne was halfway through her second year at Oklahoma State when her father died of a stroke at the age of forty-eight.

Parked beside the highway, she took out her phone and called the number on the sign. "I want to buy your boat," she said.

. . .

In a windowless room in a city on the edge of the Eurasian steppe, six men sat around a table drinking tea and smoking cigarettes. A seventh man stood by the door with an automatic rifle to make sure they were not interrupted.

"We are in danger of becoming irrelevant," said the oldest, a scholarly looking man who had spent his younger days teaching eager volunteers how to build bombs. "Oil is no longer the world's lifeblood. Which means the great powers no longer care to involve themselves in our affairs. No secret arms shipments, no bags of cash, no leverage."

"The Indians care," said a younger man. "They've got ships from Africa to Singapore now, and their drones and planes go as far as Russia."

"I'd love to know what idiot planned the Delhi operation," said a third man. "It did nothing but give the Hindus a justification for doing whatever they please."

"Never mind about that," said the oldest man. "What is done cannot be changed. We must look to the future."

"The future looks bad," said the youngest and fattest of them. "Our people are getting old. The birth rate keeps dropping, and the cleverest go off to Mumbai or Texas. Our economy has been stagnant for half a century now. It's not just Christians and Japanese—even Africans are getting richer than we are!"

"I see the rot spreading," said the fifth man. "The parliament is a lost cause. Every election brings more secularists, more 'reformers.' They will demand constitutional changes soon. I'm not sure we can count on the Army, either. They might side with the politicians."

"It is time for a bold stroke," said the last man. "Time to show the world we cannot be ignored."

"You have a suggestion?" asked the oldest.

"I do. The Americans and Indians think they can turn their attention away from us by mining the Moon. The United Nations lets them do it. The Russians are too busy selling rockets and fusion reactors to complain. China is falling apart."

"What do you propose?"

"I want to show them we can strike anywhere, even beyond the sky. I want to hit their lifeline in outer space. We can disrupt the supply of helium-3, frighten the great powers into concessions, and inspire a new generation of fighters."

"They can strike back," said the third man. "Who would object?"

"They cannot strike back if they don't know which enemy to hit. We won't send a rocket plastered with flags."

"How, then?"

"Pirates. The perfect deniable asset. The corsairs of the Maghreb once claimed tribute from every kingdom in Europe. We can do that again."

The argument lasted another hour, but in the end, the six men agreed.

2

In the spring of 2023, Elizabeth was finishing up her master's in astrophysics at MIT. For two years she'd been pretty much buried in work, powering through a heavy course load and spending all her vacation time on Air Force training. But once she submitted her thesis on gravity coupling effects in orbital rendezvous operations, she suddenly found herself with several hours of free time every week.

"Take a break. Go to some parties. Meet some people," recommended her roommate, Andy. He was another newly commissioned Air Force officer in grad school (plasma physics) but had no romantic interest in anyone but his new wife in Miami.

So she did. There was a semi-regular physics department booze and discussion session at the Miracle of Science Pub in Cambridge. Elizabeth wound up talking to a smart and intense kid named David who knew a heck of a lot about orbital mechanics.

"I'm amazed I haven't bumped into you before," she told him over her second mojito. "Who's your advisor?"

He blushed. "I don't have one. I'm not technically a student."

"Not technically? What does that mean? Postdoc?"

After a slight hesitation, he laughed. "It means I can't afford the tuition and couldn't get a loan, so I just made myself a fake student ID and show up for class like I belong there."

She felt a mojito-boosted rush of sympathy. "Why can't you get a loan? You sound like a natural for physics."

"Oh"—he waved a hand airily—"it's complicated. No undergrad degree, some black marks on my record. Never mind." He laughed again, and she laughed, too, and she bought them another round of mojitos.

The morning sun on his sleeping face made him look so young, she thought fondly about ten hours later. Almost like a little boy.

Then a weird thought struck her, and she found his jeans where he'd ditched them on the floor. His very convincing-looking MIT student card gave his age as twenty-three, same as hers, but his New York driver's license said he was only twenty. Not quite jailbait, then.

She ought to be angry, she thought. He had lied to her. But the sheer audacity of it was kind of charming. She was still making up her mind when he woke up, so she took him to Sunny's for pancakes.

For the next few weeks, it was a perfect relationship. They talked about physics and programming, screwed like teenagers, played games, and ate out every night. David never seemed to have any money, but Elizabeth's Air Force pay was enough to supply him with Thai food and beer.

He tried to get her interested in his favorite game, a multiplayer online world called *Against All Flags*. "It's awesome," he said. "You can be a pirate or a privateer or whatever you want. The whole Caribbean is rendered, and you can sail around, look for treasure, capture ships, cool pirate stuff like that. Plus there's ruined temples and pyramids in the jungle if you want to do dungeon crawls, and port cities. Clockpunk inventions, voodoo magic. You can even run businesses if you want."

"Can you play the Royal Navy or the Spanish?" she asked.

"If you want to. The Brits get to hunt pirates and search for the secret base where the Jacobites are building their submarine. The Spanish can go after anyone, but they have mutinies all the time. Here, check it out," he said, holding up his pad for her to admire. The display showed a black brigantine with scarlet sails and a bare-breasted figurehead. "The good ship *Scabby Whore*, terror of the Spanish Main. Want to join my crew?"

"Not tonight. I got an email from my CO. He wants me to go to a meeting at the Pentagon with him in a couple of weeks, and I need to get ready."

"Screw that. Say you can't make it. Tell him you're sick."

"Don't be ridiculous. I'm a little lieutenant and they're asking me to sit in on a meeting full of colonels and generals and civilian spooks. High-powered stuff. If I turn this down, I may as well go see if McDonald's is hiring."

He laughed a little. "You're serious about this whole Air Force career thing? I thought it was just a way to get the military to pay for grad school."

"Of course I'm serious! It's—" She groped for words. Explaining the "Air Force career thing" to people in Cambridge was like talking to her grandmother about orbital dynamics. The vocabulary wasn't there. "I'm on a fast track. In ten years, I could be a colonel."

"Whatever," he said. "In ten years, I'm going to be working on my second billion."

. . .

Five days later, Elizabeth woke up late on a rainy morning and was surprised to find herself alone in bed. She got up and wandered out into the living room, where David was already dressed and stuffing things into a duffel bag.

"What's up?"

"Oh, hey. Get some clothes on. Something waterproof."

"What for?"

"You'll see."

Two hours later, the two of them crouched on the roof of Building 54 at MIT. The sun had come out, which meant the puddles on the tar roof were steaming, and Elizabeth felt as though she were in an outdoor sauna. She kept her Air Force PT jacket knotted around her waist in case the rain started again.

David had set up his computer on top of an air-conditioning unit and mounted a salvaged satellite-TV antenna on a motorized telescope tripod. A cable ran from the computer to a modified police-band radio, and a fatter cable ran to the antenna. An extension cord snaked away across the roof and down the stairs to an outlet inside.

"Can't we do this some other time?"

"No," he said, staring at the screen and turning the salvaged satellite-TV antenna until it pointed south. "It's got to be today."

"You keep saying that, but you don't tell me why. We could be in bed right now." She leaned closer and made her voice seductive. "I could be sprawled naked on my bed right now."

"Save it," he said. "Do you see anything in the air that way? My glasses are all smeary."

Elizabeth squinted at the Boston skyline. "In the air? No—wait, yes. There's a little blimp over by the Hancock Center."

"That's what I want." He adjusted the antenna again. "There it is. Come to Daddy." He typed some instructions, shooed away a bothersome Japanese beetle trying to find out if his screen was edible, and typed some more.

"What are you doing?"

"It's a drone—some low-wage idiot in the traffic control office flies it around looking for accidents and traffic jams. Cheaper than a helicopter, and quieter. And oh by the way, it means the Boston cops have a camera in the sky all the time, looking at people's backyards and rooftops for pot plants or illegal barbecues, reading license plates, and probably taking videos of sunbathers."

"Welcome to the Third Millennium, David. There's cameras everywhere you look."

"Well, I just took control of that one."

"You did? How?"

"Hacked the control channel. I've been snooping it for a while. Dumbasses didn't even bother to secure it. It's amazing what you can do if you just crawl through the frequency bands and see what you get. Now I'm changing the channel and installing encryption so the cops are locked out."

"Very nifty," she said. The little blimp was coming toward them across the Charles, and she waved as it passed overhead. The image appeared on David's screen. "Too bad it's such a wet day," she said. "There isn't much to look at."

"How about a baseball game?"

"What?"

"The Sox are playing some other bunch of steroid-pumped millionaires at Fenway, and every drunken jackass in New England is sitting in the stands, spilling nachos on their souvenir T-shirts. The game just started. I'm going to have a look."

She peered off to the south, where the little blimp was crossing the Charles again. "You're losing altitude," she said.

"I want to buzz the stands. Otherwise nobody will notice."

He orbited Fenway Park a couple of times, then took the blimp in low over the Green Monster, following the foul line toward home base.

A rumbling sound caught Elizabeth's attention. A State Police helicopter thundered past overhead. Elizabeth could see a man with a sniper rifle through the open side door. She watched it circle the stadium. A second chopper approached from the east—Coast Guard, from the look of it. She heard sirens. Lots of sirens.

"David, I think this just got too serious. They don't know this is just a hack. You've got a blimp about to crash into a stadium full of people."

"Well, duh! Look at them—Black Sunday!"

She crouched next to him and looked at the screen. The view from the drone camera showed pure chaos: people climbing over seats, over one another, packing the aisles.

"David, stop it! People are getting hurt!"

"Bunch of Neanderthals. Who cares?"

Elizabeth didn't hesitate. She got to her feet and yanked the cable from David's laptop, then kicked over the antenna.

"Hey!" He looked up from the screen.

"That's enough."

He stood up, fists balled. "You ruined it!"

"Oh, for God's sake, David. People were panicking. Someone could get hurt. It's over."

She looked over toward the city. The blimp was climbing, back under police control. The helicopters still flanked it.

"Come on. We'd better get out of here. This won't be campus police taking the cow off the dome. City cops and FBI and half a dozen others will be all over Cambridge."

David stayed sulky until they were riding the elevator down. Then his mood turned triumphant. "But it was still a great hack!"

In the end, nobody died. David grudgingly admitted it was reckless, and against her better judgment, Elizabeth forgave him again. After all, it had indeed been a great hack.

. . .

That night she propped herself up on one elbow and watched him playing his pirate game in bed.

"David?"

"Where did you get all that stuff for this afternoon?"

"Oh, here and there. I found most of it. You know, Dumpster-diving, unclaimed property, that kind of thing."

"Even the telescope mount? Those things aren't cheap."

"I bought that one a while back."

She hesitated for a moment, then kept pushing. "How did you buy it?"

"The usual way. I exchanged money for goods and services like a good little consumer."

"What money?"

That actually made him pause the game and look at her. "*My* money. I do have some, you know. More than you, in fact."

"What do you *do*?"

"Stuff." He turned back to the game, but she put a hand over the screen.

"I'm serious. You don't have a job, I've never seen you do freelance work, and you're not a student so you can't be getting a stipend. Where do you get all this money, if it exists?"

He put the tablet down. "Okay, I'll tell you. But it's a secret, okay? Promise you won't tell anyone else?"

"I promise."

"Okay. My money exists. Some is in accounts, some in cash, some offshore. I get it by . . ." He seemed to be hunting for the right words, then shrugged and said, "I steal stuff."

"What? What kind of stuff?"

"Cars, sometimes. When I see one in self-driving mode with nobody on board, it's not hard to hack the guidance. A lot of them automatically reset when you take them in for repairs, and most people are too dumb to put in new keycodes when they get their cars back. So, lock on, feed it the current manufacturer override, and steer it someplace where I can strip it and sell the parts. There are still plenty of parts guys who don't give a shit where their merchandise comes from. Especially the ones who do black-market mods."

"That's terrible!"

"No, it's not. Some rich dude's car goes missing for an afternoon, and his insurance buys him new parts. Nobody loses anything but a big corporation, and who cares about them?"

"It's against the law."

"So? Are you going to turn me in?"

"I don't know. What else have you done?"

He seemed almost eager to tell her, as if he was enjoying the chance to brag about his cleverness. "You know how I hang out in coffee shops and the library so much? I've got a sweet little remote keylogger to eavesdrop on wireless links. I can swipe people's passwords and their typing styles. Then I order stuff and ship it to a dummy address—I like to use departmental offices at Harvard, because they still have these open pigeonholes for incoming mail. I get the loot, the person whose account I used can tell the bank they got hacked, and the corporation eats the loss again. That's where I got the Celestron. It's freelance economic justice."

She sat up. "I can't believe you're telling me this."

"You asked." He was smirking.

"Aren't you ashamed?"

He shrugged and didn't look the slightest bit ashamed.

She sat for nearly a minute, just looking at him as he restarted his game. "David," she said at last.

"Mm?"

"What do you want to do?"

"Now? I want to beat this fucking Spanish captain who keeps chasing me. Then I think I'm going to catch the treasure ship. Then sleep, then sex again, then breakfast. How about we go to S&S?"

"I meant what do you want to do with your life?"

"Oh, make a lot of money, maybe go to Thailand. Keep doing stuff I like."

"You can't spend the rest of your life just doing short cons and petty theft."

"Why not? When I need money, I get it."

"You're *stealing*."

"So what? Everybody steals. When you pay for a hamburger, McDonald's is stealing half of what you give them."

"That's not the same thing," she said. "It's a choice. You just take things."

"I don't take things that people care about. No real harm done."

"It's still wrong. Do you even know what that means?"

"Morality's just a set of rules people agree to follow. I don't agree with their rulebook. It's up to them to stop me."

"They will, you know. You only have to screw up once."

He laughed at that. "Me? I screw up all the time. My failure rate's about forty percent. I'm just smart enough that nobody catches me."

"You can't be smart enough all the time."

"Sure I can. Remember, I don't have to be really smart,

I just have to be smarter than a lot of really fucking stupid people."

She rolled onto her back and sighed in irritation. "David, you're wasting yourself. You really are a very intelligent man. You could do almost anything—start a company, design things, change the world. How are you going to make this fortune you want if you don't do anything? There's nothing you can steal that's worth more than a few hundred bucks."

"I'll figure something out. Now, hush, I'm about to grapple and board."

She kicked off the covers and crawled over his legs to get out of bed. "I want a drink," she said.

"Make mine an iced mocha," he said.

"Get your own damned coffee," she said. Andy was away, so she didn't bother to put anything on. In the kitchen she found the rum and poured herself a generous shot, then sat down to drink it by the fire escape security light shining through the window. She discovered that her bare skin stuck to the vinyl chair seat so that she had to stand up to make even the slightest change in position.

She wondered when David was going to come out of the bedroom and tell her he was sorry. By the time she finished her second shot of rum, it dawned on her that he wasn't going to apologize.

The rum was starting to hit her when she got up and walked—carefully, not drunkenly—back to the bedroom.

"Go home," she told him.

"Now? It's one forty-five."

"Go. I'm too tired to argue."

"You're too drunk, you mean."

"And I don't want to share my bed with you tonight. Get out."

"You're serious? You're seriously kicking me out because I stole some car parts?"

"Yes!" she said, a little too loudly. "I have to spend tomorrow getting ready for my meeting and I want to get some sleep and I don't want you around. We can talk when I get back."

"Maybe," he said, but he got up and pulled on his shorts and stuffed the tablet into his duffel bag. Neither of them said anything else until the door shut behind him.

Elizabeth could barely keep her eyes open, but before she tumbled into bed, she fired up her own computer and changed all her passwords. How did he know how much money she had?

. . .

She went down to Washington by bus, an eight-hour ride from Chinatown in Boston to Chinatown in D.C., and spent the night on the government's nickel at a hotel in Alexandria. The meeting was typical Pentagon—a windowless room, lots of bullet-point slides, and all the important stuff happened in the elevator during the lunch break.

The focus of the session was a seemingly trivial change in appropriations, and a new subcommand within SPACE-COM, to be called Orbital Command. She got the feeling that this was the end of some long battle, and all the senior Air Force people at the meeting looked very smug about it. The complete absence of the Navy was suggestive.

On the way out, Colonel McEwan asked her, "Where are you headed, Santiago? I can give you a lift."

"Um—I have to catch my bus in Chinatown, but it's right by the Metro."

"No, I asked where you're headed. Cambridge, right? I've got a trainer and an empty seat. We can talk on the way."

So Elizabeth borrowed a flight suit and stowed her bag under her feet and rode in the rear seat of a T-38 for an hour's flight up the coast to Hanscom. In the air, McEwan offered her a job. "Did you follow any of the talk today?"

"Not really," she said. "It was all policy-level."

"It means we're moving up and out. State cut a deal with the Indians and Japanese and bought off the Russians, so the Moon's open to commercial development. Helium-3 for fusion power plants. Westinghouse and Planetary Resources claim they can mine it cheaper than anyone can make it on Earth."

"I don't see what that means for us."

"It means there's going to be a lot of traffic in cislunar space pretty soon. Right now, our power projection stops at low orbit. We're going to have vital resource extraction happening in a place our military can't operate. That's a problem, which means it's also an opportunity. I'm putting together a team to design a low-cost platform that will extend our reach past geosynch. Here's the pitch: You've got the right skills, and your academic background is very impressive. Interested?"

"Absolutely," she said without hesitating.

She heard his chuckle in her headphones. "Don't let me twist your arm. Good. Now, this isn't even a real project yet. Just a study. But in the long term, it's going to be big. I expect we'll have something flying in about two years."

For the next half hour, he outlined the plan to create a robust, reusable unmanned orbiter that could get anywhere in cislunar space and be outfitted for a variety of different missions. By the time they landed, Elizabeth was already noting down ideas and suggestions on the knee pad of her suit. She was sold.

"Colonel, there is one thing I'd like to know. What kind of offensive capability are you envisioning for this vehicle?"

"Right now, nothing. It'll just be a recon and inspection platform."

"How can you do power projection without a weapon?"

"Networked battlespace. This bird will be the eyes, something else will do the hitting. Don't want to violate any treaties by putting up munitions. Nobody wants to start an arms race up there."

Elizabeth nodded, but on her knee pad she circled the word *WEAPONS* and then added a question mark.

It wasn't even rush hour when they landed. She bummed a ride to Concord and took the train into town. Her body had to navigate its way to her apartment on its own; her brain was still thinking about spacecraft.

Keycard lock on the building door. Sixteen steps up to the landing. Two dead bolts on the apartment door—her attention snapped back to the physical world. The door wasn't locked. But Andy was supposed to be in Florida.

She felt in the bag for her lockbox and silently worked

the combination. Her personal Beretta was identical to the service pistol, so she could stay in practice even off duty. She slipped in the magazine and chambered a round.

Holding the pistol aimed at the floor in a perfect two-handed grip, she nudged the door open with her foot and peeked in. Nothing was disturbed; no sign of a robbery. Had she gone off to Washington without locking the door behind her? Or had Andy come back early?

"Hello?" she called out. "Is anyone here?"

The door of her bedroom popped open and Elizabeth raised the gun, snapping into a target-shooting stance. Shoulders hunched, knees flexed, weight on the balls of her feet. Her instructor would have applauded.

It was David. *"Hey!"* he said, eyes wide at the sight of her aiming a pistol at him. He was wearing just a pair of jeans and hadn't bothered to zip them up.

"What are you doing here? How did you get in?" She flicked the safety back on and lowered the pistol, but didn't pop the magazine. Not yet.

He shut the bedroom door behind him. "Hey," he said again. "I thought you were supposed to get back late."

"I got a plane ride. How did you get in here?"

"Oh, right. I meant to tell you. I got your landlord to give me a key. It's quieter here than my place. Better for working. Do you want to go out for dinner? My treat. You can tell me all about your trip." He still looked pale.

"Sorry to scare you," she said. "It's kind of early for dinner. I've got some things I want to look up. Let me just stow my—"

"I'll get it. You go sit down." He came over and made an awkward grab for her bag.

"Stop it. What's gotten into you, David?" She popped the magazine out of the pistol and ejected the live round from the chamber.

"Nothing," he said, still keeping an eye on the gun.

"It's safe now," she said. And then she figured it out. "There's a girl in my room, isn't there?" Oddly, she wasn't angry. It was all too silly to be angry about. She started to chuckle, and then the startled look on David's face made her laugh aloud.

"You're afraid I'm going to shoot you because there's a girl in my room! Come out, come out, whoever you are!" she called. "I know you're in there, dear."

After about thirty seconds, a frightened Korean girl, an undergraduate by the look of her, came out of Elizabeth's room and stood awkwardly beside David. She was wearing a T-shirt and shorts, and was carrying her shoes and socks. She stared resolutely at the floor.

"We were just studying," he began, then shut up as Elizabeth laughed again.

She locked the gun back in its box. "Get out of here, both of you. And leave your key behind, David. I've got work to do."

The girl made a panicky dash for the door, but David still just stood there.

"Aren't you mad at me?" he asked at last.

"A little," she said. "But it's my own damn fault. I should have known better than to get involved with you.

You're still just a kid. Now, please, just go. I really do have work."

He got his shirt and shoes out of her room and went to the door. He was blushing the whole time. Elizabeth couldn't tell if he was angry or embarrassed. Probably angry.

At the door, he stopped and turned stiffly. "Are you really going to throw away everything we had together?"

She couldn't keep herself from laughing again, and he fled down the stairs.

. . .

JULY 13, 2023

David Schwartz sat curled up in a seat at the back of a Greyhound bus cruising westward along the New York State Thruway. He'd bought a ticket for Seattle, and had vague plans of looking for a job there, either in software or aerospace. Or maybe games. Or something. Time to start making that first billion.

The bus ticket had cost him all the cash he kept stuffed in the hidden pocket of his laptop bag. He had actually bought a plane ticket using Elizabeth Santiago's credit card number, but when he reached the last confirmation screen, he'd canceled the whole thing and used his own money. While burning her would have been fun, it seemed a bit petty.

Elizabeth had been right about one thing: He was wasting his time on petty scams. David Schwartz didn't want to do petty things; he wanted to do *awesome* things. At least, that was the new plan.

When it got too dark outside to see the towns and vine-yards streaming past, he looked at the little screen on the back of the seat in front of him. Some story about the Lunar Resources Initiative. A sound bite caught his attention: Each shipment of helium-3 from the Moon would be worth at least a billion dollars.

You could do a lot with a billion dollars, he thought. It wouldn't even be very hard to hack something like that. The big problem would be finding a way to sell the helium. He remembered a dude he'd met back in New Jersey who sold bootleg software. He'd bragged about his contacts in the Russian Mafiya and La Familia. Bill Benedict. David wondered if it was all bullshit. If not, those guys could probably find a way to fence a billion dollars' worth of helium-3.

David got off the bus in Cleveland just after midnight and walked four miles to the Case Western campus. He sat on a loading dock behind the Smith Library and found an unsecured wireless network he could use. As the sky grew pale and the campus came awake around him, David sketched out a plan. It could work. If Bill Benedict was only 50 percent full of shit, this could work. David Schwartz could steal a billion dollars from space.

"What do I want to do?" he asked the air around him. "I want to be the supreme badass of outer space!"

He'd need a handle. Something cool. Have to think about that.

3

Icarus Propulsion Systems was located in an industrial park on Grissom Parkway, just across from the airport in Titusville. Off to the northeast, Elizabeth could see the titanic bulk of the old Vehicle Assembly Building looming above the pine woods of Cape Canaveral. After the thin dry atmosphere of Colorado Springs, the summer Florida air was like trying to breathe boiling milk.

The glass doors were wet on the outside, but not locked, so she stepped inside and got a blast of antarctic cold air. Working for the government, she had become used to rooms that were always slightly too warm in summer and too chilly in winter. But this was private-sector Florida air-conditioning, good enough to turn any room into a meat locker.

The reception area was done up in faux wood paneling coming un-laminated despite the climate control, with a surprisingly good painting of Icarus silhouetted against a spiral galaxy on the wall opposite the door.

Nobody was about, so Elizabeth tried the inner door. That opened into a short corridor of unpainted wallboard, with a couple of unoccupied offices on either side. "Hello?" she called.

Now slightly irritated, she opened the door at the end of the corridor, and stopped. Beyond it, the building was a single vast open space. There were test stands, robot milling machines, and prototype printers, but the thing that held her attention was the spaceship in the middle.

It was small, obviously unmanned. The central body was a simple aluminum can about the size of an oil barrel, but a pair of giant curving silver wings spread out on either side. Each wing was shaped exactly like the bowl of one of her grandmother's old silver tablespoons. Beneath the body of the spaceship was a small matte-black egg, slightly bigger than a basketball, with a rocket nozzle sticking out of it.

"We call it SOTHIS," said a voice. A tall man with a shaved head emerged from behind the spacecraft. He kept squeezing a tennis ball with his left hand as he spoke. "Solar Thermal Impulse System."

"I know," she said. "I'm here to fly it for you. Elizabeth Santiago, 614th Space Operations Squadron."

"Jack Bonnay," he said, wiping his right hand on his pants before extending it to shake. "I'm not really an employee, I just come around to help out. Mike and the rest are at lunch."

"What kind of helping out do you do here?" He looked kind of old for an intern.

"Robotics," he said. "That's kind of my specialty. When I'm not training back in Houston, I've been helping Mike debug the servos."

"Wait, you're John Bonnet!" She pronounced the *t*, and then corrected herself. That was a name she recognized.

He just grinned and switched the tennis ball to his right hand.

"Sorry, I didn't make the connection at first. You didn't look like an astronaut."

"I could wear my Moon suit, but it's still up at Babcock Crater."

There was a slightly awkward pause, and then she asked, "So, where's the operations center for this mission? Are we going to control it out of Kennedy?"

"Actually, I believe the plan is to run the experiment from right here." He gestured to one corner of the factory building, where a dozen cafeteria folding tables bearing workstations faced an array of old flat-screen televisions across a floor tangled with cables. Hand-lettered signs on the backs of the desk chairs indicated the different mission control stations.

Liz thought it made the bare-bones Air Force control center in the Pit in Colorado look like the bridge of the Starship *Enterprise*. "This is an operational setup? Not just a simulator?"

"Absolutely," he said. "We've got a line to the Space Center so we can uplink to the TDRSS network. You could run any spacecraft in near-Earth space from here with the right software."

Between the air-conditioning and the primitive equipment, she began to think McEwan hadn't really been joking about Siberia.

She turned around to look at the spacecraft. "This is your bird?"

"Mike's bird. I'm just a volunteer."

She knew perfectly well he was a founding partner of the company, but didn't argue. "I read the project summary. You really expect to get nine klicks of exhaust velocity just by solar heating?"

"The mirrors are the key," he said. "Mike borrowed some techniques from adaptive-optics telescope design. They change shape to maximize the energy on the rocket chamber, no matter what the sun angle."

"And that's why you're debugging servos."

"Right!" He had the delighted look of a teacher whose students are smarter than expected. "The mirrors are really the only part of the system that's experimental. Everything else is just plumbing and off-the-shelf electronics."

"Whatever he's trying to sell you, don't buy any!" boomed a very Texan voice from across the cavernous interior.

Jack waved at the couple approaching. A very large man in a very sharp-looking Italian suit and cowboy boots was walking toward them, hand in hand with a tiny woman in cutoff jeans and a tank top. "You must be Captain Santiago! I'm Mike Levy, and this is—"

The small woman shook Elizabeth's hand. "Yumiko Shima-Levy." She didn't look like the cofounder of a space propulsion company; she looked like she should be hanging around a skateboard park.

"And I see you've already met Jack," Mike added. "The

boys are still finishing up lunch. You need any food, Captain Santiago? I brought back some ropa vieja and plantains, and I think there's a quart of curry in the fridge."

"Has Jack shown you SOTHIS yet?" Yumiko asked her.

"We were just looking at the control center. Are you sure it wouldn't be simpler just to borrow time at Kennedy?"

Mike's laugh made the room echo. "You don't like our homeschooler science project setup? I told Jack we should get in some people from Disney to make it look all slick and professional. Fact is, we don't have the budget for anything else. But I'll tell you what: You go over our little command center here, try some simulator runs, whatever you like, and if you actually think it'll impair our ability to test out SOTHIS in space, I'll see if we can get out the tin cup and beg NASA for enough to cover the cost of renting their room. Deal?"

"Michael, save the haggling for later. She just got here," said Yumiko.

"Go ahead, sweetie. Show her your engine. Jack, we still having problems with the rotation?"

The two men went to poke at one of the mirror wings while Yumiko led Elizabeth under the spacecraft to the matte-black motor.

"Don't touch!" she said, even though Elizabeth's hands were still folded behind her back. "Sorry, but everyone tries it, and it could damage the surface."

Even from only a meter away, the spherical motor was impossible to focus on. It was absolutely black, without any highlights or reflections, like a circle cut out of reality. The only way Elizabeth could even measure the distance to it was by looking at the fuel lines connected to the top end.

"How do you get it that black?"

"It's not paint," said Yumiko. "It's a pseudorandom arrangement of carbon nanotube segments. Reflectivity is less than point-oh-five percent. We should get over four thousand degrees K in full sunlight."

It seemed absurd that something so fragile-looking could handle that much energy. Yumiko must have read Elizabeth's expression, or maybe it was a common reaction, because she added, "I can show you our static test videos if you don't believe it."

"What's the payload?"

Yumiko shrugged. "Right now, nothing. Just the control and comm systems. Mike's been trying to line up a couple of science experiments to help defray the cost, but nobody's knocking down the door."

The rest of the crew got back from lunch then, so there was another round of introductions. Icarus Propulsion Systems was a young company, and most of the employees were grad students or engineers fresh out of college. The only person over forty in the whole building was one grizzled machinist in a faded Rocketdyne cap.

She did manage to buttonhole Mike Levy when he and Jack took a break from making SOTHIS flex its wings. "Are you really on track for a launch in August? That's only six months."

"Hell yes!" he said with a big grin, and wrapped a massive silk-clad arm about her shoulders. "Captain Santiago, we're all betting our careers on SOTHIS. The last thing I want to do is screw things up by trying to launch a vehicle that isn't ready. We're due to crate her up July Fourth weekend, and she'll be ready to fly."

"You're sure?"

He laughed. "You're the one who gets to make the call—you know that, right? When we deliver her, you're the last one on the sign-off list. If you don't like the way we've prepared your bird, you can send it back to the kitchen."

* * *

Elizabeth spent that first day at Icarus putting names to faces, getting a company computer account and keys, and building a pile of things to take home and read. She was trying to make sense of the operational plan for the first test mission when Jack Bonnet tapped her on the shoulder. "You don't have to do it all in one day," he said.

"Oh, I'm just getting my bearings," she said. "Learning what I need to know in order to ask the right questions."

"Are you hungry?"

"I had lunch, but thanks."

He laughed. "I was actually thinking about dinner, if we can find anyplace still open."

Liz checked her watch. It couldn't be nine thirty. She must have forgotten to reset it from Mountain Time. No, wait, that would make it midnight. "I guess I can knock off for the night."

They wound up at a taqueria on US-1, right on the edge of the lagoon. Over the drink dispenser hung autographed photos of astronauts from as far back as the Shuttle program. Jack had an adolescent's appetite, loading up his tray with one of each type of taco the place offered—bean, beef, chicken, chorizo, egg, catfish, pulled pork, kimchi, shrimp, crab, and yuca—plus a plate of beans and rice and a couple of spare tortillas. Liz just had soup to buffer the ice-cold Bohemia she drank. As the beer hit her bloodstream, she could feel the muscles in her neck and shoulders lose their stiffness.

"I guess this is a big change from ORBITCOM, huh?"

"The food's better," she said.

"God, yes. I was in the Army for ten years, and that was the part I never got used to."

"Where were you?"

"Mideast, mostly," he said. "Plus a couple of years in Africa. It all kind of looked the same: air-conditioned trailers in the middle of some dusty hellhole. I fixed robots, and then I commanded people who fixed robots, and eventually they sent me back to the States to help design robots. How about you?"

"Oh, I'm Air Force all the way. At the Academy I did really well in physics, and they paid for my master's at MIT. Then a couple of years at Vandenberg, and then Cheyenne Mountain."

"And now here. You were on the MARIO program, right?"

"Mission director."

"That's a pretty high-powered spot for a captain."

Elizabeth didn't answer. She finished her first beer and got a second while Jack put away a couple more tacos. When she sat down, she spoke again. "So, why am I here looking after some garage-band project when I used to be on the fast track at ORBITCOM? Because I screwed up and lost the spacecraft."

"I read the official report," he said. "Enemy action, it said."

"I still screwed up. I got overconfident and greedy, and it literally blew up in my face." She took a long drink from her second bottle.

"I wasn't trying to be nosy," he said. "I just meant you must be pretty good at what you do."

"Not as good as I thought."

"Oh, don't say that. The other guy had a bomb on his orbiter. You had no way of knowing that."

"I should have guessed. I should have been ready. When I first transferred to ORBITCOM, McEwan put me to work thinking about tactics and methods for space combat operations. I came up with a big long list of risk factors to consider, and I even put target self-destruct as one of them. But in action I got greedy and screwed up."

He wiped up the last of his beans and rice with a tortilla, ate it in three bites, and took his tray over to the dirty-dishes bin. "Are you done with your beer?"

She drained the bottle and put it in with the dishes. "Let's go."

He pulled into the Icarus parking lot and gave her a worried look. "Can you drive? I could run you home, pick you up in the morning."

"I'll be fine."

He didn't argue. She drove very carefully to the apartment she was renting. It was on one of the few streets that didn't seem to be named after a dead astronaut. She'd rented it sight unseen from Colorado, and furnished it with a futon and a crummy particleboard desk and a couple of plastic lawn chairs. She'd shipped everything else she owned to her uncle's place in Texas.

The clock on the microwave said 11:14 when she got in. Elizabeth poured a shot of rum into a cold glass of Sprite and sat down on the floor with her back against the wall and her pad on her lap. There was a file she kept encrypted on a keychain drive, never allowing it to touch her machine's permanent memory. Its file name was a random string of characters, but when opened, the top of the page read PIRATE HUNTER PROJECT.

She'd pestered everyone involved in the antipiracy initiative, fingering David Schwartz as Captain Black, but that was as far as she could go without any proof. She knew it was him, but an old role-playing game character name and a vague feeling about someone's personal style weren't enough for law enforcement. They needed hard evidence, and apparently David was exceptionally careful about not leaving any traces the FBI could find. He barely existed at all.

So Elizabeth had been amusing herself by designing a way to fight pirates directly. Now she dumped almost everything she had created into a separate file, and copied all the technical information on SOTHIS from her main drive.

The team at Icarus Propulsion Systems were nice people. They had a cool spaceship. And Captain Santiago wanted to use it to destroy Captain Black the Space Pirate.

. . .

SEPTEMBER 9, 2030

Special Agent Dominic Yu read through the Schwartz file on the drive out to Long Island while the car smoothly navigated through New York traffic. Yu hated driving himself; it was such a waste of time to sit and stare at the ass of the car in front of you and try not to crash into things. The only time he'd actually enjoyed operating a car manually was during the Law Enforcement Emergency Vehicle Operation course down at Glynco. Screaming tires around obstacles on the training track was a blast, but that didn't make Yu any more fond of normal, tedious driving. Let the car do that.

Most of his fellow FBI agents claimed to dislike self-driving vehicles. They wanted their hands on the wheel and their feet on the pedals. Dominic had once checked the records out of pure nosiness and was amused to see that all the most vocal defenders of human driving had the greatest number of operating incidents.

The Schwartz file didn't have much in it. The only thing connecting David M. Schwartz to any helium piracy operation was a tip from an Air Force officer who'd known him in grad school and claimed that the online rants by "Captain Black the Space Pirate" sounded like him. She'd been unable to furnish any samples of anything written by Schwartz for comparison.

Agent Yu never liked it when military people tried to do law enforcement. Even the intelligence specialists always got things wrong. The kind of "solid intel" they trusted when planning a drone strike or whatever was absolutely useless when you were building a case that would stand up in court.

The car parked itself in front of a 1970s split-level ranch house in Massapequa. Agent Yu tightened his tie and put on his suit jacket. With his tablet in his left hand, he marched up the steps and knocked firmly.

Jordan J. Schwartz was sixty-two, according to the file, employed as a senior evidence technician for the Nassau County Police Department. Agent Yu decided to approach him as one law enforcement professional to another.

"Good afternoon, Sergeant Schwartz," he said, taking off his sunglasses and smiling. "I'm Dominic Yu. May I come in?"

"Um . . ." Schwartz glanced over his shoulder. "My wife's asleep. Can we talk on the step?"

The room behind Schwartz looked a little shabby, with old IKEA furniture and a framed Shepard Fairey print on the wall. No sign of any illegal drug lab or teenagers trussed up, so maybe the wife really was asleep.

Keep it friendly and informal. "If you like," he said. Schwartz pulled the door shut behind him and followed Dominic down the steps. He took a seat on the top step, squinting in the glare, while Dominic remained standing.

"You said this was about David?"

"That's right. We're trying to locate him." Dominic held his tablet under his arm, recording everything.

"Good luck with that," said Schwartz. "I haven't seen him in . . . six years now."

"No contact at all?"

"He sends birthday cards, but that's all."

"Do you know where he is?"

"Nope. They come from all over. Miami, Seattle, Japan. He never puts a return address on them."

"Do you have any samples of anything he might have written? A diary, schoolwork, anything?"

Schwartz looked even more unhappy. "When David left home, he built a fire in the backyard and burned all his stuff. The only things we have left are some old toys and some school photos I had in storage."

"What about electronic media, or online?"

"Nope. He wiped out everything. I downloaded some video of the school play from when he was in fourth grade. He got everything else."

Dominic waited a moment before continuing. "Mr. Schwartz, would you mind telling me why David might have done that?"

Schwartz stared at the struggling lawn, then sat up straighter. "We had some problems with David. When he was younger he was a very good kid, very bright. Hardworking—you don't see that very much in kids. When he found something that interested him, he'd work on it nonstop. He tested in the ninety-eighth percentile, right across the board. I thought he'd be a scientist or a game designer or something."

Dominic waited.

Schwartz chuckled a little sadly. "It was girls," he said. "David hit thirteen and all of a sudden that was all he cared about. He started going out, skipping school, sneaking out at night. Turned out he was borrowing cars to go see his girlfriend."

"But no arrest," said Yu.

"Nope. He didn't even know how to drive. The guy across the street—that house, but he moved—had a self-driving car. First one on the block, I think. He had seizures. David figured out how to key it to his thumbprint so that he could use it. He was going over to see this girl down in Amity Harbor, and—you know. Fourteen years old."

Did Schwartz sound a little proud? Dominic wondered. Maybe.

"Anyway, the guy who owned the car saw him coming back early one morning and came over here. He was a good guy, didn't really want to see David in juvie court, so Jen and I promised it wouldn't happen again."

"Did it?"

Schwartz sighed and looked sad again. "I don't know. We thought he was straightened out, but I guess he just got better at hiding what he was doing. When he was a junior in high school, my wife tried to get a transcript from the school for colleges, and we found out he hadn't been going to school for more than a year. He'd faked up an email account and was sending us report cards, announcements, all kinds of stuff. All fake. I don't know what he was doing all that time. He said he was just going to the library, studying on his own. But there had to be more to it, right? I mean, why go to all that trouble if he was just going to the library?"

Schwartz suddenly tensed and glanced behind him, as if he'd heard something. When he started speaking again, Dominic could barely hear him.

"So we had a long talk with him. Jen talked with some

of the doctors at work about medicating him. Nothing major, just something to help him control himself so he could finish school. We sat him down at dinner and explained it, and he said it sounded like a good idea. The next day there was a pile of burning paper in the yard and no David."

"Did you see him after that?"

"Just a couple of times. He never called or anything, but he did visit. The first time he showed up out of the blue one Saturday morning. That was in 2020, I guess, in the summer. He said he was living with some friends in the city, working at a game company. We had lunch, and then he called a cab and left. A couple of weeks later, I tried to contact him and it turned out the number and address he gave me were bogus. Nobody at the game company had ever heard of him."

"Was that the only time?"

Just then the front door opened, and Schwartz jumped to his feet, as if he were trying to hide Dominic. His wife was drying her hands with a dish towel. "Jordan?"

"Hey, Jen. This is . . . this is Dominic Yu. He stopped by to say hi."

She took in the Bureau ID on a lanyard around Dominic's neck, and her face turned fearful. "What's going on?"

"I'm just trying to locate your son, David, Mrs. Schwartz," said Dominic.

"Is he all right? Is he in trouble?"

Mr. Schwartz looked at Dominic with a pleading expression.

"We're just trying to get in touch with him right now," said Dominic. "All I want is to get some information from him. That's all. Mr. Schwartz—you were saying?" Try to wrap this up and get out. Avoid an ugly emotional scene.

"Oh, right. The last time I saw him was about six years ago."

"That would be 2024?" Dominic asked.

"November fifteenth," said Mrs. Schwartz.

"I was just getting off shift at work when he called me, asking if I could meet him at the sushi place down the street. He called Jen, too. She came over from the hospital and I drove us. David bought dinner. He said he was working at a little technology start-up, making good money."

"Did you believe him?"

"Nope. I . . . I don't know what he was doing. Not drugs," he added quickly. "I can tell you that. I've seen enough users and dealers. Definitely not drugs." He looked at his wife, who nodded. "I kind of figure he's doing some kind of, you know, nothing job somewhere and doesn't want us to know. Wants to seem like a success. I mean, he's smart, but he didn't even finish high school. Probably just mooching off a girlfriend."

"Did you tell him about the cards?" asked Mrs. Schwartz.

"Already covered," said Mr. Schwartz. "That's it, really."

"What about the money?" she asked.

The resulting silence lasted about half a minute. Schwartz looked very unhappy, about as unhappy as you'd expect a local cop concealing information from a federal officer would.

Dominic didn't want to spook them. "Remember this is all off the record," he said, though of course that meant nothing legally.

Mr. Schwartz sighed. "Okay, he's been sending us money. It started about four years ago."

"January of 2026," said Mrs. Schwartz.

"A mailer full of cash," said Mr. Schwartz. "A thousand bucks in old twenty-dollar bills, and a little note saying 'From David.' No return address."

"Since then, it's been every few weeks," said Mrs. Schwartz. "About ten times a year."

"May I see one of the mailers?" asked Dominic.

"I don't keep them," said Mr. Schwartz. "I throw them out. We use the money for groceries, fixing up the house. Stuff like that. Just to help make ends meet."

"Return address?"

"Nothing," said Mr. Schwartz. "They come from the city; the zip was . . . 10018, I think. That's all, really."

The two of them watched him. They were both in late middle age, with retirement coming up. She was a nurse, he was a cop—decent civil service pensions and benefits, but nothing lavish. Not like the old days. An extra ten K a year was a nice bonus. But it wasn't enough to support them.

More to the point, it wasn't helium-pirate money. A crook like Captain Black the Space Pirate would be pulling millions. You'd expect him to take better care of his parents. Send over a new car or some tacky jewelry if he wanted to show off. A Starbucks manager could spare ten thousand a year.

"Thank you for your time," he said, and the two of them visibly relaxed when he said it. "If you have any contact with your son, please let me know at once, and don't throw anything away. And—be sure you start reporting any gifts to the IRS. You know how picky they are."

On the ride back into the city, he checked over his notes. Was David Schwartz secretly Captain Black? No proof.

Dominic Yu was a careful man. He didn't want to go off on a wild-goose chase on nothing but an Air Force officer's hunch, but he wasn't ready to give up any potential leads. For now, keep the file open, keep sifting for information about David M. Schwartz—and the fifty or sixty other people who might be Captain Black.

· · ·

MESSING ABOUT IN MY BOAT

March 16, 2031

Location: 30° 9′ 58″ N by 89° 44′ 13″ W (Fort Pike, Louisiana)

Well, this is it.

I'm down to my last twenty bucks in the bank. I think there's maybe another twenty on the boat, if I dig under the seat cushions for change. That's it. I have enough fuel to get to Bay St. Louis, but I can't afford to fill up *Carina* again.

The voyage is over.

Damn. I wanted to get to Florida. Or at least Alabama.

I can stretch this out as much as I can. Today I'm going to head east, out to Isle au Pitre or maybe Cat Island, and spend one last night on the water. I'm running low on food, but I don't see any point in buying more supplies. *Carina*'s cruise is over.

I've got some granola bars left, and I refilled my water bottles at the fuel station. If I run into any fishermen, maybe I can cadge a couple of beers or a fish. I'm sure I'll see someone. People around here are lunatics about fishing.

(I always thought of it as something old guys did on weekends, but here you see whole families out at the crack of dawn, even on weekdays, ready to stay on the boat until sunset. Fishing here is like football back home.)

I want to thank all the people who hit the tip jar over the past couple of months. Your donations made it possible for me to . . . have dinner last night. You've extended this voyage by a good eight or ten hours. Thanks!

No, I shouldn't be snarky. I really do want to thank everyone who donated. This voyage wasn't the exciting adventure I promised when I started, and I can't really blame the readers who gave up along the way.

What I've learned: I've been too timid. When I look back over my entries since I left Oklahoma, there's way too many nights when I just hung out on my boat by myself, and too many days when I just list the mile markers and islands I passed. Who wants to read about that?

What's next? I guess I can try to sell *Carina* in Bay St. Louis. I'm probably going to lose a bundle on the deal since I can't very well hang around and wait for a good offer. I'll find a boat dealer and get the best price I can.

And then, back to OSU. Find a job somewhere to pay the bills, and beg the university to let me finish my degree.

Going around the world on my own was a crazy idea, and now I guess I have to go back to real life.

4

Captain Black the Space Pirate sat under an umbrella on the beach in Tortuga Pirate World™ with a tall chilled Bloody Mary beside him and a newly downloaded journal in his hands. His suntan was perfect.

Tifane dropped into the chair next to his, toweling her hair. "You should go swimming," she said. "It's nice."

"Maybe later. I want to finish this."

She put aside her towel and lay back in the deck chair. Her tan was perfect, too. The micro mesh bikini she wore didn't block anything. David had bought her a dozen and didn't let her wear anything else.

"What are you reading?"

"This." He held up his pad so she could see the screen, and clicked back to the cover art.

"*Proceedings of the Royal Society?* Is that about the King and Queen?"

"No." David clicked back to the paper he'd been reading.

"Well, what's it about, then?"

"It's scientific papers. The one I'm trying to read is on new propulsion concepts for spacecraft." He started to read the abstract for the third time.

"I thought you gave up all that stuff."

"It's still interesting. Now, do you mind?"

She finished drying her hair, sat still for about a minute, then started to fidget. Finally she stretched herself, arching her back and thrusting out her chest, then glanced sidelong at David from under her sunglasses.

"Davie," she said in a little-girl voice. "I need some lotion."

He handed her the tube without taking his eyes off the screen.

"Can you put it on me? *Pleeeease?*"

A gorgeous former exotic dancer wearing less than thirteen square centimeters of bathing suit was begging him to run his hands all over her hot skin, and David's chief emotion was annoyance.

"Davie?" the little-girl voice had a slightly harsh edge to it.

He sighed, put down the pad, and squirted half the tube into the palm of his hand. He covered her legs in four swipes, smeared a gob across her stomach, and left a white handprint on her chest. "There," he said. He picked up her towel and cleaned the rest of the lotion off his hand before picking up the pad again.

"What do you want to do tonight?"

"I want to finish reading this."

"Don't you want to go out? We don't go anywhere anymore."

"Not tonight. Maybe tomorrow."

"Can we go see Prospère?"

"No."

"Why not?"

He put down the pad again. "Because—Prospère's a busy man. He doesn't have time to hang out with us." Inside his head, David was thinking a very different answer. *Because Prospère's an illiterate thug, and so are all his friends, and the only reason you like to visit him is because he gives out blow like it was Halloween candy.*

But he couldn't say that out loud. Someone might hear, and it might get back to Prospère, and Prospère might be unhappy. Prospère Malouin was a very useful person to have as a friend. He'd gotten David settled in Tortuga, and his contacts in the island's security force and local police made sure nobody interfered with David's comfortable retirement. David's opinion of him was best kept safe inside David's head.

Tifane didn't interrupt again, and David could concentrate on his reading. When he looked up again, she was gone. He eventually spotted her over by the cabana bar, drinking something bright pink and flirting with a couple of Turkish-looking guys.

He ought to feel jealous, David thought, but he didn't. If the Turks could put up with Tifane's demands for attention, drinks, and presents, they were welcome to her.

As he watched them, he saw one of the two men look over toward him and nod politely. David nodded back and went back to his reading. The paper was really quite elegant, and he enjoyed the sensation of *understanding* something complex. That didn't happen much in Tortuga Pirate World™. It wasn't a place that catered to complexity.

"Excuse me, are you Mr. Schwartz?" The older of the two Turkish-looking guys sat down in Tifane's beach chair next to David.

Panic! "Uh, no. No, my name is Williams."

"Oh, yes. My mistake. My name is Ghavami. I am looking for someone who can help me with a project I am supervising. Someone with experience operating orbital vehicles. Do you know anyone who can help me with that?"

David's mouth was dry. Was this the moment he'd been dreading, when the men with badges finally showed up? But this Ghavami didn't act like a cop.

"This is a funny place to look for people with space operations experience."

"And yet I have been told I can find just the man I need right here in Tortuga."

Time to quit fooling around. "Who are you?"

Ghavami laughed. "If I were a policeman, would I tell you? Actually, I suppose I might. The Americans have all sorts of absurd rules they must follow. No, I am not here to arrest you, Mr.—"

"Williams."

"Mr. *Williams*, yes. Pardon my curiosity, but what sort of passport do you carry, Mr. Williams?"

"I'm a citizen of Tanzania."

"You don't look very African."

"I get that a lot. Where are *you* from, Mr. Ghavami?"

The other man laughed again. "I presented an Afghan

passport when I arrived in Haiti. And I would bet Swiss francs I can tell you more about my hometown in Afghanistan than you can tell me about your birthplace in— Zambia, did you say?"

"Tanzania. I've lived abroad since I was a little kid."

"Mr. Schwartz, let us put aside this nonsense. I know who you are, and I am not going to put you in jail. I want to hire you."

"What for?"

"Space piracy, of course."

"I'm retired."

"I can offer you five percent of a payload. Fifty million francs, after laundering. That's a lot of money, even nowadays."

"I've got enough money."

Ghavami looked over at the cabana bar, where his younger companion still had Tifane rapt in conversation. "Are you happy here, Mr. Schwartz? You live in a tropical resort, you have a pretty girl to sleep with, you can spend all your days on the beach and drink as much as you like. Most men would envy you. But does it really *satisfy* you?"

"Fifty million more wouldn't change anything," said David. A little bitterness crept into his voice; a little more than he intended.

"What do you want, then?"

"If I was really a retired helium pirate, here's what I'd want," said David. "I'd want your five percent *and* a solid new identity. The kind of thing some intelligence agency could provide. Solid enough for me to live in Europe or

America without getting picked up. Solid enough to get a doctorate or start a company. I'd want that in advance—if I was a crook, that is."

"I can provide that, if you wish. But not in advance. Only when the job is done."

David looked out to sea. He had already made up his mind, but he didn't want Ghavami to think he was jumping at the offer. "Tell you what, Mr. Ghavami. Let me know where I can get in touch with you, and I'll think about what you've said. You'll hear from me in a few days. Okay?"

"Go ahead and check my identity, trace the accounts I used to pay for my hotel, and make whatever inquiries you like. I will be here for a week." He handed David an old-fashioned paper business card, lettered in Roman and Arabic. *MAHMOUD GHAVAMI,* it said, *CONSULTING.*

Ghavami got up and walked off down the beach. At the cabana, his companion said good-bye to Tifane and followed him. She looked a little puzzled, then brought her shocking-pink drink back to where David was sitting.

"Change of plan, sweetie," he said. "We're going to see Prospère tonight after all."

Her eyes lit up. "Is it a party?"

"Something like that," said David.

. . .

Anne Rogers woke just after dawn, at anchor off Isle au Pitre, between the Mississippi coast and the Louisiana delta. She finished the last of the granola bars and decided to have one last walk on the beach before using her remaining fuel to get to Bay St. Louis.

Anne got into her little inflatable dinghy and rowed ashore. Isle au Pitre was the last of the chain of islands she'd followed heading east from Lake Borgne, and she wanted to get in a little exploring before the place got too crowded with fishermen.

She made landfall at the island's northern tip. To her right, the sound stretched off toward the mainland, and she could just make out the lights on the tall bridge where Highway 90 crossed Bay St. Louis. To her left was the Gulf of Mexico; nothing but blue water until you hit Florida. Anne made sure her little dinghy was well above the tide line, then set out along the Gulf side of the island.

Isle au Pitre had a pretty good beach, though all the jagged oyster shells embedded in the silt made her glad of her sandals. Beyond the beach was about a square mile of marsh, all brackish ponds and clumps of scrubby tall grass. The air was full of gulls and pelicans waiting for fishing boats to turn up.

The breeze off the Gulf was strong, but the sun was already warming up the sand. It felt good to stretch her legs after a day and a night on the *Carina*.

Ahead she saw a beat-up pontoon boat on the beach. It was in such bad shape she wondered if it was a wreck, cast there by the tide. The thought of coming this far out in that was pretty daunting. But then she saw a man beyond it, wearing a windbreaker and a wide-brimmed hat, methodically working a metal detector over the beach.

He didn't notice her until she passed him. "Good morning!" he called out, shouting over the wind. He had a white mustache and his nose was thickly smeared with sunblock. Below his cargo shorts his legs were skinny.

"Morning," Anne said pleasantly. She was torn between the enjoyment of her solitary walk and the desire for a little human interaction. She decided on humanity. "What are you looking for?"

"Pirate treasure!" he shouted, grinning.

"Find anything?"

"Beer cans!"

"Well, keep looking," she said, and turned to go on.

She walked all the way to the southern tip of the island, keeping an eye on the tide. All Anne's boating had been on lakes and rivers, where high and low tide were about as relevant as the Shanghai stock market. She'd learned enough to be nervous—how much of this island would be above water at high tide? According to the little tide calculator app on her boat's nav system, the water was still going out.

By the time she began walking back toward the north end of the island, she could see a couple of boats on the landward side, maybe half a mile off. They were close together, which suggested they'd found a good spot.

Up ahead she saw the old man, but he wasn't scanning the beach anymore. He was on his knees. For a second, Anne worried that he was having a heart attack or something, but then she saw that he was digging in the sand with a garden trowel.

He looked up and waved as she approached.

"Find something?"

"Don't know! Big, though." She knelt next to him and used her hands to scoop away sand. They cleared away the sand until they'd exposed a metal box about the size of a suitcase. It was wrapped up in steel cable and locked with a combination lock.

"It looks like you did find some treasure after all," she said.

"We found it," he said. He stuck out his right hand. "George Adorno."

"Anne Rogers." They shook hands. "But it's really yours," she added. "You had the metal detector."

"You're my good-luck charm," he said. "Never found anything but junk until today."

"Can you open it?"

"I got some bolt-cutters on my boat," he said, getting stiffly to his feet.

"I'll get them," she said, and ran toward the old pontoon boat while he was still dusting sand off his knees.

Mr. Adorno kept all his gear in heavy plastic garbage bags, so she had to peek into all of them. One held a half-melted sack of ice and a six-pack, another had a first-aid kit and sunscreen, and the biggest bag was full of sandy, tide-scoured old beer cans. The tools were in a bag under the pilot seat.

She ran back with the bolt-cutters. Cutting the cable was an epic struggle. The cutters got through the plastic sleeve coating the cable easily enough, but then Anne and Mr. Adorno had to take turns squeezing the long handles, gradually cutting through the wound steel fibers a few at a time. When the cable finally parted, they exchanged high fives and then the old man cleared it away while Anne went back to his boat for a crowbar.

"Never thought I'd need this," he said, working the end of the crowbar under the latch. With a pop, he broke it open and then threw back the lid.

Neither of them said anything for several minutes.

"Who the hell would leave something like this here?" he said finally, picking up one of the ziplock bags full of bundled cash.

"There's a lot here." She dug down and tried to count the bags. They were stacked three deep. "There must be fifty bags."

He had opened the first one and was riffling through the bills. "Tens and twenties," he said. "Comes to . . . a thousand bucks, I think."

Anne had opened another bag. "So is this one. That means fifty thousand dollars! Maybe more!"

"Must be real pirates," he said. "Drug smugglers or some kind of crooks."

"I wonder how long it's been here."

"Could be years. That lock's pretty rusty. Maybe somebody dumped it when they saw the Coast Guard coming, or maybe somebody was supposed to find it but didn't."

"Look at this!" Underneath the bags of cash was a bag containing a fancy-looking automatic pistol. It was chrome-plated with gold crosses set on the handle.

"Can't believe anybody'd just leave something like that," he said. "Maybe they wound up in jail before they could come back for it. Maybe dead."

"What are you going to do with it all? Can you keep it?"

Mr. Adorno looked around. Aside from the boats on the

water, they were alone. "You're supposed to report stuff like this. The government takes it. I heard about a guy in Florida who found Spanish gold—they grabbed it all."

Anne didn't say anything.

"This—this is cash money," he said. "Don't have to sell it or anything. You could just walk into a store and spend it. Who's going to know?"

"You don't want to break the law," she said, not very emphatically.

"Why not? Why the hell not? Why should I give it to the government? They didn't bury it, they didn't dig it up. Spent my whole damned life paying taxes to the government. Call the St. Bernard Parish police, and you know some deputy's going to stuff it all in his pocket. No," he said. "This is my treasure. *Our* treasure."

"Be careful," she said. "If you spend too much at once, somebody might notice."

He got to his feet again. "Where are you heading, Anne?"

"Me? Bay St. Louis, I guess."

"If you don't mind going slow, I'll join you," he said with the air of one who has made a decision. "I'm going to take you out to dinner. The fanciest dinner we can find."

"All I've got is clothes to wear on my boat," she told him.

"Then we'll go shopping," he said. "My treat."

. . .

Bay St. Louis reminded Anne very strongly of reservation resort towns in Oklahoma—the same slightly cheesy casinos and gambling boats, the restaurants heavily promoting early-bird specials for retirees, the billboards for musical acts that were past their prime before she was born. The only difference was the Gulf of Mexico.

Mr. Adorno paid the fee for both their boats at the marina in the shadow of the Hollywood Casino. They were both starving after the two-hour voyage from Isle au Pitre, so her first meal in Mississippi was a burger at the theme diner on the casino floor. But then Mr. Adorno called for a cab, and the two of them went off to the mall for some shopping.

"Are you sure this is a good idea?" she asked him again as he paid the cabdriver. "Shouldn't you save some?"

"I'm saving plenty," he said. "I've opened only one bag so far. Maybe I'll get into a second. Don't worry about me. I'm an old penny-pincher from way back." He handed her a roll of twenties. "Buy yourself something nice. I'll meet you back here in an hour and we'll go out to dinner."

As soon as he was out of sight, she divided the roll in half. Even if Mr. Adorno managed to run through the entire trove in the next few hours, there was still enough cash here to put him on a bus back to Chalmette.

With the remaining half she went to Target and looked for something cheap but nice. She found a simple knee-length hot-pink skirt, a pair of sensible sandals, and blew the rest of the money on a lovely silk blouse.

Mr. Adorno was waiting at the mall entrance, dressed very sharp in a new seersucker suit, saddle oxfords, and a straw hat. He looked a little disappointed when he saw her. "You didn't get anything?"

"I did," she said, holding up the bags. "But I want a shower before I change clothes. Could we maybe find a truck stop or—?"

"Forget about that," he said. "I already called the hotel. We've got us a suite!"

An hour later, Anne stepped out of the shower and surveyed the bathroom. There was a shower, a separate soaking tub (with Jacuzzi jets), two sinks, and a whole closet full of towels as thick as sleeping bags. She dried off, wrapped herself in one of the massive complimentary bathrobes, and padded off to her room. The whole suite was about as big as the apartment in Stillwater she shared with three other women.

Finally, with dry hair and her new clothes, Anne presented herself in the sitting room. "I'm ready."

"Great. I got us a reservation for dinner at the steak place downstairs in half an hour. We can go down and have some drinks. You can play the slots if you want."

"No, I don't gamble. What about you?"

"Never did like slot machines. Always liked pinball better. And cards—you can forget that. My uncle used to play poker, made more than he lost, and he said if you're doing it right, it's the dullest thing in the world. Like I said, I'm a penny-pincher."

Like everyone she'd encountered south of Vicksburg, Mr. Adorno fancied himself an expert on food and drink. He insisted on ordering for her, and Anne had to admit he chose well. The meal was huge—steak, pasta with crawfish, tiny peas, and profiteroles for dessert. The wineglasses were oversized, and they went through a bottle of champagne and a bottle of Malbec during the three-hour meal.

Both of them were staggering a little by the time they went upstairs. Ever the gentleman, Mr. Adorno waited until the door of the suite closed behind them before he tried to grab Anne's ass.

"No," she said, and pushed him away. For a moment, the two of them stood about a yard apart, uncertain what to do next.

"Hey, sorry about that," he began. He looked sad and desperate and a little frightened. "I thought maybe—"

"No," she said again. "You're very sweet, but it's just impossible."

His face fell when she said that. Then he got an odd, almost wild look in his eyes. "You can have the money," he said.

"What?"

"You can have all of it. There's still more than forty-five thousand. You can take it all if you stay with me tonight."

"I said no." Anne hurried to her room, grabbed her boat clothes and stuffed them into the Target bag, and came out again.

Mr. Adorno was slumped in one of the armchairs in the big sitting room, crying silently.

"I have to go," she said. "Thank you for a wonderful time."

. . .

Prospère Malouin lived over in Plase Nepre, in the western part of Île de la Tortue—the half that wasn't owned and operated by Tortuga Pirate World™. David and Tifane signed out an electric car on his room tab and drove along the north coast road.

The resort complex filled the easternmost quarter of the island with half a dozen hotels, entertainment centers, and condominium developments. They ranged from the very family-friendly Tortuga Bay resort, through the more grown-up-oriented Port Royal Harbor, to the no-kidding adults-only Voodoo Cove. Tortuga Pirate World™ boasted rides for the kids, casinos, duty-free shopping, beaches, gambling, diving, riding stables, gambling, a marina, dozens of bars, gambling, a nude beach, and top-quality restaurants. And gambling.

The whole place was owned and run by a Macao syndicate, which had waved boatloads of cash in front of the Haitian government in exchange for what amounted to sovereignty over half the island of Île de la Tortue. They brought in shiploads of white sand, dug lakes and an entire river, and blasted a boat harbor out of rock. In a country as poor as Haiti, even the bottom-level cleaning and landscaping jobs were good money, and the company reserved a bloc of well-paying management jobs for Haitians. To no one's surprise, those all wound up being filled by relatives of Haitian political bosses, and the company very nicely didn't ask them to show up and do anything.

Part of the deal involved transforming half the Pirate World tract into a nature preserve, painstakingly restoring the pre-Columbian ecosystem of the island. It shut up any

well-meaning Yankees who might otherwise have objected
to kicking all the Haitians out of half the island to make
room for Asians and white people. Ten years into the project, the trees were getting to be good-sized and rainfall was
up by almost 10 percent.

The contrast at the boundary was startling. The Tortuga Jungle Adventure preserve was deep green and smelled
of flowers and damp earth. Crossing back into the real world
of Île de la Tortue plunged David and Tifane into harsh
late-afternoon sunlight and dust. There wasn't a tree taller
than David between the preserve boundary and the western tip of the island. The boundary fence was six meters
high, topped with razor wire and patrolled like a prison
wall.

They motored along the smooth blacktop road—paving
the whole island was another service provided by the Pirate World management—through the straggle of slapped-
together housing where all the service employees lived. A
posse of skinny brown kids ran alongside and David tossed
them a handful of Tortuga Doubloons. After a couple of
kilometers they turned inland.

The young man sitting on the porch of the Malouin
house with a machete in his lap glanced at David, spent
more time looking at Tifane, who had wrapped a transpar-
ent sarong around her hips for the outing, then went back
to watching the road.

On the outside, Prospère's place looked like a large but
not particularly fancy farmhouse, built of cinder blocks just
like all the newer structures on the west side of the island.
Inside—David privately thought it looked like the place

living room sets went after they died, if they were bad. There were about two furniture stores' worth of couches and armchairs crammed into the place. Prospère's *maman* kept all the furniture covered with plastic sheets to protect the shiny print upholstery from spilled cane liquor, marijuana ash, and food drips. Unfortunately, that was where her housekeeping stopped, so it was prudent to wipe the seat before you sat down at Prospère's.

As the day started to cool off, the house was filling up. American and Cuban pop music blared from old stereos, and the TV wall showed a Nigerian horror movie. About forty people were sitting on the horrible sofas. David recognized some of them—time-share-owning hipsters here to buy coke and weed so they could show off their "connections" at the nightclubs later on. They sat tensely and laughed a little too much. The rest of Prospère's guests were locals and relatives, and they were all working hard at being cool and dignified.

Prospère didn't give a damn. He was sprawled on the biggest, ugliest sofa in the house, right by the door to the kitchen, with a couple of girls beside him and a shirtless boy with a pistol jammed in the waist of his cutoff jeans standing nearby. Prospère was no larger than David, physically, but he *seemed* big. He took up a lot of room. The scars on his muscled chest and arms were real.

"Daveed!" he hollered over the dueling stereo systems, and waved them over. "Good to see you, man. Sit down here. What do you have?"

"Nothing for me. Tiff?"

For a second he was afraid she was going to come out

and ask for cocaine, but she kept it cool. "Beer," she said, and accepted a plastic cup full of foam.

David waited patiently while Prospère had a brief conversation with one of his nephews, which concluded with Prospère handing the boy a wad of hundreds. "Kids," he said at last, as if it explained something. "So, you don't visit now much, Daveed. I think that you want something."

"No, not really. I just wanted to talk with you about some stuff."

"Stuff?"

"Business."

Prospère shook his head and laughed. "I don't understand all that shit from Wall Street," he said. "It's too crooked for me." He repeated it louder in Creole, and the girls laughed along.

When David had settled in Tortuga, he got in touch with Prospère because the man had excellent connections in the local government and the resort security branch. David wasn't stupid enough to let anyone know he was the notorious Captain Black, but he did have to explain why he did all his business in cash and needed it kept secret. So he'd told Prospère his money came from embezzling in a New York brokerage house, and tried to keep their relationship strictly professional.

He leaned closer to Prospère, wishing the room weren't so noisy. "I just need to know if anyone's been looking for me. Cops, anybody like that. Have you heard anything?"

"No. You want that I ask?"

"Would you mind doing that for me?"

"Of course, of course! You're my *friend*, Daveed. Prospère Malouin cares for his friends."

"Thanks. I owe you one," said David. Up till now, he'd been very careful about getting too close to Prospère, but his encounter with Ghavami that afternoon had spooked him. He might need a friend with plenty of well-armed nephews.

And if Ghavami's offer was for real . . . then he could promise Prospère ten billion francs and a blow job every morning, because he'd never set foot in Haiti again once the mission was done.

The next couple of hours passed about as David had expected. He waited for Tifane to get properly wasted, then asked Prospère to keep an eye on her until he got back.

He drove the little electric through the deepening twilight down to Trou Basseux on the seashore and got the hourly water taxi to Port-de-Paix over on the main island. As the center of Haiti's new resort industry, Port-de-Paix was growing by a couple of hundred people a day. The rich white people lived in tall concrete buildings along the seashore, while the poor dark people lived in shorter concrete buildings in the hills. From time to time one of the buildings in the hills collapsed in a heap of substandard concrete, insufficient rebar, and dead dark people.

Stores in Port-de-Paix stayed open late; most people with money to spend were working or playing during the day. David found an electronics shop and bought a cheap pad, then took a table in a café in the Old Town with free wireless. With his pristine computer and anonymous public connection, he established some perfectly virgin addresses and accounts.

Then he went to work. One of the first things he always did at a new hotel was to find out the admin passwords for the computer system, so getting into the database back at Tortuga Pirate World™ was quick and easy. He quickly located Ghavami, who was staying in one of the luxury bungalows at Voodoo Cove; he'd checked in under the name of Ali Amiri, which was about as useful as if he'd called himself Bob Jones. The fact that Ghavami hadn't even bothered to give David his cover name suggested there wasn't any point in tracing that any further.

Follow the money. David traced the credit card Ghavami had used to check in. That was a little harder. The card number got him as far as Zaman-Bank in Kazakhstan, at which point the security got very tough and all the text was in Cyrillic. His translation software started giving him things like THE SKY BANK ? THE ARCS WITH MORE ENORMOUSLY THE CONSTANT SECURITY DECLARATION IS THE COMPLETE ECONOMIC SERVICE, so he gave up on that.

The phone number Ghavami had given David was from Somali Telecom, which made him raise his eyebrows. However, a little more digging revealed that the company was based in Dubai, so that didn't tell him much either.

David got himself another espresso and wished for some Thai iced coffee. Nothing he'd found contradicted what the man had told him. If Ghavami really was planning a helium-capture operation, and really was some kind of black-ops dude, it was all consistent. If he was an American or Indian cop, his cover was shockingly good. The phone was especially convincing. A cop would just have bought a disposable phone in Miami or wherever.

He tossed back the coffee like a shot of whiskey. Did he really want to do this? Just asking himself the question gave him the answer. Of course he did. He could feel himself getting excited at the thought of running another pirate mission.

Ghavami answered on the second ring. "Okay, Mr. Ghavami, I'm in," said Captain Black the Space Pirate.

. . .

MESSING ABOUT IN MY BOAT

March 19, 2031

Location: 30° 20′ 8″ N by 89° 21′ 16″ W (Bay St. Louis, Mississippi)

Change of plan! The cruise of *Carina* continues!

I woke up this morning and found some extra money in the donation account. I won't say how much, but it's all I needed. I can keep going, to the Florida Keys at least. I've got fuel, I've got food, the toilet tank is empty, and I'm ready to brave the high seas!

To my anonymous donor: I know who you are, and thank you very much. You're one of the sweetest people I've ever met, and I enjoyed our time together.

To everyone else: From now on, I'm going to go out and look for adventure instead of waiting for it to find me.

I'm leaving Bay St. Louis tomorrow morning, and my next update should be from Pensacola!

. . .

JANUARY 6, 2031; 20:10 GMT

As soon as the plane from Havana to Madrid reached cruising altitude, David pulled out his pad and got to work. Ghavami had given him a very broad outline of the mission, and he was brainstorming ways to accomplish it. The flight would give him six hours of uninterrupted thinking time.

"Don't get predictable" was his mantra. The first time he stole a helium payload, it had been straight hacking—he interrupted the uplink and diverted it to the pirate drop zone. That had netted him only a couple hundred thousand, but as proof of concept, it was priceless.

The second time was his first venture into space, with a probe that matched velocities with the falling helium payload, clamped on, and diverted it by brute force. His most recent capture had been a combination of the previous methods—hard docking and then waging electronic warfare with the onboard control systems. The next one would have to be different.

The corporate and government people were good at patching security holes after the fact. None of his previous methods would work anymore; that was the way to bet, anyway. Ghavami had insisted that this hijacking had to work perfectly the first time, so now David was working out how to do that. He got the hot Spanish stewardess to bring him a freshly made iced espresso with condensed milk and a chocolate croissant, and wondered if it would be worth his time to make a play for her phone number.

No. No way to follow up on it. His budget was simply "a lot." No way to tell if Ghavami really meant that or would start pinching pennies when David presented his ideas. So as he worked, he noted lower-cost alternatives whenever he thought of them.

If money was abundant, time was scarce. The launch date was already set: It had to go up before August 23, in order to catch the Lunar payload launch on the twenty-sixth. Seven months from design to launch. The booster was already paid for. That meant he had to fit a very specific mass limit and use off-the-shelf tech—but of course, he'd never been able to afford anything else, so that wasn't a problem. He was good at bargain-basement engineering and just-in-fucking-time production.

Mass was decent. The booster was a knockoff of a knock-off of a Russian Soyuz, descended through a couple of bastard links from the mighty pencil of Sergei Korolev himself. It would throw a ton to Lunar orbit, enough for a pretty good vehicle. Still—keep it small. Any spare mass could always go for more maneuvering fuel.

There was one final design constraint that David wouldn't mention when he made his pitch to Ghavami. The new mission had to be *awesome*. It had to be unexpected and clever and ballsy and elegant and remind everyone how Captain Black the Space Pirate was the baddest ass in outer space.

5

Elizabeth Santiago shivered in the subarctic air-conditioning of the Icarus office. Even in what passed for winter in Florida, the place was like a pen for polar bears. The technicians in their cleansuits appreciated the cool air, Mike Levy had a fat man's loathing for heat, and Yumiko seemed utterly impervious to temperature.

Jack Bonnet had the most entertaining reaction. "Think of it as an inverse sauna," he told her. "Stay outside until you're too hot, then dash inside wearing nothing but a hat and sandals. This being *Central* Florida, I'm afraid I can't recommend switching yourself with birch twigs. People might get the wrong idea. Down in Key West, it's pretty much routine."

"You go first," she said.

"Okay—oh, darn. I left my hat and sandals back in Houston."

She put aside the thought of Jack running around the parking lot bare-assed and tried to focus on her work. The original mission plan had been pretty simple: just some maneuvering in low orbit and then boosting into a free-return trajectory that would take SOTHIS around the Moon and back to Earth. And then the whole thing would drop neatly into the South Pacific to avoid cluttering up orbital space. But Elizabeth had a better idea.

Mike Levy was at his desk when she knocked on the door. As always, he was dressed to the nines with his tie neatly knotted. "Hey, come on in!"

"Are you busy right now?"

"Nothing too big. The Brazilians are asking for bids on an optical telescope in orbit—and since it's their Air Force that's suddenly all hot to do space astronomy, it's a pretty safe bet it's really a spy sat. I thought I'd put our name in the hat. The SOTHIS wings are really telescope mirrors anyway."

Elizabeth was curious despite herself. "Can you really get an image with the wings? They're just silver film and cables."

"See that?" Mike pointed at a print on the wall. It was slightly blurry, but the orange and green disk was obviously Mars. "Jack and I set up the portside wing out in the parking lot one night, put my phone at the focus, and took that picture. Blame the air for the blurring. We have to deliberately de-focus to keep from burning holes in Yumi's motor."

"That's pretty amazing." She forced herself back to her original train of thought, then sat down. "Mike, I've been wondering about the mission plan. Is there any reason to do the maneuver experiments in low orbit?"

"Well, there's the propellant issue. Burn off some mass

before we shoot for the Moon. Keeps the launch weight down. But if you've got a better idea, let's hear it!"

Elizabeth's mouth was suddenly dry. She had absolutely no authorization for what she was about to do. "You know I was working on the MARIO project before they sent me down here, right?"

"Everyone says you did a damn fine job, too."

"Thanks. When we put together the MARIO vehicle, the mission was power projection. ORBITCOM wants to protect American and allied assets in cislunar space."

"That's no secret."

"This is off the record now: I happen to know that the Air Force is looking for a lower-cost replacement for the MARIO vehicle. Losing number 5 cost way too much. Ion drives are expensive hardware."

"While SOTHIS is cheap. Got it. Go on, I'm listening."

"So . . . why not show that SOTHIS can do what the Air Force needs? Fly it up to L_1, do some station-keeping, maybe practice approach on some objects there."

Mike tapped his own pad and raised his eyebrows. "Delta-v's nearly the same either way, so we have to carry the propellant as payload. . . . It cuts into our maneuvering test propellant by about a third, but I designed in a ten percent margin on the launch weight, so that's doable, barely."

"What do you think?"

"I don't know, Liz. There won't be much left to play with when we get up to L_1. I make it about half a klick of delta-v left, and we'll need some of that to deorbit her."

"You can do aerobraking, right?"

"Oh, yes. The wings are great for that. Just get her back into low orbit, and they'll bring her down." He frowned at the numbers on his pad, then looked up at her. "Air Force is really interested in this?"

"It's not official, of course." She didn't add that the Air Force's interest in a replacement vehicle wasn't just nonofficial; it was nonexistent, as far as she knew. If the Air Force really *were* developing a new vehicle, Liz wouldn't be trying to repurpose Mike's bird. Everything she had just told Mike was a lie.

He smacked his palm down on the desk, making her jump. "I'm sick of pissing around in low orbit like everyone's been doing since Sputnik! Okay, Liz, you've sold me. I can squeeze another quarter-mil out of the investors. That ought to be enough to launch the extra propellant. Can you draw up a list of test maneuvers that'll look good for the Air Force?"

"I'd be delighted," she said. Her conscience didn't bother her at all.

That evening Jack caught up with her in the parking lot as the sun went down in the hazy Florida sky. "Are you busy?"

"Not really."

"Buy you dinner?"

"I don't know—that sounds like a conflict of interest, Mr. Bonnet." She said it with such a straight face that for a second he looked disappointed. "But I won't tell if you won't."

He got it then, and tried to play along. "We'd better go someplace where we can't be recognized. Do you like crabs?"

They wound up at a crab shack down in Palm Bay. The place was an old house with a windowless concrete annex, all painted bright blue. They got a dozen boiled crabs and sat on the porch. Jack showed Elizabeth how to crack open the crabs and pick out the meat. Not the most efficient meal, but with a couple of cold beers, it was very relaxing.

Once his first couple of crabs were reduced to fragments of chitin, Jack sipped his iced tea before asking, "So—why the new mission profile?"

"I want to do a good job. The Air Force wants to project power out to Lunar space. The old plan didn't really demonstrate that capability. A ballistic free return doesn't let you *do* much while you're up there."

He took another crab from the platter and pried off a claw. "True enough, but that's asking a lot from a proof-of-concept vehicle. I mean, I'm sure the SOTHIS system will work fine, but it hasn't been tested in space yet. It could just sit there in orbit, dribbling hydrogen."

She shrugged and busied herself with a crab leg.

"What kind of approach maneuvers do you want to try at L_1?"

"Nothing fancy. Pick a target and try to maneuver close to it, then move off. A standard rendezvous."

"Any targets in particular you want to check out?"

Did he know? He was smart and well informed. She decided on a diversion. "Well, there's one target I've noticed orbiting around for a few days now," she said.

He frowned, not getting it. "Which one?"

"Never mind, I just realized that what we were saying

sounded like some kind of innuendo. You know, approach and *rendezvous* with a *target*."

"Oh," he said, and then blushed. "Oh, gosh, I'm sorry if—"

"No, no. It's all right. I just have a weird sense of humor sometimes."

He busied himself with getting the meat out of another crab for a couple of minutes before speaking up again. "So what's the target you meant? A real object at L_1, or something else? I'm kind of confused now."

Now it was Elizabeth's turn to blush. "Well, you have invited me to dinner four times now. Plus lunch. That's what I meant by orbiting. Never mind—it was a dumb joke."

"Oh." He picked up a fourth crab but just held it. Then: "Are you free Friday night? I think we should have a real date."

"Sure! What do you want to do?"

"Some friends of mine are having a star party out on the cape. Amateur astronomy. We can see the wonders of the Universe, eat some barbecue. Are you interested?"

"That's not what most people would think of for a date."

He shrugged. "When I was younger, I tried to make a good impression on dates. I'd take girls out dancing, bribe the bouncers to get us into trendy clubs, follow all the rules on the pickup artist sites. And one day about five years ago, I realized something: I suck at dancing, I hate trendy clubs, and the women who fall for the standard pickup techniques are airheads. So now I do stuff I like to do anyway. If my date doesn't like it, then we're probably not compatible anyway."

"That's probably the least romantic way of asking a girl out I've ever heard. I would be delighted to go to the star party with you on Friday."

. . .

"I like it," said Colonel Ghavami.

Inside his head, David gave a whoop of triumph and relief. Outwardly, he just smiled confidently.

The colonel looked at the other two men sitting on his side of the conference table in a windowless room in Albania. David didn't know their names; neither had said a word during his presentation. The one on the right looked like he might be Ghavami's uncle or something—straight nose, dark hair, awesome black hobo/wizard beard. Turkish? Iranian? Something like that. He was older than the colonel, and sat in his chair with the perfect posture of an equestrian medalist. He hadn't looked at the screen display at all during David's talk, but David had felt his dark eyes burning a hole in his skull the whole time. They didn't shift by so much as a degree as he nodded.

Ghavami turned to the other man. He was small and plump, unmistakably Southeast Asian—maybe Thai or Malay. He'd been full of questions, interrupting and taking lots of notes as David spoke.

"This could work!" he said, sounding almost surprised. "It is very clever. I like it."

"Do you agree with his cost estimates?" asked the colonel.

The plump man grinned and shrugged. "Everything always costs more. I think maybe twice what he said."

David winced inside but didn't argue. He'd been low-balling the cost all the way through; he knew that and they knew that. But his numbers weren't complete bullshit, just optimistic.

"Note that it will take them some time come up with good countermeasures," David pointed out. "We can probably use this method a couple of times, so the cost gets spread out some."

The plump man shrugged again. "Maybe yes, maybe no. They have smart men, too. But this is good. I say go ahead."

The colonel smiled then. "Congratulations, Captain Black," he said. "I think we will begin right away." He gestured at the big guy standing by the door with a gun stuck in his waistband. The big guy opened the door, and an old man in a waiter's uniform came in with a carafe and sixteen little glasses of crushed ice on a tray, followed by a younger waiter with a platter of hors d'oeuvres. The old waiter filled four glasses with something that turned milky and handed them out; then Ghavami lifted his glass in a little toast. "To our mission!"

The stuff in the glass was strong and tasted like licorice. The old waiter filled new glasses and snatched away the empties. When everyone was in a jolly mood, Ghavami leaned over to David. "There is someone I want you to meet."

A gangly blond kid with a ponytail and weird glasses came in and shook hands all around. "Captain Black, this is Halfdan," said Ghavami. "He will be your assistant on this project."

Now that he was close enough, David could see that Halfdan's glasses were an elaborate custom set of data spex, anchored to a stud in the bridge of his nose. "Halfdan honors you," said Halfdan before David could get a word in. "You are a fucking hero. A warrior! Halfdan has explained in many comments on your site how—"

"None of those sites are really mine," said David. "I don't read them."

"Oh," said Halfdan, and looked almost hurt. "Well— Halfdan thinks you are a hero to a lot of people. Fighting against the corporate kraken, taking the wealth of the sky for yourself. You have reclaimed the role of the reaver for the modern man, showing how we can break our shackles. You are a fucking inspiration!"

"It's really nice of you to say that. Here, have some of this stuff. The meatballs are great. I need to talk with the colonel for a sec." He practically pushed Halfdan toward the food tray and then put his arm around Ghavami's shoulders and drew him away from the others. "Who the fuck is that? I don't need some fanboy drooling on my shoulder the whole time."

"He is very good," said Ghavami. "He has a doctorate in physics and was employed by the European Space Agency for a time. They fired him for political reasons. I think he will be a great help to you."

"I don't need any *help*," said David. "I've stolen more payloads than anybody else, all on my own. I *invented* this, remember? I certainly don't need Halfass the Barbarian for anything."

"This mission is too important to depend on one

man," said Ghavami. "What if the American police find you?"

"The feds aren't even looking for me. They're looking for half a dozen crazy fanboys like Halfwit there who pretend to be me online."

"You could choke on an olive or fall down the stairs. He is your backup. You need a backup."

David glanced over his shoulder at Halfdan, who was stuffing his face with hummus. "Shit. All right, how about this: I'll let Halfdick hang around while we get the mission ready, but when I'm actually running this thing, he gets to shut the fuck up and sit in the corner."

"Of course. He is your subordinate and should respect you."

"Right. Hey, Halfdan! You're on the crew."

"Halfdan is honored," said Halfdan. "Halfdan will fight at your side, like true Nordic shield-brothers."

"*Oy gevalt,*" David Schwartz muttered to himself.

. . .

MARCH 21, 2031

For once Elizabeth and Jack left the Icarus Propulsion workshop promptly at 5 P.M. on Friday. "Have fun, you two!" Mike Levy bellowed as they went out the door, which made Elizabeth blush.

In Jack's pickup truck, he handed her a stick of insect repellent. "Put this on. We're going to be next to Mosquito Lagoon on a summer night. The bugs will pick you up and carry you away if you don't have lots of deet."

They drove easily through the desultory rush hour traffic in Titusville to the NASA Causeway, and crossed the lagoon to the cape. The roads inside the Space Center perimeter were huge, like highways for a city the size of Orlando, but there were weeds as tall as Jack growing in the cracks in the shoulder pavement, and once they had to swerve around an alligator sunning itself in the right lane. The Vehicle Assembly Building loomed up on their right, and Elizabeth could see the gaps where hurricane winds had blown out parts of the building's skin. They did not pass a single car. It felt to Elizabeth as if they were driving through the remains of a lost civilization.

They turned off the titan boulevard onto a smaller blacktop road that turned into another causeway, and then suddenly there was nothing but beach and ocean in front of them. Jack followed the road north until it was just a strip of pavement with beach on one side and lagoon on the other. He parked by a clutch of other cars and trucks in one of the old launch viewing area lots. There were more big weeds growing in the cracked concrete. To the south, the towers of the old Saturn and Shuttle launch gantries were rusty against the blue sky.

They walked through the scrub grass and ground-hugging live oaks to the beach. The breeze carried a scent of mesquite wood and beef, and just at the high-tide line, half a dozen people were setting up telescopes and tending a couple of portable barbecues.

Jack made introductions. "Hey, Mel—I want you to meet Elizabeth Santiago. She's the Air Force liaison at Icarus. Elizabeth, this is Mel Koenig."

Koenig was a short man with a long gray beard and only three fingers on his right hand. "Hey! There's beer in the cooler and we're cooking ribs and chicken. So you're the young lady Jack's been talking about."

She glanced at Jack, who looked like he wanted to run away and hide. "Jack's been talking about me?"

"Can't shut up about you," said Koenig, chuckling evilly. "Actually, I think he mentioned you once, which is a lot for him. So you're in the Air Force—you fly fighters?"

"No. I fly satellites."

"Not much difference these days, is there? Sit in a control trailer somewhere. Hell, even the goddamned Army's all automated."

"It's safer," she said.

"Everything's too goddamned safe already," said Mel.

More cars and trucks pulled up as the sun went down. A married couple with twin ten-year-olds set up a launch stand and fired off half a dozen model rockets. That started many of the older guests reminiscing about their glory days at NASA, DARPA, or projects they couldn't talk about.

Elizabeth ate some beef ribs and corn on the cob, tasted some chili that tried to replace meat with pepper, and drank beer to keep from dying of heat exhaustion.

The sky began to turn purple after eight, and the party broke up into about a dozen little knots of three or four, each gathered around someone's telescope. The scopes ranged from a basic department store Meade refractor through increasingly expensive Celestrons and a couple of handmade Dobsonians to a 180-millimeter Takahashi with a high-sensitivity infrared camera. She stayed away from that one, because she could look at space on a screen anytime she wanted.

Saturn and Venus were close together above the setting Sun in the west, so naturally those were the first targets. Venus was a little crescent, but Saturn was a tiny white ringed disk. Elizabeth was always amazed that Saturn looked just like Saturn.

The smaller scopes stayed on planet-watching duty, but the owners of the big ones soon pointed them at nebulae and galaxies. The Pleiades and the Orion Nebula were right near the two planets, so everyone lined up to ooh and aah over them. Nobody looked at stars. Even through the biggest scopes, they still just looked like stars.

When her feet got tired, she sat in a lawn chair next to Mel Koenig, who wasn't interested in any of the telescopes. "I'm here for the beer and chili," he said. "Got my own observatory down in Kenansville. Three hundred acres of cow pasture with a dome I made out of an old silo top."

"What kind of telescope do you have?" she asked, more to be polite than anything else.

"A piece of history. A twenty-inch Super-Schmidt from the old ground-tracking network. Built to keep an eye on Russkie hardware in orbit. I got it from a surplus dealer who didn't know what he had. Took me five years to get it fixed up with a CCD instead of a camera plate. The mount's fully automated—I can sit at home and run the whole thing from my laptop. The resolving power is fantastic. I've got pictures of the Chinese base at Fra Mauro, they look like you're right there."

"That's pretty amazing. Are you an astronomer?"

"Not professionally. I used to be a lineman for Kentucky Utilities, till I retired. Always liked watching the sky, started buying telescopes. Told my wife it could be worse, I could be spending it on lap dances or model trains."

Jack stopped next to Elizabeth and put a hand on her shoulder. "Found any aliens yet?"

The two of them chuckled and Koenig leaned over to Elizabeth. "I've got my own SETI project, too. Remember those big old satellite dish antennas? I've got six of them synched up to make a synthetic-aperture antenna. Every night, they track Saturn as long as it's up. Jack here helped me with the motors."

"What are you listening for?"

"Well, a while back I got this crazy notion I wanted to try out. See, everyone else in SETI wants to listen for aliens in other star systems. But that takes a big antenna to do right. I started thinking, what if there's an alien presence right here in the Solar System? You know, like the monolith in *2001* or something? Or even just a Bracewell probe? You know what that is? Whatever, it would have to call home sometime, and that signal would be detectable. So I've been monitoring each of the planets for six months at a time, see if I get a peep."

"Any luck?"

"Not yet. But it's like fishing. If you're sitting out on your boat with a box of chicken and a six-pack, who the hell cares if you get a bite?"

Elizabeth and Jack settled into a kind of transfer orbit of their own. They'd spend some time out in the dark, looking through telescopes, then swing back to the dim red light by the barbecue for more beer and another helping of chips or homemade cookies. She had long since given up trying to count calories; to work off this binge, she'd have to ride her bike to Key West and back. Maybe twice.

The two of them were orbiting each other, too, and as the night went on, the distance decreased. In defiance of all physics, that also made them move more slowly. During the passages through the darkness, they spoke of random things. He described one summer he'd spent in Japan during college; she gave him her opinion on titanium versus carbon-fiber bike frames.

She could feel herself fading and checked her phone. Just past midnight. Mars was well up in the southwest, and Jupiter was just rising.

"Hey," she said. "I think I need to go to bed now."

"Okay. How about a look at Jupiter first?"

"One, but that's all."

He got the telescope aligned and stepped back so she could have a look. Even through a cheap telescope, Jupiter was impressive. She could make out colored bands and the Great Red Spot.

"When are you going up?" she heard someone ask.

"July," said Jack. "Right after the holiday."

Elizabeth finished her turn at the eyepiece and tapped him on the shoulder. "Let's go." On their way to his truck, she said, "You didn't tell me you're going to the Moon."

"Sorry. I have this phobia about saying anything that sounds like bragging. I'm doing a standard tour at the base. Commercial shuttle to low orbit, meet the Crew Transfer Vehicle there, and drop down to Babcock about a hundred hours later. Then I spend three months in the Moonbase fixing robots. It's not as exciting as it sounds."

"You'll be on the Moon, for God's sake! Of course it's exciting."

"Well, yeah, okay." He started up the truck and they bounced along in darkness until the dunes blocked the star party from stray headlight glare. They rode through the Space Center in silence, until the causeway back to Titusville. Then she heard Jack take a deep breath before speaking.

"Would you like to stop at my place?" he asked her. "It's a lot closer than driving all the way down to Icarus to get your car."

"That sounds like a good idea," she said. "Just to be clear, though: I'm not having sex with you tonight."

"Oh, I didn't—," he began.

"I want to wait until tomorrow and spend all day at it." She leaned over and kissed him on the cheek.

. . .

Sixteen hours later, Elizabeth stepped out of Jack's shower and wished she'd brought some clean clothes with her. The shower, like the rest of Jack's place, was impressively neat. The polished surfaces could be the work of an efficient hired maid service, but the uncluttered and perfectly organized closet and cabinets were definitely Jack's own doing. The easiest things to reach were the ones most often needed, and the things that weren't needed simply weren't there.

Among the many things that weren't in Jack's bathroom

were any traces of prior female visitors. Either Jack Bonnet was ruthless about getting rid of things left behind, or he was coming off a long dry spell. Or both.

She picked through the heap of clothes she'd left on the bedroom floor, feeling almost guilty about how untidy they looked. The pants could be used again. The underwear was all she had. But the shirt reeked of sweat and mosquito repellent.

"Do you have a T-shirt I can borrow?" she called out.

"Chest of drawers, third drawer down," he called back. "Then come get your eggs Benedict."

Nice guy, kept his place clean, strong arms, smart, good lover, and he could cook. Why was he sleeping alone?

She found the T-shirts and picked one bearing the slogan I WENT TO THE MOON AND ALL I GOT WAS THIS LOUSY T-SHIRT with the Consortium logo on the sleeve. She put it on. It reached almost to her knees, which made her consider leaving her jeans on the floor. The memory of a kitchen chair sticking to her bare legs made her pull on the jeans.

Just then her phone buzzed. The screen said MINUTEMAN ARMS.

"Shit," she muttered. It would be easy to ignore it. In fact, it would be very smart to ignore it. She tapped the screen. "Hello?"

"Hey, is this Ms. Santiago?"

"That's right."

"Sidney Tanaglia, Minuteman Arms. I've got the ammo you were looking for. Came in this morning."

"Great," she said. "I can't get over there today. Are you open tomorrow?"

"Closed Sundays. Sabbath is for church and fishing."

"Okay. I'll be there Monday, then."

From the kitchen she heard Jack call. "Coffee or tea?"

"Coffee!" she yelled back. To the phone, she said thanks and ended the call.

Jack's apartment didn't have a dining room, but the kitchen had space for a big table. He had set two places across from each other and was already halfway finished with his eggs.

"Coffee's on the stove. Were you talking to somebody?"

"My father," she said. "He calls me every weekend." To change the subject, she said "Shouldn't this be dinner?"

"We just woke up. That makes it breakfast. We can go out to dinner in an hour or so."

. . .

Anne was getting a little sick of trees. Ever since leaving Panama City, she'd been following the Gulf Intracoastal Waterway through mile after mile of forest. The occasional clear-cut patch was a welcome break from the endless pine trees.

There were plenty of animals about, though. She saw deer drinking from the canal, and once a bear with cubs. Otherwise, she had the waterway to herself for a good twenty miles.

She should have spent the night at Panama City, she decided. It was getting dark, and she didn't relish the thought of trying to navigate Lake Wimico and the Apalachicola River in the dark. For one thing, the mosquitoes would probably devour her, boat and all.

So when she got to the junction of the Intracoastal Waterway and the Gulf County Canal leading south to Port St. Joe, she decided to stop for the night. The Florida air turned clammy in the night, and even with every square inch of her body slathered in deet, the bugs still whined in her ears and threatened to fly into her nostrils.

Carina's cabin was (mostly) bug free, but even with the tiny screened windows open, it was as stuffy as sleeping inside a plastic bag. She sweated and tried to read, and eventually fell asleep.

When she woke again, the moon was shining through the window over her bunk, right into her face. Anne grumbled and tried to prop up her book to block the light, even though it meant giving up the faint breeze. The noise of frogs and crickets was almost deafening.

Just then she heard a sound from outside—a splash, followed by a gentle bump. By now she knew that feeling: something had nudged *Carina*. A manatee, maybe? Or an alligator? She grabbed her camera and went to see what it was.

When she opened the companionway that led up into the cockpit, Anne froze. A man was standing on the open rear deck of her boat. She could see him clearly in the moonlight—not much more than a teenager, shirtless despite the chilly night air. He gestured, and a second young man scrambled aboard, also shirtless, with tattoos on his torso dark against the moonlit skin.

Anne's heart started beating very fast. She had no idea what to do. When the first intruder turned on a flashlight, she reacted more by reflex than thought. "Hey!" She tried to keep her voice from shaking. "Get off my boat!"

The flashlight shone in her face, and she heard the intruder take a step forward. "Hey, it's cool. You got a phone?"

"I'm calling 911 right now if you don't get off my boat!"

"Come on, Bobby," the second boarder whispered.

"We got lost," said the one with the flashlight, presumably Bobby. "I just want to call my mom. That's all. Help us out?" He took another step closer.

Panic welled up in Anne. She ducked back into the cabin and slammed the door—only Bobby had moved at the same moment she had, and was pushing the other way. He was bigger and could put his weight against it.

She got her leg braced against the toilet and her back against the door and pushed back with her whole body. The door started to close, but something was blocking it. She pushed harder and heard a loud yell from the cockpit. He wasn't pushing anymore; he was kicking and shouting.

Anne glanced over her shoulder and saw what was blocking the door: his arm, still holding the flashlight. Her hands were both braced against the cabin ceiling, but she could lean over far enough to get her face against the arm.

When she bit him, the shout turned to a scream and he dropped the flashlight. She relaxed for a second, then slammed herself back against the door with all her strength. This time his arm wasn't in the way and she heard the latch click. She turned the dead bolt and then caught her breath.

"I called the cops!" she yelled. "They're coming right now!"

The intruders gave the cabin door a couple of hard kicks, and then she heard more thumps and the sound of glass breaking, and finally silence.

She had a gun in a lockbox under her bed. It had belonged to her father, and she'd never gotten around to selling it. There was no ammunition in it, and right now she really really wished there were. She opened the box and checked, but the cylinder of the revolver was empty and there were no rounds in the box.

Anne waited until the sky was turning light outside before she unlocked the door. Shards of the smashed windscreen covered the deck, and her GPS unit was gone, but otherwise, *Carina* looked intact. When she turned the key in the ignition, the engine started right up.

. . .

Special Agent Dominic Yu held his service pistol in the approved grip with the muzzle pointing at the ground. He nodded, and two of the SWAT officers he'd borrowed from the Minnesota State Police charged forward with the battering ram.

The door of the mobile home smashed inward. Yu and the Stearns County deputy sheriff rushed inside. "Police! Nobody move!" the deputy shouted.

"Mama's not here!" came a childish shout, and a boy of about twelve came into the living room. "She's at work."

"Is there anyone else in the house?" Yu asked the boy.

Meanwhile, the deputy and the SWAT officers began searching the rooms.

"Nope," said the boy. The presence of half a dozen men with pistols and M4 carbines in his home seemed to be only mildly interesting to him.

Yu holstered his weapon. The boy was tall enough that Dominic didn't have to kneel down to talk with him. "Was there anyone here just now? Just before we came in?"

"Nope. Mama's at work."

"Why aren't you at school?"

The boy shrugged. "I got suspended."

A vague horror was growing inside Dominic Yu. "What's your name?"

"Mark Hauptman."

"Mark, I'm looking for Captain Black the Space Pirate."

That got a reaction. The kid's eyes got an oh-shit look in them. "I'm not him! I just post stuff on the forums!"

The SWAT officers began drifting back into the room, shaking their heads. "House is clear," said the deputy sheriff.

The horror was nearly overwhelming now. I have just royally screwed up, Yu thought. He tried desperately to salvage the situation. "Mark, the posts coming from this address show an unusual knowledge of space piracy operations. Is there anyone else who has access to the computer here? An adult? Maybe a friend of your mother's?"

"No, it's mine!" said the boy, a little scornful. "I have to tell Mama how to open her mail every time. I just know a lot about Captain Black. I read all the sites. At school they put me on suspension because I was reading about space mining when we were supposed to be doing group crafts and shit like that."

"Christ, isn't there even some meth or something in here?" asked the deputy.

"Mama doesn't keep anything in the house anymore," said Mark.

Dominic could feel the eyes of the local cops on him. The big fancy FBI agent chasing space pirates, and he screwed it up. Before the raid, he'd spent fifteen minutes briefing them on the importance of recovering any computers and data storage devices, but the only thing in the house was a very old and obsolete laptop. They'd be snickering about this for years to come.

"Do you have any friends who borrow your computer sometimes? Or who come over and use your connection?"

"I don't have any friends," said the kid, matter-of-factly.

"Okay, Mark, we're sorry to disturb you like this. Here's my card, tell your mother the Bureau will pay for the damage to your front door."

No space pirate at this address. Not yet, anyway. Dominic wondered if he'd be busting Mark Hauptman for real in another decade or so. He kept calm through the extremely sarcastic after-action debriefing, he turned down the offer of a beer from the sympathetic SWAT captain, and after sunset he put on his sweats and running shoes and ran and ran until the embarrassment and humiliation turned to sheer exhaustion.

. . .

APRIL 7, 2031; 15:12 GMT

Elizabeth was waiting in the parking lot when the gun shop opened. Minuteman Arms was a metal building in Brandon, just east of Tampa on the highway to Orlando. A repurposed fiberglass Midas Muffler giant stood in front of the store wearing a sheet-metal tricorne and rather awkwardly holding a pair of pistols made from PVC pipe. Elizabeth picked it because she had never been to that part of Florida before and didn't want to be recognized.

Sidney Tanaglia was already there, but didn't unlock the door until ten precisely. Elizabeth had never met him in person before, but it was easy to recognize him. There weren't very many firearms dealers in Florida with achondroplasia. As soon as the dwarf opened for business, Elizabeth hurried in. She stood by the checkout counter while Tanaglia made a final circuit of the store, turning on lights, checking the locks on cabinets, and picking up bits of trash. He had a revolver in a shoulder holster over his MINUTEMAN ARMS T-shirt.

"Morning," Tanaglia said at last, hauling himself up into a captain's chair behind the counter.

"Good morning. I got a message Saturday that my special order had come in. The name is Santiago."

"Oh, yeah. It's here." He dropped to the floor again and unlocked a big safe. He took out a bulging padded mailer, closed the safe again, and got back into his chair before opening the mailer.

"Here you go. Fifty rounds of eleven-millimeter Gyro-Jet ammo. This stuff's hard to find. All handloads. No guarantees."

"And it's legal?"

"Under fifty caliber it is. ATF calls it a 'curiosity.' Fifty or bigger's a 'destructive device.' I don't sell stuff they don't like. These'll still fuck you up, though. Guy who makes them says they've got as much power as a forty-five at seventy yards."

She opened the box. The rounds were shiny brass, obviously hand-turned on a metal lathe. "Electrical ignition?"

"Yep. He also makes a centerfire version, but you said—"

"No, this is perfect."

"Now comes the part you aren't going to like," said Tanaglia. "With tax, that box of fifty comes to thirteen hundred bucks."

"That's twenty-five dollars a shot!" She wasn't actually surprised, but she didn't want Tanaglia to know how much research she had done.

"If some guy had to hand-turn and handload every round, all ammo would cost that much. You want cheap ammo, get a smoothbore. Mix your own black powder and cast your own shot in the kitchen."

"Can you give me a cash discount?" she asked innocently, pulling the thick bank envelope out of her back pocket. It held nearly her entire last paycheck after rent and taxes, with no bills bigger than a twenty.

He squinted at her, and Elizabeth realized that a gun dealer probably had to deal with people trying to be cunning and sleazy all the time. Her earnest efforts weren't fooling anyone. "Why not?" he said with a shrug. "Twelve hundred cash."

She counted out a stack of tens and twenties and waited

patiently while he checked each one. There were a couple of forms to fill out, and then he handed her the ammo in a red-white-and-blue MINUTEMAN ARMS bag.

"Mind if I ask you a question? I'm kind of a nosy SOB," said Tanaglia.

"You can ask," she said.

"You got a launcher for that ammo? They're pretty rare nowadays."

"Not a problem. I'm going to build my own."

6

Captain Black the Space Pirate saw the little nod out of the corner of his eye and tried to keep his temper.

The little nod was given by Vladimir Draganovic, a Serbian exactly David's height and exactly twice his weight. Draganovic didn't have a gram of fat on him, and the only hair that wasn't trimmed precisely to five millimeters was his elaborate mustache. The 'stache wouldn't have been out of place on a Civil War general, and Draganovic kept his carefully waxed and curled.

Draganovic gave the little nod every time David gave an instruction to one of the technicians building his pirate spaceship. The techs were a mix of Pakis, Chinese, and Kazakhs, with a sprinkling of assorted whiteboys like David. They worked in a big sheet-metal oven of a building outside Gwadar in southwest Pakistan.

What was really starting to bug David about Draganovic's little nod was the fact that the technicians said "Okay" or "Yessir" or "Right away" to one of David's instructions only *after* they saw the little nod.

He'd be talking to Hamid or Phuong or even Erwin, explaining something, and they'd be nodding, or making understanding grunts, or whatever, and everything would be just fine. Meeting of minds across cultures.

But then David would say something like "I think we need to cut some more mass off the VOS. I want to go with a three-point-two megapixel camera. That's plenty of resolution for what we need to do, and we can get away with smaller actuators as well."

And invariably Hamid or Phuong or even Erwin would glance off to David's left, where Draganovic stood about half a pace behind him with his thumbs casually stuck in his waistband. And Vlad would give the nod, and then Hamid or Phuong would smile (Erwin never smiled) and nod repeatedly, and say, "Yes, I will get that done before Friday."

Twice so far, the nod had not been forthcoming. The first time was when David wanted to ditch the crap-ass Chinese gyros and actually spend some goddamned money on a decent set from UniTech. Not only would they save a full kilogram, but the things would actually, y'know, *work*.

Phuong's eyes flicked to Vlad. "Uhh . . ."

Vlad's head didn't move. There was an awkward pause.

"C'mon, Phuong, you can order them through the shell company in Cyprus."

"Uhh . . ."

And then the bulky guy with the awesome mustache said, "Check with the colonel about that," and Phuong nodded vigorously and David gritted his teeth and went on to the next item on the Big List o' Tasks.

The second time, it was with Hassan, the guy who'd replaced Hamid. "Look, you're a nice guy, Hassan, but you just don't know anything about hypergolic rockets. Why don't you take over the pyrotechnics and let Erwin handle the maneuvering system?"

Eyes left. "Uhh . . ."

That time, David didn't even wait. "Yeah, yeah, I know. Ask the colonel. But until we can do that, Hassan, I want you to work on the pyros and get them working right, okay?"

Nod.

"Of course," said Hassan. "I will work on that right away!"

No point in complaining to Ghavami. Vlad was his man. When the colonel wasn't in the fenced compound, Draganovic was the ultimate authority. And when neither of them was on hand, everything got really slow. Without that little nod, nobody did anything.

It bothered David more than he expected. He usually thought of himself as a free spirit who didn't play the whole primate troop hierarchy game. Hell, that was one of the big reasons he'd gone into freelance space piracy rather than a corporate job. He didn't like people bossing him around. David Schwartz was not a cog in anyone's machine. So every time Vlad gave his little nod to let one of the techs know it was okay to go ahead, it reminded David that on *this* job he was hired help. *Still.*

He worked his way down the list of today's tasks for the team, and today Vlad gave the little nod every time. The second-to-last item was about dirt. "Erwin tells me he found more dust inside the bird this morning. I know we're working in a desert and there's dust everywhere, but that's why we put those stupid shower curtain air lock things on all the doors. It really is important. A lot of the crew have worked in electronics, they know all about clean rooms. So from now on, we keep the vehicle covered with the vinyl sheeting at all times. Even when someone's working on it, only the sheet covering what they're messing with should be moved. Mr. Draganovic will be coming in to check on that," he added. Vlad didn't even hesitate before nodding. Good. Make the big motherfucker do something besides hang around and act menacing.

"And finally," he said, trying to keep the reluctance out of his voice, "I'd like to meet with Halfdan about the new flight software. That's it, everybody, let's get going."

David would have liked to have his meeting in the air-conditioned trailer used for electronics work, but he wanted privacy for his little talk with Halfdan, so they used David's room instead.

Back when the Chinese were pouring money into Gwadar, this complex was going to be some kind of sweatshop factory, and the builders had set up big barracks for the workforce. David's room had originally held four double bunk beds, but he'd dragged all of them out to the scrap pile himself and bought a big old rope bed. With a futon on it, the thing was almost comfortable, and it was high enough off the ground that David didn't worry much about rats.

Once the two of them were in the room, David carefully closed the door. "Okay, Halfdan, what the fuck?"

"Halfdan doesn't ken your meaning."

"You keep fooling with the guidance software! And you don't put in any comments, so I don't know what you're doing!"

Halfdan's face took on the slightly smug expression that made David want to strangle him. "Halfdan didn't see that it was needful to explain. It's simple physics. The laws of nature aren't secret."

"Yeah, but I don't want to have to spend half an hour watching an MIT tutorial just so I can figure out why you've made an operation change. Just a little note is all you need. And why are you fooling with it, anyway? You stole this stuff from ESA yourself. It should be good enough!"

"Halfdan thinks of ways to do things better. When he thinks, he acts. There is no wall between the will and the world. His mind flashes like lightning and his arm strikes like fucking thunder."

"It doesn't have to be better. It has to be good enough to do one simple job. Like this crap you put in about measuring the rate of change of the signal Doppler. What good is that?"

"It will tell us when our reaver is at a local velocity maximum or minimum. The best times for energy changes. Simple physics."

"I know all about that. Just because I never bothered to get a degree doesn't mean I'm—" David felt himself about to lose his temper. Halfdan had that effect on him. "What I mean is, why do we need that at all? Why not do the fucking work I asked you to do?"

"Colonel Ghavami asked Halfdan to do it—in case the reaver needs to do orbital maneuvers you didn't plan for."

"Look, Ghavami doesn't know shit about physics or orbital mechanics. He's probably been watching that Turkish *Star Wars* knockoff and wants to be able to zoom this thing around like it's Darth Vader's TIE fighter or something. Ignore him. This is a one-shot mission. The only maneuvering we're going to be doing is the close approach stuff—and that's what isn't ready yet. I want automatic station-keeping without any input from the ground. I need to be able to park this vehicle next to the target and have it hold position without demanding my attention. That's not too hard, is it? Not for a smart guy like you."

"Halfdan will make that ready. The reaver will fly at the appointed time."

"And, Halfdan—can I ask you a question? Why can't you talk like normal people? Would it fucking kill you to just say 'I' or 'me' once in a while?"

"When Halfdan speaks of Halfdan, he speaks for the warrior within, the essential male, the animus. But the female side there is, too, in all. The Goddess, the anima. Halfdan does not speak for the Goddess within."

"You know what? Never mind. I've just realized I have no desire to hear from your feminine side. Just get to work."

. . .

Anne left *Carina* moored at the marina in Port St. Joe, Florida, and walked three blocks to the nearest sporting-goods store. She was still trembling a little.

"I need some bullets for a gun," she said to the first salesman she could find. He was a very fat black man with a big white beard, making him look like a dark-skinned Santa Claus. "It's a Smith and Wesson Model 10. What kind of bullets does it use?"

"Ammo's right over here," he said, leading her to a row of locked cabinets. "You want hollow point? FMJ?"

"I don't know," said Anne, feeling even more panicky. "Whatever's best."

"Well, it depends on what you're planning to use it for," he said patiently. "Target shooting? Personal protection? Pest control?"

She almost said "Pest control," and the thought of blasting away with a pistol at the palmetto bugs and mosquitoes made her want to laugh. But she didn't want to start giggling hysterically right there in the store, so she swallowed and said "Protection."

"Then I'd recommend hollow-point rounds, 125-grain." He looked at her with some concern. "You scared of somebody?"

"No, no," she said. "I just—I'm on a long boat trip by myself. Last night someone tried to break in while I was on board."

"Well, that's just good sense," he said. "I always make sure my daughter's carrying when she goes off by herself. You never can tell."

"I guess not," she said. If even Santa Claus was arming his family, maybe this wasn't such a crazy idea.

"Two things," he said, "and you didn't hear this from me, okay? First, I don't know if you got a carry permit at home, but if you don't, you should leave that firearm locked up on your boat. Understand? Get yourself a permit if you're going to be here for a while. Second, you ought to practice up some. Even if it's just shooting cans off a stump or something. Take a class if you can. Don't be learning how to use it the first time you need it. And remember that thing's always loaded."

. . .

MESSING ABOUT IN MY BOAT

May 26
Location: 29° 43′ 31″ N by 84° 59′ 32″ W

I'm anchored right now across the Apalachicola River from Apalachicola, Florida, in the shadow of the Highway 98 bridge. There's a marina, but I'm going to save my money and sleep aboard *Carina* tonight. You can read my last entry to see what the town is like. (Executive summary: small, trying hard to be charming, good seafood.) In the morning I'll top off the fuel tanks and begin the epic high seas voyage to St. Petersburg.

No kidding—if I keep on hugging the coast, it's 250 miles to Tampa Bay—and just about all of that is swamps and wildlife refuge, with no towns at all between Saint George Sound and Jug Island.

I've already seen plenty of swamps. I've been going through swamps ever since I left the Mississippi River. I know swamps are important for the biosphere and all, but I'm kind of tired of swamps right now.

So I'm going to cut across Apalachee Bay. The coast here makes a big wide curve to the north and I'm going to go straight across, out on blue water. I figure I can save a whole day of travel, and get to Crystal River by sunset.

This will be the first time I've ever taken *Carina* out of sight of land. For the first time, finding where I am will take more than just watching for mile markers and looking at the chart display. I'm not just going to rely on the GPS, either: I'm going to figure out my compass bearing and do some real navigating!

All that high seas adventure means I need a good night's sleep, so I'm knocking off now. My next update should be from Crystal River!

. . .

The big metal building was located on a grand and empty boulevard near Gwadar International Airport. It was part of a huge industrial park composed of nothing but rusting skeletons of buildings left unfinished when the Chinese investment money dried up suddenly. Beyond the empty park was nothing but desert.

The Pakistani technicians could at least go off to their rental housing in Gwadar proper and enjoy what passed for nightlife. David and the other foreigners were stuck inside the compound, both for secrecy and because two of the Koreans had gone out looking for fun and come back in a police car with bruises and bloody noses.

So the four white guys—David, Erwin, Halfdan, and Franklin—spent most of their free time in the air-conditioned trailer used for electronics work, drinking smuggled bottles of Kingfisher and bitching about everything.

"I want to go away from here," said Erwin one evening, completely out of the blue.

"Why bother? Gwadar's a pit. We've probably got more liquor in this fridge than in the whole town, and you can't even talk to any of the women."

"There are some hookers down by the port," Franklin put in.

"I hope you're not that desperate," said David.

"They are not worthy of your seed," said Halfdan.

"No," said Erwin. "I do not want to go to town." He took a big swallow of beer. "I want to go to my home."

"We're not done yet. We need you."

"My work on the power system is finished. That is what you hired me to do."

"I still need you here, Erwin. You and Franklin and Hassan are the only real engineers on the whole project. The rest are just glorified technicians. They can follow instructions, but that's it. You saw what happened when I asked Phuong to kludge up some way to read the gyro spin rate. Deer in the fucking headlights."

Franklin shook his head sympathetically.

"You and Franklin can still manage the work without me. The vehicle is almost completed," said Erwin.

"We're at the debugging stage. That's the hardest part, when I need people who can really think."

"Why do you want to go?" asked Franklin. "Heat getting to you?"

Erwin lowered his voice and leaned in toward the other

two. "I am afraid. In Munich at school I studied a little Hindi. Urdu is very close to Hindi."

"The only real difference is the writing system," said Halfdan. "Urdu uses—"

"Anyway," said David, cutting him off. "You were saying, Erwin?"

"When the security guards speak to each other, I can understand some of what they say. It makes me afraid. I think they hate us. One of them said the *kuffār* smell disgusting, and the other one called us pigs."

"You're just being paranoid," said David. "It's just a more macho culture out here, that's all. These guys feel like they have to act tough all the time. Just ignore them."

"That is not the only thing. Do you know for who we are working? Really? Obviously, this Colonel Ghavami is some kind of intelligence agent. But what is his country? Turkey? Iran? Uzbek? He must have connections in the Pakistan intelligence office if they let him run this place here."

"So what?" said David, maybe a little too loudly. "Queen Elizabeth used to invest in Francis Drake's pirate ventures. If the Iranians and the ISI want to do the same, it's fine with me. Why should the U.S. and the rest of the helium cartel hog all the profits?"

"We are fucking warriors for hire, like the Varangians. We do not care about the quarrels of kings so long as there is blood, ale, and gold," said Halfdan.

"I want to go, David. I do not anymore care about my share. I am afraid all the time and I do not like it. I want to go back home. If you are smart, I think you will do the same thing."

"Okay, fine. Leave, then. Go right out the gate if you want to. Go back to stealing power for a bunch of squatters in Hamburg. I'm going to get a cut of the biggest helium haul ever. And when you're trading weed for blow jobs from some skanky Coptic chick, I'll be getting backrubs from supermodels in Thailand."

Erwin went over the wire two days later. Actually, he didn't go over anything; he bicycled out through the main gate in his work clothes with rubber bands around his ankles to keep his pants legs from catching in the chain. He left all his gear behind—everything except his money, his passport, and his bottle of diarrhea medicine. The guard shift changed at sunset, so it wasn't until midmorning the next day that anyone but David and Franklin noticed he was gone.

Vlad Draganovic put a meaty hand on David's shoulder as he tested the control interface. "Where is Gruber?"

"Who?"

"Dr. Gruber. Erwin. He is not in the compound."

"I think he left last night."

"Did he tell you where he was going?"

"He told me he wanted to get out of here. Relax, man—he probably just went down to Gwadar to find a hooker."

"No," said Vlad. "I would know if he had."

David kept his surprise at *that* little remark to himself, but his mouth was suddenly dry. "Shit, I don't know. Maybe he went back to Germany. It's okay with me. The power system is up and running, and if he wants to bail now, he's only hurting himself."

Draganovic stared at David, and David found he couldn't meet the other man's eyes. "Tell me what you know," he said at last.

"I told you, man! He said he wanted to leave, and I guess he did. That's all he said to me."

"I must find him. He might talk."

"No, no. Erwin's an okay guy. He knows better than that. It'll be fine. Like I said, relax."

Vlad looked at him silently for another few seconds, then strode rapidly away.

All that day, the guards searched the compound, and after dinner, a pair of SUVs with blacked-out windows drove in through the gate. Colonel Ghavami jumped out of the rear vehicle as soon as it came to a stop and spent about five minutes inside the electronics trailer with Vlad.

He invited David to sit with him in plastic lawn chairs on the north side of the big metal building. The evening breeze from the hills was hot and dusty, but any moving air was better than the baking workshop floor.

"Captain Black, please! Sit down! Drink!" He passed David a cold Kingfisher. The two of them sat for a moment. David opened his beer and Ghavami lit a cigarette. "So," he began. "Why didn't you tell Mr. Draganovic that Dr. Gruber was talking about leaving?"

"I didn't think he was serious. All the guys bitch about this place all the time. Except the Koreans. And Halfbrain."

"This is a serious matter, you know. Gruber could expose us."

"I told Draganovic, it's okay. Erwin's cool. He wouldn't go to the cops. He's an anarchist."

"I don't want to rely on the sincerity of his beliefs. Did he say anything about his plans? The least little thing may be important."

"He didn't say much. Just that he was scared of your guards and wanted to go home."

Ghavami took another long drag on his cigarette and let the wind carry away the smoke. "He left yesterday. When did you realize he was gone?"

"I don't keep track of everyone in the compound, you know. I didn't see him around after dinner, but I figured he was just in his room reading or something. This isn't a jail. If someone wants to go off by himself, I'm not going to stop him."

Ghavami looked pained. "We discussed the importance of operational security. You know the dangers we risk. Even if Dr. Gruber says nothing about his time here, someone in the Indian or American intelligence community might notice him. They would not hesitate to kidnap him, interrogate him in some secret bunker, and then make him disappear forever. You must know this is possible."

David didn't say anything. While he had often railed about the brutality and injustice of the corporate-dominated governments, it had always been a lot more *theoretical* than it was right now. The thought that someone he knew, someone he had been drinking beer with only three days ago, might actually be snatched by CIA-backed contractor goons in mirror shades and get waterboarded or worse had never really occurred to him before.

While that was certainly alarming, he also felt a slight elation at the prospect—the satisfaction of finding out his worst fears were *right all along*. In his more self-aware moments, David had wondered if his justifications for helium payload piracy were just excuses for stealing stuff. Now here was a real-life deep black secret agent man telling him *it was all true.*

"I really don't know where Erwin went," he said at last. "If I hear from him, I'll tell you right away."

"Of course, of course," said Ghavami. "You want this operation to succeed. Now, please tell me: Are there any others on the staff who are unhappy?"

"I can't think of anyone. Heck, until he brought it up, I didn't know Erwin was having second thoughts. I mean, nobody likes being stuck here, but it's only for a few more weeks."

Ghavami finished his cigarette and tossed the butt aside. "That reminds me of something I have been meaning to bring up. For greater security, I would like to run this operation from a facility in Kazakhstan. Tasbuget. It is a very nice town."

"Kazakhstan," said David. "In *August?*"

"It is dry heat, not like here," said Ghavami, not at all convincingly.

"I ran my last mission from a luxury hotel in Thailand. This isn't the twentieth century. You don't have to put everyone all in one control center somewhere, with a big screen like the bridge of the *Enterprise.*"

"I am concerned about security."

"Then you shouldn't put everyone together in one place and hang up a big sign saying PLEASE RAID HERE. Decentralize. Go native. No footprint."

Ghavami considered this. "If you don't want to use the secure facility, there are some very comfortable hotels in Qizil Orda."

"I don't even know where that is."

"It is in Kazakhstan. The capital city of the province where Tasbuget is located. It is very close to the Russian cosmodrome at Tyuratam."

"Great. Luxurious Soviet-built hotels in bustling Qizil-whatever. Look, Colonel: I have some basic requirements when I'm working: good coffee, hot skinny women in short shorts, Thai food, and a *reliable* gigabit data pipe. I can get those things in a lot of places, but if you can find all that in a provincial capital in Kazakhstan, I will let you shove any object of your choosing up my ass."

"The facility has excellent data connections. The other things are—"

"*Essential.* If I'm stuck in the middle of the steppes without them, I'm not going to be doing my best work. I might screw up at a key moment during the mission. You don't want this project to fail, do you?"

Ghavami stared off into the middle distance for a moment, his face utterly blank. Then he turned to David and gave him a big smile. "You can run the mission anywhere you like. Tahiti! Monaco! But I do wish that you stay here in Gwadar until the vehicle is actually ready to ship out for launch. Will you do that for me?"

"Uh, sure. It's only a couple more months. I'll survive."

"And then you will go off to—where, may I ask? Back to Bangkok again?"

"I haven't decided yet. It'll be prime beach weather in Sardinia."

"When you do make up your mind, be sure to tell me."

"Absolutely," said Captain Black the Space Pirate.

. . .

MESSING ABOUT IN MY BOAT

May 27

Location: 28° 54′ 1″ N by 82° 35′ 38″ W (Crystal River, Florida)

Made it. Barely.

I left Apalachicola at six thirty yesterday morning, passed out of St. George Sound into the Gulf by eight, and set my course at 120 degrees, southeast by east-southeast. With the throttle open all the way, I figured I'd make landfall at Cedar Key on the other side of Apalachee Bay by early afternoon.

Didn't happen.

I forgot about the wind.

On the river, wind was never a problem. Motoring along the Intracoastal Waterway, wind was never a problem. On the ocean, wind is . . . a huge fucking problem. Even a gentle ten- to twelve-knot breeze is a huge problem if it's blowing from the direction you're trying to go. It slowed me, so I didn't make landfall until four o'clock, and I wasn't at Cedar Key, I was thirty miles north of there at a place called Bull Cove.

I was never gladder to see any place than I was to see

Bull Cove. It will always have a place in my heart. I may marry Bull Cove.

From there I hugged the coast, right at the one-fathom depth line, for the next four hours, battling the fucking wind the whole way.

Oh, and throwing up. Did I mention the throwing up?

I thought I had pretty good sea legs. I've lived aboard a boat for a couple of months now. I've been out in the coastal waters between Louisiana and Mississippi. I've been out in Mobile Bay and Santa Rosa Sound and Choctawhatchee Bay. I thought I was a real sailor.

Turns out all those sheltered bays, and all the canals and rivers and bayous I've been on, have one thing in common: They're calm. Even when they look rough, they're calm.

Out on the ocean, in a ten-knot breeze, you get waves. The boat bounces into them, up and down, up and down, up and down . . . for *seven fucking hours.*

Excuse me, I have to throw up again.

Okay, better now.

So when I finally got to Crystal River, it was past eight, I was shaking and exhausted and dehydrated, I wanted nothing but a big cold drink and a box of seasickness patches. I tied up, signed everything they handed me, swiped my card, and got a room so I could spend the night on dry land.

What I learned:

• Pay attention to wind speed and direction when you're planning your course! Now I understand why all the navigation guides say that.

- Seasickness meds! I'm going to get a giant box of patches.
- Pack extra Gatorade!
- More seasickness meds! Maybe TWO giant boxes.
- When you've been out at sea all day, the bed feels like it's going up and down as you fall asleep. I learned that last night.

▪   ▪   ▪

JULY 25, 2031

June gave way to July, and the heat in Gwadar didn't abate at all. The big metal building was still an oven in the middle of the day. It hadn't rained for weeks, but at night there was dew, and sometimes mist in low-lying spots.

David spent as much of each day as possible inside the electronics trailer, and that was where Franklin found him on the last Friday in July. He didn't say anything, just put down a folded newspaper and sat.

The paper was the Karachi *Daily Times,* three weeks old. David hadn't read a print newspaper since his teens, so he browsed through the pages, wondering if Franklin had anything in mind or was just done with the section.

BODY IDENTIFIED, a small filler piece read.

QUETTA—Balochistan Police have identified the body found on the N10 Makran Coastal Highway near Pasni on June 30. The body was that of Dr. Erwin Gruber, 31, a German tourist. According to the medical examiner in Quetta, Gruber probably died of injuries caused by falling onto the roadway from a moving vehicle. Police believe Gruber may have tumbled from the back of an open truck or motorcycle while hitchiking. No wallet or identification documents were on the body when it was discovered, which led to the delay in establishing its identity. Dr. Gruber's remains will be returned to Germany for burial.

"Aww," said David. "That really sucks. Poor Erwin."

"Do you think it was an accident?"

"I don't know. Really, I don't know. Was it an accident? Somebody hit his bike and didn't stop? Or maybe someone robbed him and threw him off a truck. Did some Indian Intelligence goons do it? I have no way to tell."

That seemed to satisfy Franklin, but David did make some changes in his daily routine. He began taking walks around the compound at intervals during the day. He began watching the guards and paying attention to the daily routine. And at night, lying in his bed with his headphones on, he began making plans.

They were starting the last week of tests before shipping the pirate probe to Biak Island in Indonesia for launch when David dragged Franklin out to the edge of the compound with a couple of folding chairs and a cooler of beer.

He opened the first can and handed it to Franklin. "Can you see anybody watching us?" he said quietly, with a big smile on his face.

"No, I don't think so."

"Good. We're leaving tomorrow morning."

"Does Colonel Ghavami know about this?"

David popped a beer for himself. "He'll know once we're gone." He caught sight of Franklin's alarmed expression. "Relax; we're still going to get paid, and I'm still going to run his mission for him. I just don't want the colonel to try anything cute and drag us off to Kazakhstan or wherever for our own protection."

"I thought he said it was okay to leave?"

"He did. But you know, Franklin, a man in his line of work may not be completely truthful all the time. So we're going to sidestep the entire problem by leaving early."

"What if Vlad doesn't let us go?"

David felt himself tense up. "We're not going to ask him."

Their conversation died down for two minutes while one of the guards moved across their field of view. David raised his beer in a toast to the man, who looked away.

"How do you expect to get out of here without anyone noticing?" asked Franklin when the guard seemed out of range.

"You'll see." David laughed. "Hey, calm down. I'm not just being an asshole here. The less you know, the less chance you'll give anything away by accident. Like the colonel always says, 'Preserve operational security!'"

"I just don't want to get shot."

David raised his hand, palm out. "I swear by . . . by the bones of my spiritual ancestor, the Dread Pirate Bartholomew Roberts, that nobody will even think of shooting at you."

Franklin still looked dubious.

"Are you in or not? I need to know."

It took Franklin nearly a minute to decide. "Yes, count me in. I don't want to stay here. I want to go back to my sweetie in New Orleans."

"Good." David took a swallow and then tried to sound conversational. "Will he still be there? It's been, what, four months? That's a long time in boyfriend years."

"He won't leave, if that's what you mean. It's his house."

"Yeah, but will there be someone else there when you show up?"

"Oh, no. He's the old responsible one. I'm the cute guy everyone flirts with. He forgives me every time."

"That's the way. Be a player! Okay, so be sure you're up by five tomorrow morning, and have your money and passport on you, and anything you can get in a shoulder bag. Stick with me, don't say anything, and you'll be cheating on your sugar daddy again in a week."

. . .

MESSING ABOUT IN MY BOAT

June 22

Location: 25° 47′ 36″ N by 80° 17′ 25″ W (Miami, Florida)

I'm writing this aboard *Carina,* anchored (not quite legally) in the Miami River near the airport. Someone nearby has a wireless hub and didn't bother to use password protection. Thanks, whoever you are!

I just got back from the supermarket, and now the cabin is stuffed with supplies. There's enough room for me to sleep, but that's it. The fuel and water tanks are full, I've changed the oil and filters, I've got a backup radio and a flare gun, and now I just have to make a decision.

I hate making decisions.

Should I go east from here, or north?

If I go north, I can follow the Intracoastal Waterway up the East Coast. Cape Canaveral, St. Augustine, Savannah, Charleston, Virginia Beach, Chesapeake Bay—I can motor right up to the Jefferson Memorial! Baltimore. I can follow the Susquehanna up into Pennsylvania, or cruise up past New Jersey and look at the lights of Manhattan when I sleep. According to the chart, I could even follow the Hudson and the Erie Canal and explore the whole Great Lakes basin. Sure, I'll have to pull *Carina* out of the water in winter, maybe get a job somewhere to pay the rent until spring. But I can sail through America, and eventually go back down the Mississippi to where I started.

Or I can turn east.

It's fifty miles to Bimini, and from there, I can island-hop through the Bahamas, then work my way south through the Antilles to Trinidad.

And then? There's no Intracoastal Waterway along South America, but I'll be in the tropics. I know I could go up the Orinoco. Maybe even reach the Amazon and spend a couple of years exploring tributaries. Learn to samba!

Or . . . I keep joking about sailing around the world, but it's not quite a joke. If I can figure a way to get *Carina* from Recife to Monrovia, I can work north along the coast of Africa and then into the Mediterranean. And from there, it's coastal waters all the way to . . . India? Singapore? China? Maybe New Zealand?

I keep looking at the Aleutians. People sail among them in boats not much bigger than *Carina*. I'd have to wait for summer, of course, but ... *I could do this*. I could sail around the world.

Before you all start telling me I'm crazy, relax. I'll probably run out of money before I get to Trinidad.

Nevertheless, I've made my decision. North is the sensible choice, the sane choice, the obvious choice.

Which is why I'm going east. As soon as I post this, I'm casting off for the Bahamas. Trinidad, here I come!

. . .

AUGUST 1, 2031; 23:00 GMT

Franklin Snyder was up at four. His bag was packed and he'd slept in his clothes. Since he normally didn't get up until seven, he had no idea where he should meet Captain Black the Space Pirate for their unscheduled departure. Finally the tension got to be too much for him, so he slung his bag over his shoulder and tiptoed down the hall past Draganovic's room to Captain Black's door. He tapped lightly, then a little less lightly, then risked turning the knob.

No one home. Now fighting panic, Franklin looked into the bathroom, then stepped outside into the cool dawn air. The sky above was pale purple, shading to pastel red in the east. The bugs were out in force, and Franklin was mildly surprised to see how many people were up and about in the compound. He had never realized how much got done while he was asleep.

"Hey, Franklin!" Captain Black came strolling up, looking like he'd just finished a night of hard partying in his Hawaiian shirt and cargo shorts. His glacier mirror shades were perched on top of his head. He checked his watch. "Let's grab some tea before we head out."

Trying to stay calm, Franklin tagged along behind Captain Black as he wandered into the dining room and filled cups from the tea urn. He was still acting like the life of the party, waving to the Pakistani technicians and security guards eating big piles of scrambled eggs with roti.

"Did you run the final mass check?" Captain Black asked Franklin as they stood sipping tea.

It took Franklin a second to put his brain in the right gear. "Yes, uh, yesterday afternoon. We're twenty grams over."

"That's fine. Well within the margin. Good job." He checked his watch again. "Hey, time to get moving. We don't want to be late. Oh, fuck."

Franklin followed Captain Black's gaze and saw Halfdan coming toward them. He was shirtless, wearing yoga pants, sandals, and his bolted-on data spex. Franklin thought Halfdan's skinny cyclist build and deep tan decorated with Maori tattoos were actually kind of attractive, and he briefly regretted missing the chance to make a pass at him.

"Morning, Halfdan," said Captain Black, sounding just as cheerful as before. "You're up early."

"Halfdan chose to greet the dawn today. We are all avatars of the Sun's power."

"Ain't that the truth. I was just saying the same thing

to Franklin here. Well, time I was going. Come on, Franklin. We're burning daylight."

"Halfdan has a question."

"Make it quick."

"Halfdan needs the command encryption key."

"And just why does Halfdan need that?"

"Halfdan needs to edit some of the installed guidance software."

"I thought that was all done?" Franklin could hear the panic under Captain Black's annoyance. "You said it was done! What else isn't done?"

"All is well. But Halfdan got some new code from a friend at ESA. It is better than what we used. Halfdan wishes to switch it and test it."

Captain Black's eyes flicked down to his watch. "Look, I'm busy right now. Talk to me later."

"Why are you busy?" Halfdan sounded genuinely puzzled. "You never start work before nine."

"Special day today. Gotta run."

"What is special?" Halfdan persisted.

"I can't—," began Captain Black, then stopped. After a pause he smiled and spoke much more calmly. "Okay, Halfdan. Go right ahead. The command encryption key's a big long random string, but I keep it filed in a document called 'Song Lyrics.' The keyword for *that* is 'hip hop banjo roku porkchop'—all lowercase, no spaces, no dashes. Got it?"

"Halfdan understands."

"Great. Go crazy. Now, we've all got stuff to do. How about you meet with me at lunch and give me a status report?"

"All will be ready by then."

"I'm counting on it. Get moving!" As he spoke, Captain Black the Space Pirate began walking briskly toward the door. He favored some of the technicians they passed with smiles and cheerful waves, dismissing Halfdan from his attention.

Outside, it was already warming up. The captain led Franklin across the compound to the parking area, where he pushed the button on a car key and was answered with the welcoming *chunk* of doors unlocking in a black Mercedes SUV.

"Hop in," he said, taking a seat behind the wheel and putting on his sunglasses.

"This is Vlad's car," said Franklin, now close to genuine terror.

"That it is. And Count Fucking Dracula just got back from his morning run, which means he'll be in the shower for three minutes and then spend another three minutes shaving himself with his badass straight razor."

Captain Black started the car, then spent what seemed like an agonizingly long time working the power controls to get his seat adjusted and the mirrors properly aligned. Then he cranked up the air-conditioning and plugged his music player into the stereo. To the gentle strains of Stereolab they peeled out of the parking area and barreled toward the main gate. As they approached it, he leaned over to Franklin. "Remember my promise about nobody shooting? This is where we find out if I'm a liar."

. . .

After leaving Crystal River, Anne spent an afternoon anchored at Deep Creek, in the middle of the wildlife refuge stretching along Florida's west coast. She waited until no other boats were in sight, then took up a position about ten yards from a dead cypress tree. She put on the hearing protectors she'd gotten at the hardware store in Apalachicola, held the revolver the way the instructional videos showed, and began firing at the dead tree.

Only one round of the first dozen shots she took even hit the trunk. By the time she finished a box of fifty, she could pockmark the tree about half the time from twenty yards away. Her thumb and her wrist were sore, her ears were ringing, and the tree trunk looked . . . well, it looked like some Oklahoma redneck in a boat had been shooting at it.

That night she cleaned the gun before locking it up. She made sure it was empty, but she put the unopened box of ammo right next to the lockbox in the storage space under the bed. Because you never knew.

7

Franklin tried not to look as scared as he felt as the car roared up to the gate and David lowered the window to talk to the guard.

"Hey!" he said with a wave. "Gotta pick up a package at the airport."

The man with the AK-47 slung over his shoulder and no shoes looked at him blankly. Franklin held his breath.

David honked the horn. "Come on, open up! I gotta get to the airport before some dumb fuck steals my gyros!"

The guard looked at the other guard, and then Franklin exhaled as they undid the padlock and swung the gate open.

David gave them a cheery wave and floored it. They turned south and sped down the empty boulevard toward the airport, shot past the entrance, and kept on going.

"Where are we going?" Franklin asked.

"The bus for Karachi leaves Gwadar at six."

"A *bus*? We're going to get away by *bus*?"

"Yes, a bus, with sixty or seventy witnesses if anyone

wants to try anything rough. And as a bonus, we're going to be driving through a big dead zone east of here, so there's no way for anyone to call the driver and make him stop or turn back."

"What if they have someone waiting for us in Karachi?"

"Then they're going to wait a long time and go home cranky, because we're getting off in Hub Chowki. Franklin, I've *thought about this*. I'm not just making shit up. I even made a room reservation in Karachi and bought plane tickets in our names from there to Dubai to throw off any snoops. That should keep Vlad and Ghavami amused while we head on up to Lahore and catch a plane to Bangkok."

"And then?"

"*Bangkok*, Franklin. Ever been there? It's awesome. I'll show you around. And then . . . we go wherever. You said you want to go back to New Orleans, right?"

"Yes. What about you?"

"I'm not sure. Maybe back to Tortuga. Kind of like the purloined letter. Hide a pirate in a pirate resort."

*   *   *

APRIL 13, 2031

Elizabeth took the box of GyroJet rounds to work with her on Sunday, tucked into her gym bag under her Air Force PT sweats. She had hoped that the Icarus Propulsion workshop would be empty, but Yumiko was there, wearing a cleansuit and attaching hoses to the tightly packed plumbing of the motor.

"Oh, hi," she said when she heard Elizabeth. "I'm afraid I have to make some noise here. I hope you don't mind."

"No, no. What are you doing?"

"Pressurization test on the fuel system. Mike bought these old valves from a salvage outfit in Tucson, and I'm afraid they're kind of touchy."

"Touchy? How?"

"That's what I'm trying to determine. The response curve doesn't match the specs, and I want to make sure it won't cause any problems."

"Well, if you need help, I'm here," said Elizabeth.

"No, no. You do whatever you came for. I'll finish this. But—put these on, just to be sure." She handed Elizabeth a pair of hearing-protection earmuffs. "It does get a little noisy."

Elizabeth put them on and sat at the control station for two hours, pretending to work while Yumiko connected a pressurized nitrogen tank to various parts of the motor and tested the valves. The result was an earsplitting series of roars and whistles. Even with the earmuffs on, Elizabeth soon had a hammering headache.

Yumiko finally quit for the day at six. "Want to come over for dinner? We've got cold lamb left over from Passover, and Michael's making fingerling potatoes and grilled eggplant to go with it. And a Greek salad, I think."

"How do you stay so thin eating with Mike?"

"Swimming, mostly. And if he didn't cook for me, I'd forget to eat. Back in college, I was eighty pounds."

"I'm afraid I can't make it tonight. I've still got some things to do here."

Yumiko suddenly smiled, but didn't say anything else as she peeled off her cleansuit and left.

Elizabeth didn't take any chances. She went to Mike's office and peeked out the window to make sure Yumiko had gone. Then she got to work.

The Icarus workshop had plenty of metalworking tools, and Elizabeth had read all the manuals she could find, not to mention the hours she'd spent watching videos. But her mouth was still dry when she started work.

The shop had aluminum tubing in every possible size, so Elizabeth was able to find some eleven-millimeter without any difficulty. The equipment bay inside the SOTHIS spacecraft she was planning to use was twenty centimeters by ten by five, so she went ahead and cut thirty-one segments of tube, each ten centimeters long. When she was finished, she loaded one of her overpriced rocket cartridges into each tube.

Every instinct was telling her that the tubing was far too thin-walled to act as a gun barrel—which was entirely true but irrelevant. She found that as long as she mentally called the tube segments "launchers" she could keep from worrying about the whole thing blowing up.

With her little miniature Katyusha loaded, the next step was to wire up the igniters. She didn't have the time or equipment to do anything complicated, so she went ahead and used conductive space-rated epoxy to simply glue the ultrathin igniter leads to the cartridges.

Then she got to work with CAD/CAM software, crafting a casing to hold the tubes. The exterior exactly matched the empty experiment bay in the spacecraft, while the interior cradled the thirty-one tubes stacked in three rows, embedded in solid plastic. She made a laser scan of them to ensure a perfect fit. When she was satisfied, she sent the design to the three-dimensional printer and set it to work making the thing out of high-impact plastic.

The print job was halfway finished when she heard the front door close. Her pistol was at home in its lockbox. She pulled out her phone and held a finger over the emergency icon. "Who's there?" she called out.

Jack Bonnet opened the door into the assembly floor. "Hello? Hope I didn't scare you."

"No, no," she said. She put her phone away, but she could still feel the adrenaline pumping. Elizabeth was acutely aware of the noise the 3-D printer was making.

She put her computer on top of the loaded tube segments as he came over to the worktable. "I just stopped off to get my tool kit. What are you doing here so late?"

"Oh, catching up on some things."

"What are you making?" He nodded at the printer.

"Yumiko had to go home for dinner, so I offered to stay here until it finishes. I'm not sure what it is."

He wandered over to the CAD/CAM workstation and peered at the screen. "Looks like a casing. Did she say what it was for?"

"No. She was doing pressure testing on the fuel system, so we couldn't really do much talking."

There was a long pause while they both listened to the staccato buzzing of the printer.

"Elizabeth," he said suddenly, "what are you planning to do?"

"What do you mean?" she asked, trying not to panic.

"Long-term," he said. "Are you going to stay in the Air Force? Private sector, academia?"

She relaxed a tiny bit. "Well, I want to finish this project, of course. After that . . . I don't really know." As she said it, she was a little surprised to realize it was true. "I always figured on staying in the service, at least until I make my twenty years."

"What if you got a good offer? Something that might pay a lot better than an O-5 retirement benefits."

"Well—it depends on what the job is. I didn't join the Air Force for the money anyway. I wanted to fly spaceships."

"Icarus. You'd be a partner, starting at five percent and vesting up to ten percent after five years. There'd be a salary, too. It's not great, but as the company grows, your dividends could be serious money. Or if we sell it, you get a big wad all at once."

"Are you offering me a job here? Formally?"

"I talked about this with Mike and Yumiko, and they're both on board. We don't want to do anything formal until the SOTHIS test is finished, of course. If it fails, there's no reason for you to trash your career."

She could still hear the printer working away in the background, and for once, she didn't know what to do. The urge to say yes was very strong. She could throw the GyroJet launcher into the nearest canal, tell McEwan she was going private sector, and maybe . . . move in with Jack?

No more pirate hunting. Of course, her plan was pretty crazy anyway. Putting an armed vehicle up at L_1 in the hope of taking out a pirate was more than a long shot. But giving up would mean letting Captain Black win.

"I—," she began, unsure of how she was going to end the sentence.

"No rush, no rush," he said, and she realized he was almost as nervous as she was. "Take time to think it over. Wait until after the launch."

"Okay," she said. "And . . . thank you."

The printer beeped to let them know it was finished. The two of them hesitated; then Jack gave her a wave and headed for the parking lot while she put on safety goggles and gloves before opening the printer.

The tubes fit perfectly into their new casing. A little more work, and she'd have a weapon for her pirate-hunting ship.

* * *

AUGUST 9, 2031; 14:50 GMT

The night before his flight was due to take off from Bangkok to Amsterdam on the way to the Caribbean, David had one last swim in the hotel pool, poached himself for half an hour in the spa, then went upstairs for his scheduled massage before bed.

But when he answered the brisk knock at the door of his suite, it wasn't the hot young masseuse, or even the older woman who actually knew what she was doing.

It was Colonel Ghavami, looking very dapper in a white suit and straw hat. "We must talk," he said.

For an instant, David considered slamming the door and calling hotel security, but presumably if Ghavami wanted to kill him, he'd have done it by now. So he opened the door wider and turned his back on the colonel. "Come on in. Want something to drink? Tea? There's some in the minibar," he said, trying to sound casual though his mouth was dry and he suddenly had a powerful need to urinate.

"Why did you flee Gwadar?"

"Didn't you find my note? I told you, I don't want to wind up stuck in some Central Asian shithole."

"You are putting the entire operation in danger."

"No, it's cool. I've done this before. There's no way anyone can trace where I'm located."

"You will attract attention."

"I've done this before! You're not talking to some amateur here. I *invented* this game, remember? Why doesn't anyone remember that? It's all going to be fine. The only danger is that I might get distracted and unhappy because of all this fucking around, so that I won't be able to do the job well."

"That is not an issue. If you do not come to Qizil Orda, you will not be part of this operation at all."

"You can't do that! You need me for this!"

"I have other people who can operate the vehicle."

"Who? Halfwit? Give me a break."

"He is very skilled, and he has a doctorate in physics. You are just an ignorant American from a suburb."

"Who is the supreme badass of outer space. Quick test, Colonel: Before I left Gwadar, I gave Halfbrain the master command key for the onboard software. Now, right now, I bet you're thinking you should have someone go over the code to see what he's fucked up. Am I right?"

The colonel was silent for only a second. "A sensible precaution. I would do it anyway."

David just laughed. "Come on. You need me."

"Security is too important. I need you in Qizil Orda."

"Not going to happen."

"Then I bid you good evening," said the colonel.

"Oh, well," said David in a tone of exaggerated unconcern. "I guess if I'm not in your little club anymore, then maybe I should earn myself some brownie points by sending everything I know to the cops. And I know a hell of a lot about this operation, especially when you consider that I thought it all up myself."

Suddenly there was a charcoal-colored automatic pistol in Ghavami's hand, pointing right at David's face. "I cannot let you put the operation in danger."

David took a step back, fighting to keep from pissing. "Hey, wait! Don't be crazy. If you kill me, the whole plan's screwed. I put copies of all my files on this mission into a secure site, with a Dead Hand system. If I don't enter the right password from time to time, it'll dump everything into a mailing list of all the cops, intelligence agencies, and space operations people I could find addresses for. Nobody will launch your bird, and the Indians and Americans will fucking *pave* the sky over Gwadar and Qizil-whatsit with drones."

"That is very unwise," said Ghavami, but he lowered the gun.

"No, I think it's pretty smart, really. As long as I'm happy and healthy, this operation can go ahead. Piss me off, and it's ruined. I'm good to go, you're the only one causing problems."

"What if something happens to you by accident?"

"If I'm dead anyway, what do I care?" David could feel his heart pounding, but the need to pee was fading. He was back in charge of the frame.

"If this information does get out, I will kill you," said Ghavami calmly.

"Relax. As long as we trust each other, everything will be fine. Don't you trust me?"

Ghavami stared at David for several seconds, then said, "I want to be sure you can protect yourself. This 'Dead Hand'—if the Americans or Indians arrest you, they can make you talk."

"I'm not gonna get arrested. And if I do, I've got lawyers."

"They may keep you hidden. These things do happen. Here," said Ghavami, "I want you to take this for your own protection." He wiped the pistol with his floral-print silk handkerchief before passing it handle-first to David. "It is a SIG Sauer nine millimeter. Very good quality, and it was made in the days before palmprint locks or identifier chips. All serial numbers have been removed. My gift to you."

David took the gun, trying to look casual about it, like he handled pistols all the time and it was no big deal. In point of fact, he had never held one before. It was lighter than he'd imagined.

"I trust you. Now, will you trust me?" asked Ghavami. "I only wish to make sure everything goes as we have planned. Take the gun, keep it with you. Protect yourself."

"Okay, sure. Thanks." Now David felt kind of like a dick. "Look, I'm sorry about running out on you. I just don't like people trying to boss me around. So, am I still part of the project?"

"You have a flight to Curaçao. Where are you going after that?"

"Back to Tortuga. I mean, hell, I bought the condo, I may as well get some use out of it."

Ghavami looked thoughtful, then nodded. "Tortuga is . . . acceptable to me. You can run the operation there. But be careful."

"Absolutely."

And with that, Ghavami just left, without another word to David.

He was still standing in the middle of his room wearing a bathrobe with a pistol in his hand when the masseuse knocked on the door. It was the hot one.

. . .

JUNE 14, 2031; 11:45 GMT

It was already getting too hot and muggy when Elizabeth finished her morning ride at quarter to seven. She pulled into the parking lot and coasted toward the staircase up to her apartment. But halfway there, she squeezed the brakes and came to a stop.

Jack's truck was parked right next to her car, and he was sitting on the tailgate. His head hung down and his elbows rested on his knees, and he looked worn out.

She pedaled over more slowly and stopped right in front of him. "You're up early," she said.

He looked up with the saddest expression she'd ever

seen. "What's the payload?" he asked without any pre-amble.

Her mouth went dry. She looked around and got off the bike. "Let's talk about this inside."

He followed her up the metal stairs and held her bike while she unlocked the door. The shabbiness and emptiness of the place embarrassed her. He'd never been inside before.

"Want something to drink?"

"What's the payload?" he asked again. "You've been going into the mass estimate and hiding twenty-six hundred grams. When Mike cut the science payload, out you changed the structural mass, and when Yumiko fixed that, you put it into thermal insulation. You used other people's computers, but I checked the times against the keycard logs, and you're the only one who was there both times."

She had never seen Jack so upset.

"I . . ." She had prepared a couple of cover stories, but his eyes were locked on to hers. She couldn't lie to him without looking away.

"It's a weapon," she said at last. "A launcher for Gyro-Jet ammunition. You know, little rockets. Want to see it? I rigged up a control unit so I can fire any number of barrels at once. Minimal recoil so the bird won't tumble."

"Why?"

She was calm, just as when she'd taken MARIO into battle. "I need a weapon at L_1 to fight pirates," she told him. "Right now there's nothing anybody can do if Captain Black steals another payload. SOTHIS can fight pirates."

"That's—"

"Don't say it's crazy. What's *crazy* is that this country's building fusion power plants that depend on helium-3 from the Moon and we're letting one in sixteen payloads get stolen. What's *crazy* is that we're letting the bad guys funnel billions into other crimes, terrorist support, corruption, all kinds of shit, because it's too expensive to follow the stupid rules we've saddled ourselves with!"

"Elizabeth, I understand. I know how frustrating it is. I don't like it either. But there are treaties, laws, FAA regs. Icarus can't send up an armed spacecraft. They'd shut us down."

The two of them stared at each other in silence. She cracked first.

"Dammit! I've screwed everything up again, haven't I?"

"Only a little. Mike and Yumiko don't know about it yet. I'll go in and fix the mass estimates, we'll crate up SO-THIS with an empty payload bay, and no one will ever know."

"What about us?"

"We can keep on the same as before, only—you can't lie to me. Ever. Promise?"

"I promise," she said.

■ ■ ■

AUGUST 11, 2031; 17:11 GMT

When David unlocked the door and stepped into his Tortuga condo, his first reaction was to check the number on the door to make sure it matched his keycard. The place was entirely changed. Back when he moved in, he'd furnished it by picking stuff out of a catalog and hiring a guy to assemble it all. Captain Black the Space Pirate didn't have time to worry about furniture.

But now the room had a fancy Mexican-style rug, and a bunch of hanging ferns and potted elephant ears, and a big wicker couch covered with brightly printed cushions. It looked . . . *nice.*

"Davie!" It was almost a shriek. Tifane stood in the doorway to the bedroom, looking very fit in a T-shirt and yoga pants. Her face lit up, and she hurled herself at him with arms wide. "Why didn't you call? I've been so worried!"

"I—" I thought you'd hook up with someone else and leave, he thought. "I was off in this crummy town in Pakistan, and there wasn't any phone service. It was business."

She knew that "business" meant something he wasn't going to talk about. "I'm so glad you're back! I missed you!"

"Yeah. Um, I like what you've done with the place."

"I bought it all myself," she said, looking proud of herself. "With my own money."

"Was there enough in the Doubloons account?"

"I only use that to pay the maintenance fee. Everything else comes from my account. I have a job!"

"One of the clubs at Voodoo Cove?"

"No, no. I teach dancing now, three classes every day plus private coaching. I have sixty-two students, and they all pay twenty francs a lesson. I make three thousand francs a week. It's better than the clubs! They are such nice ladies. A couple of them have grandchildren."

David let her rattle on because he absolutely could not

think of what to say. He hadn't expected Tifane to hang around more than a week, let alone get a job and redecorate the condo. He'd been mentally prepared to find the place trashed or cleaned out, but not this.

"Um . . . are you seeing anyone? I mean, it's been a while and—"

"No," she said, more decisively than he expected. "Some men flirt with me, especially the husbands of my students, but I am not sleeping with anyone."

Something in her expression and the tone of her voice made him wonder if she'd had a bad experience after he left, and he made up his mind not to bring up the subject again.

"Let's go to the beach," he said. "I'll get changed."

"Only for a little while. I have a class in forty-five minutes. Did you really go to Pakistan? I worked with a girl from there once, at the club in Majorca."

So on the way to the beach, he told her all about Gwadar, dwelling on the heat and the local food, and the rusting ships on the beach. He didn't talk about the project at all, and she didn't pry.

"And were you alone all the time, too?"

"I didn't have much choice," he said, and resolved not to mention the stopover in Bangkok afterwards.

. . .

Tifane's new career was a blessing for David. It meant that for four or five hours a day, he could work in the condo without any distraction. More than that, really, because she made sure to be in bed before eleven in order to lead her morning class on the beach at seven. "I need my rest," she told him. "I can't stay up playing games like you."

The games he was playing until three or four in the morning were practice simulations of the new pirate vehicle. It was a pretty simple setup, a lot easier to fly than the one he'd used on the last operation. That was because of his exceedingly clever mission plan. This pirate sloop wouldn't need to board and grapple the target, so he didn't spend much time practicing approach maneuvers. There were other systems to get used to, and even though he'd designed them, he still had to get the feel for how they'd work in practice.

Tifane was different; that much was obvious. Instead of wearing whatever he bought her, she'd picked out a whole new wardrobe of practical, professional-looking clothes. She taught her classes in tights and leotards rather than stripper costumes. She still wore her micro-bikini to lounge on the beach with David—but she also had a racing suit and insisted on swimming at least a kilometer every day. She had only one glass of wine with dinner, and she never once asked him to get her any blow.

He kept wondering what had happened to Tifane, and one dawn when he crept into bed next to her, it came to him that the answer was obvious: He had gone away. Without Captain Black the Space Pirate buying her nose candy and dressing her like a Japanese sex robot, Tifane had gotten her shit together in an almost epic way.

And that was the problem. Apparently Tifane had never had the slightest interest in any of the things David liked to talk about: space technology, software, and the fusion industry all left her cold. The new, improved Tiff didn't pretend to be fascinated just so that he would buy her stuff. And David, with the best will in the world, couldn't really work up much enthusiasm for the stories she told him about her dance students, the world of Tortuga's freelance workers, or the Brownian romantic dynamics of the condo-owning set.

Logic suggested that it was time to go their separate ways. Over brunch (breakfast for him, lunch for her) about a week after his return, David tried, very tentatively, to make the suggestion. "So . . . are you happy?"

"Very happy," she said. "I think this is the happiest I've ever been. Now that you're back things are just perfect!"

"Oh," he said. "Well, good."

"Are you happy, too?"

"Oh, yeah. No complaints." He dug into his eggs and rice, and washed it down with some coffee. All the Tortuga restaurants had really excellent coffee, grown in a high-tech super-green organic farm on the main island. If not for tax breaks and write-offs, each cup would have cost about twenty Swiss francs.

"I was just wondering if you want to get out more. I mean, you used to party every night."

"I got tired of that," she said. "After you went away, I did that for a month and then one night I was getting dressed to go down to Voodoo Cove, and I looked in the mirror and started crying. I felt so tired. I just didn't want to do it anymore. Staying home that night was incredibly nice. I took a bath and went to bed and it was so quiet and peaceful, I wanted it to go on forever."

"You don't miss it?"

"Not really."

"Isn't there anything you want? Anything at all?" Her contentment was almost making him angry.

"Well, there is one thing. I wanted to talk to you first about it. I think I am ready to have a baby."

"You're pregnant?!"

"No, not yet. Do you want to?" she asked him. Her voice was shy, but her eyes were as intense as lasers.

"That's a big decision. Let me think about it, okay?"

"Okay," she said, and he could tell she was trying not to cry.

. . .

JULY 6, 2031; 17:23 GMT

The concrete runway was still radiating heat an hour after sunset, and Elizabeth was very glad she'd decided to buy a sundress to wear instead of her Air Force uniform. She wasn't here in any official capacity, she was Jack Bonnet's guest, and she could be comfortable.

He'd invited her in his typically offhand way. "I'm going up next Monday. Want to fly out and watch the launch?"

"Of course!"

"I'll put you on the list."

She'd thought "the list" was just to get her a parking spot at one of the viewing areas at Mojave Space Port, but it turned out "the list" was *the* List. It put her in the last-look area the night before, standing a measured four meters away from Jack with tape marks on the concrete to make sure nobody cheated and sent a virus to the Moon.

"What did they feed you?" she asked, trying to keep it casual. There were people around. "Steak and eggs?"

"Wagyu beef," he said. "I skipped the eggs."

"I bet you went back for seconds."

"Of course! It was good, too. Like beef-flavored butter."

She didn't answer for a moment, just stood there. The carrier plane loomed behind him, its size making it hard to judge the distance.

"I'll miss you," she said. He cupped an ear, so she said it louder. "I'll miss you!"

"I'll miss you, too." It was his turn to be quiet and gaze away; then he looked straight back at her. "I love you, Elizabeth," he said quite loudly.

She had to will her feet to stay in one place. "I love you, too!" she said back, also loudly. Someone clapped and was shushed. "Take care of yourself up there. Come back!"

"I will. You take care of yourself, too."

For the rest of that half hour, they stood out on the pavement, saying little, just looking at each other under the starry desert sky.

Eight hours later, Elizabeth followed the carrier plane pilots up the very long ladder to the cockpit. Apparently Jack had put her on some kind of extra-superexclusive List with nobody else on it. None of the other "special guests" had training in midair evacuation or parachuting, and none of them owned a sweltering hot Air Force flight suit.

The Stratolaunch plane was as big as a ship—or two

ships, as it was a twin-fuselage design with the heavy-lift Falcon rocket slung between them. The titanic wing was longer than a football field, with six giant turbofans the size of school buses on pods underneath.

The flight deck was forty feet above the broiling concrete in the right-hand fuselage. It was a roomy space with seats for the pilots, a couple of flight engineers, a dozen launch techs and communications people, and four chairs for guests lined up on the left side with a perfect view of the rocket. Elizabeth was comforted by the look of the interior, a mix of bare-bones military efficiency and posh private-sector comfort. Her seat was a luxurious leather-upholstered first-class airline model, but the seat belt was an Air Force five-point restraint.

Takeoff was amazingly smooth. It wasn't like flying in a plane, or even sailing on a ship. It was like riding a building. She sat in a comfortable chair on the fourth floor of a building in Mojave, California. Outside, some distance away, a bunch of very big jet engines began to roar, and the landscape outside began to move past the windows of the building she was sitting in. The landscape moved faster and faster, and then the building she was sitting in was no longer located in Mojave, California, but in the air. At no point did she feel any movement.

The pilots took the launch plane up in big lazy circles, climbing to thirty thousand feet before steering west. They crossed the coast over the launch gantries and tracking antennas at Vandenberg, then turned south over the Pacific.

Elizabeth had a headset and listened in on the channel connecting the onboard launch crew, the three astronauts in the MoonDragon capsule at the front of the rocket hanging from the wing to her left, and the control center back in Mojave.

"Go for launch vector," someone said, and the pilot up front said, "Roger. Go for launch vector." The plane swung into a slow turn, lining up due east with two thousand miles of ocean and then Guatemala in front of it. The beach crowds at Acapulco would have a perfect view.

When the count reached five minutes and word came from Mojave to proceed with the launch, things got very busy. The plane pulled into a gentle climb, and the roar of the engines got louder as they shoved the biggest flying machine ever built up to nine-tenths Mach.

"Forty seconds to drop," said the controller back in Mojave. "Turbopump power-up check."

The digital display on Elizabeth's window counted down the seconds. "Aircraft attitude check. Range is clear. Twenty seconds. Falcon on internal power. Twelve seconds. Ten. Nine. Eight."

Elizabeth found herself mouthing the numbers as she clutched her armrests. The window display helpfully said FASTEN SAFETY BELTS.

"Four. Three. Turbopump start. One. *Drop!*"

The great big Falcon rocket hanging from the center wing dropped away and the giant plane swung into a very tight turn. Elizabeth craned her head to see the white oblong of the rocket as it continued forward on a ballistic path over the blue water, and then . . . Then she almost screamed in frustration as the turning airplane blocked her view completely, so that Elizabeth had to turn her attention to the screen in front of her, showing the feed from a chase drone.

"Ignition," said a voice, and the white rocket suddenly sprouted a tail of flame and smoke. For a moment the cloud hid the vehicle itself from the camera, and Elizabeth dreaded that the word "malfunction" would come through her headphones. But then the rocket rose above its vapor trail and she could see it climbing up, up, and away into the sky.

Five seconds after ignition, the shock wave reached the Stratolaunch plane and Elizabeth could hear the startlingly loud crackle, like God frying bacon, right through the skin of the plane. By the time the aircraft completed its turn, the booster was just a bright dot moving eastward, and a minute after that, it was gone.

The launch techs took off their headsets and slumped back in their seats. Someone broke out a bottle of champagne and some aluminum cups, and everyone except the pilots at the controls had some.

It took the MoonDragon capsule nine minutes to reach orbit, and after that, there was about an hour of maneuvering as it docked with the orbital tug that would push it to the Moon. Then came a lot of checklists and waiting for the launch window.

The Stratolaunch plane touched down on the long, long runway at Mojave just as the tug in orbit fired up its VASIMR engine and started accelerating toward the Moon. Elizabeth had another glass of champagne and some mini-flautas at the buffet laid out in the hangar, but listening to company managers congratulating everybody got old quickly. Elizabeth didn't think Jack would mind too much if she slipped away. Her bag was already in the rental car, and she could take a leisurely drive over the mountains to the Bakersfield airport for her connecting flight to Denver.

"Good afternoon, Captain Santiago." She looked up and saw General McEwan standing there, looking casual in a polo shirt and a souvenir INDIAN SPACE RESEARCH ORGANISATION cap. "Fine launch today."

"Jack Bonnet invited me to come watch."

"I know. How'd you like your ride on the Stratolauncher?"

"It's big."

"That it is. Let's take a little walk outside, Captain."

The fact that he was calling her "Captain" instead of "Elizabeth" was a bad sign. But showing up at Mojave Space Port in golf slacks meant this wasn't official, whatever this was.

The desert air was like rocket exhaust. "I ran into one of Dr. Bonnet's partners at the airport in Atlanta just the other day. Mike Levy. We had a drink together while we waited for our flights. Great guy."

"Yes, he's very nice," she said.

"Really enthusiastic about his spacecraft. He was telling me all about it."

Elizabeth suddenly felt cold in the desert sunlight. "It's an impressive system."

"He was especially keen on telling me about its cislunar capability. Apparently the maiden test flight is going to be up to L_1. Mike said he hoped I'd keep that in mind when we start the bidding on a replacement for the MARIO series."

Elizabeth knew enough not to say anything.

McEwan's voice went up a few decibels. "I told him I couldn't comment, and then I made some calls—just to be sure I'm not losing my memory. Did you know that we're not planning a replacement for the MARIO vehicle?"

She looked at the ground.

"In fact, between you and me, Captain Santiago, that last *fiasco* means we're pretty much giving up on power projection beyond low orbit. Helium piracy is a law enforcement issue, not defense. Air Force Orbital Command is not in the market for a new vehicle. So where the—*heck*—did Mike Levy get the idea that we were?"

"I never told him that."

"No? Well, you sure didn't bother to correct the *mistaken impression* he got from someone!"

She could feel herself getting angry back at him. Shut up, Elizabeth, she told herself, but it didn't work. "We're going to need that vehicle, sir. How many payloads can we afford to lose?"

"Captain, that is a policy decision, which *you* are not qualified to make!" He glanced around and lowered his voice a little. "*Darn* it, Elizabeth! You had so much potential! I could've got you back on the fast track after losing MARIO. Everybody has bad luck sometimes. But this—! This shows *bad judgment*. That's terminal."

"What's going to happen to me now?"

"Now? Levy's going to find out about the change in policy, and I expect he'll ask for someone else to act as mission director. Because he's a nice guy, he probably won't file a complaint about you, or a lawsuit. But people will know, Elizabeth. You'll get put someplace where you can't do any harm to finish your tour, and if you've got any self-respect left, you'll leave the service for good."

"I can . . . ," She stopped. She couldn't think of a way out.

"Do you feel all right?" McEwan asked her suddenly, with a slightly different note in his voice. "Having any trouble sleeping lately? Substance issues? Because . . . losing a spacecraft is pretty stressful. Could cause psychological problems. Maybe a medical discharge? No shame in that, and you keep your pension."

"I'm fine," she said. "I'm not going to pretend. I screwed up, and I'll take the consequences. I'll submit my resignation."

When McEwan spoke again, he was almost apologetic. "Look, if you need a letter of reference or a recommendation, I'd be glad to write one for you. You're really very talented. Whatever you decide to do, I'm sure employers will be standing in line to get you."

Except the employer she wanted to work for. "I have to get going," she said. "I don't want to miss my flight." As she walked away under the blazing sun in her flight suit, her posture was perfect.

■ ■ ■

AUGUST 22, 2031; 10:19 GMT

The day after their serious brunch conversation, Tifane showed David a brightly printed paper voucher. "One of the ladies in my class gave me this. It's free admission to a party at the Viceroy Club. Me and a guest."

"Sure—oh, wait. When is it?"

"Tomorrow night from six to six."

"Shit. I've got something very important going down on Saturday. But," he added as her face fell, "I can put in an appearance for a couple of hours, if you want to go."

The party was exactly what David had expected. Music too loud for conversation, a throng of douche bags trying to impress one another, and a DJ who kept assuring the crowd that they were having a good time.

David danced with Tifane for an hour or so, until the bass beat and the effect of four frozen daiquiris made his temples start to pound. He went out on the balcony to clear his head. The wrought iron was a genuine replica of old Havana, but the cobbled street below was a bizarre hybrid of New Orleans, San Juan, and the Pirates of the Caribbean ride at Disney World. The low-key lighting meant he could see the stars overhead, and he was about to check his phone to see what orbiters might be visible when he heard a thump and saw movement in the shadows to his left.

A dark-clad figure was climbing up over the railing. David felt a jolt of paranoid terror. Black-ops assassins coming for him! But then the person moved into the light and he saw it was a young woman in jeans and a nice-looking black silk blouse. She caught sight of him and smiled.

"The door guy wouldn't let you in?"

"There's a line," she said. "And I can't afford the cover, either."

"If you can't afford that, I've got bad news about the drinks," he said.

"Then you'll just have to buy me one," she said promptly.

A year ago, or even six months, David would have laughed and bought her a drink without hesitating. Now his eyes flicked to the dance floor to see if Tifane was watching. "Sure," he said, and handed her his Tortuga Doubloon card. "Get me something, too. Something interesting."

She came back with a bottle of Veuve Clicquot and two plastic flutes. "This interesting enough?"

He knew it was the most expensive thing in the bar, but did his best to act unimpressed. "I bet they're glad someone finally bought it. It's been sitting in that chiller behind the bar gathering dust since I moved here." He got the little cagework off the cork, at which point the bottle erupted, launching the cork off in the direction of Andromeda. "Victory celebration!" he said as foam gushed everywhere, including her blouse. He filled the cups and let his settle before sipping.

"You live here?" she asked.

"Yep. I've got one of the condos. How about you?"

"I'm here on my boat."

"What kind of a boat?"

"My boat. The *Carina*. It's a Stingray."

He didn't know if he was supposed to be impressed by that or not. "Where'd you sail it from? Miami?"

"Kingston."

"That's a pretty long haul." Actually it wasn't. Boaters went back and forth between Jamaica and Haiti every weekend. She probably had a professional crew on her Stingray, anyway.

"Kingston, *Oklahoma*," she said with a triumphant air.

"You sailed to Tortuga from Oklahoma? Seriously?"

"Yep. Last winter, I was driving home from OU on Highway 70 when I passed a boat on the side of the road with a FOR SALE sign on it. I stopped right there and bought it that same day. Then I withdrew from my classes, got a box of MREs, a GPS, and a bunch of books and videos about boats, and launched it on Lake Texoma."

Rich and crazy, he decided, but nice enough. "How'd you wind up here?"

"I decided to go downriver. It took me two weeks to get to New Orleans, and then I just kept on going. A month later I was in Miami, and then I worked my way down here through the Bahamas. I had to ride out Tropical Storm Bernard in Eleuthera."

"All by yourself?"

"I like being alone."

"And you never went sailing before?"

"Not really. I grew up in Oklahoma and Texas. I went canoeing a couple of times when I was a Girl Scout, but that's it. This trip has been amazing. I've learned a lot. At first I used the GPS for everything, but I got a sextant in Mobile and now I can navigate with just that and a compass if I have to. I even figured out how to fix the bilge pump on my own. The first couple of days out on the Gulf I got seasick, but now I can handle anything."

"So where are you going next? Back up to Oklahoma?"

"Nope. I figure I'll work my way down to Brazil. Then I can decide if I want to go up the Amazon, or try to cross over to Africa. I'm going to sail around the world, if I can. I've been posting updates and videos online as I go."

Very crazy, thought David, though you'd never know it from her matter-of-fact way of talking.

"What happens when Daddy stops paying the bills?"

Her grin went away in an instant. She studied him for ten long seconds with her jaw clenched, then emptied her plastic champagne flute onto David's shoes. "Daddy died," she said. She turned and walked into the crowded bar, edging her way between people until she got to the stairs.

He was about to follow her when his phone played the chorus of "With Cat-Like Tread." Ten o'clock, which meant it was 2300 Zulu time. At the launch facility in Indonesia, the last scheduled hold would be starting at T minus sixty minutes. Time for Captain Black the Space Pirate to take command of his ship.

Tifane was ready to go home, too. "Time for your big conference?"

"That's right. I'm going to be at the hotel room for the next few days. Call me if you need something, but only if it's really important and can't wait."

"Davie?" There was a plaintive note in her voice.

"What?" He tried not to sound impatient, but the clock in his head was running.

"You really have to work?"

"Yes, sweetie. I'm going to be sitting in front of a screen, eating room service food the whole time."

"Did you think about—what I said?"

"The baby thing? A lot of it depends on how this job comes out. If it comes off the way I want, we'll be set up for life." That wasn't quite true—by any reasonable standard, he was already set up for life, but it did buy him time to actually make up his mind without delaying the mission.

He gave her a dutiful peck on the cheek, and the two of them parted ways at Place des Boucaniers. She went up the hill toward the condo, he went down to the Port Royal Inn, where his command center was ready.

David's command center was a "business suite"—a bedroom, a large living room with a conference table and folding couch-bed, and a kitchenette. He had made a few modifications to turn it into Space Pirate Command. He'd taped unshielded copper wire onto the walls and ceiling in a semi-random zigzag plugged into the wall socket. That ought to generate enough static to defeat any attempts at electronic eavesdropping. He'd paid off all the maids on this floor to leave the place absolutely untouched until he moved out, and to let him know if anyone rented the rooms on either side of his. And he had moved his coffeemaker into the kitchenette along with five pounds of dark-roasted local beans.

The conference table was his new quarterdeck. He had four top-of-the-line laptops networked together, with the VR rig for interactive control. There were two phone lines, and he'd established connections to Ghavami's operation in Qizil Orda two days earlier. The telecom bill for the room would be ferocious, but with the profits from this mission, he'd be able to buy the goddamned hotel if he felt like it.

His ultimate weapon was in the kitchenette refrigerator: a box of two dozen drug patches, straight from his connection in Geneva. They increased nerve transmission rate and neurotransmitter uptake. With a patch on each side of his neck, Captain Black the Space Pirate would be the fastest, smartest guy in outer space. The downside was increased risk of Alzheimer's, but he figured there'd be a cure for that by the time he had to worry about it.

System check was nominal. The booster on the pad was ready to fly, his pirate payload was safely asleep on top of it. Weather looked good, both in Indonesian waters and in near-Earth space.

Colonel Ghavami's image appeared on the conferencing screen to his left. "Are you ready? They are going to resume the count in ten minutes."

"I'm all set. Yo ho ho, and all that."

Ghavami didn't even react to that. "Operational security is good. According to my sources, there has been no unusual activity by the American Air Force or the Indian Navy in the past forty-eight hours."

"Great! So let's light this candle."

Ghavami's image turned back into a silhouette. Evidently he had someone else to bother. David looked at the clock. Seven minutes.

On a whim, he opened up a new screen and connected to the Tortuga resort's own system. What had that girl called her boat? The *Carina*? He looked at the listings for the yacht harbor. There it was: *Carina,* home port Kingston, Oklahoma, owner Anne Rogers. A seven-meter cabin cruiser, fifteen years old.

Four minutes left in the launch hold. He took out his personal phone, the one listed to David Schwartz, harmless expat and occasional freelance space-industry journalist. He called the phone number in the hotel database and left a message.

"Hey, this is David Schwartz. I bought you a bottle of champagne earlier this evening. Listen, I don't know what I said to get you so upset, but I'm sorry. I was just making conversation. Let's get together for lunch next Thursday if you're still in Tortuga."

"End scheduled hold at 00:01 Zulu Time," said the voice of the Indonesian launch director. "Resuming the count at T minus sixty minutes . . . now."

The mission clock blinked over to 00:59:59 in the corner of David's screen. "Arr, me hearties," muttered Captain Black the Space Pirate. "Time to hoist the black flag!"

8

The Delta rocket sat steaming on the pad at Kennedy in the predawn light. Inside the payload fairing were two orbiters. One was an atmosphere research platform called AEOLUS—the name was a typically convoluted acronym made up to fit a nice classical mythology reference. The other was SOTHIS. Since it was a propulsion test vehicle, the exact orbit didn't really matter, and Mike Levy had been able to work out a bargain with NOAA and NSF to share the launch cost.

The control area at Icarus was jammed—all the employees and partners were there, along with some reporters, family members, friends, and hangers-on. Mike Levy looked magnificent in a new seersucker suit as he spoke to the press, while Yumiko nervously hovered in the flight control area, trying to do three people's jobs at once. Jack Bonnet even sent a video greeting from the Moon.

Elizabeth Santiago sat on the floor of her apartment drinking rum straight from the bottle.

Three weeks earlier, she had gotten off the flight from

California and gone straight to see Mike. As it happened, he was at home that day. Mike and Yumiko lived in an old slab-foundation ranch house from the Space Coast's glory days. Elizabeth found him in the kitchen, peeling tomatoes.

"Oh, hey!" he said when he looked up. "I'm just making some gazpacho. I've got chicken marinating to put on the grill when Yumiko gets home. Want to stay for dinner?"

"No thanks," she said. Her mouth was dry. "I'm afraid I have to quit the SOTHIS project."

"Aw, that's terrible. Air Force sending you somewhere else?"

"No. I'm resigning."

He looked shocked. "Why? What's going on?"

She took a deep breath. "I lied to you. I told you ORBITCOM was considering SOTHIS for a new inspection orbiter. There is no new orbiter planned. I just wanted you to change the mission plan so it would be testing at L_1."

"Liz, I don't understand. Why? Was this some kind of undercover project, or—?"

"No. It was just me. I wanted to have something—anything—up at L_1 to stop the next helium piracy attempt." She didn't mention the GyroJet launcher. That would bring Jack into it.

"My little bird a pirate-hunter?" He almost smiled, but then shook his head. "No, it wouldn't work without legal cover. Crash into someone else's satellite, and it's lawsuit time. Even winning in court would break Icarus right now. Did you think of that?"

"Yes," she said quietly. "I just thought it was more important to show the pirates we can still fight back."

"I see. So why'd you decide to fess up?"

"My boss talked with you at the airport the other day and figured it out. He gave me the chance to tell you first and then resign. I'm out of the Air Force, and the space business."

"God damn. Do you know how much launching that extra propellant's going to cost? Never mind. McEwan sending me someone else to fly SOTHIS?"

"Probably. There are some good junior officers who could use the experience."

"And you?"

"I don't know yet," she said.

"Well," he said, and took a deep breath. "Good luck. You can still come watch the launch if you want."

But she didn't. She did have the live feed open on her tablet as the rocket thundered off into the sunrise, and she toasted the mission with an extra-long swig from the rum bottle. Then she crawled back into bed and passed out.

. . .

AUGUST 23, 2031; 00:59 GMT

"T minus one minute," said the voice of the Indonesian launch controller in David's headphones. The controller had a great deadpan Right Stuff delivery, with just enough Malay lilt in his vowels to let you know he wasn't in Florida. The screen in front of David showed a view of the rocket standing in tropical sunshine, vapor streaming from its frosted skin.

"Captain Black?" said Ghavami, his image switching

from a silhouette to active video, "I have just received a message. The American CIA may be aware of your involvement in this operation. According to my informant, one or more of their agents may already be in Tortuga."

"Who's your source?"

"I can't tell you that," Ghavami chided him.

"I mean, how hard is this info?"

"T minus thirty seconds. Twenty-nine . . . ," said the controller.

"I would not have told you if there was any reason to doubt the report," said Ghavami.

". . . twenty-three, twenty-two . . ."

"Well, it's way too late to move, so I'll just keep the door locked." David didn't give a crap about the CIA. He kept up with intel and covert-ops news. Those assholes didn't know anything about the helium business. Now, if Ghavami had warned him about a team from the FBI or Indian RAW in Tortuga, he'd be hitting the igniter for the thermite taped to all the computers in the room and heading out the window.

". . . fourteen, thirteen, twelve . . ."

"Be careful, Captain," said Ghavami.

"T minus ten. Nine. Eight. Engine start sequence. Six. Five. Four. Thrust check okay. Two. One. Umbilical disconnect. We have liftoff." The little clock in the corner of all David's screens switched from negative to positive numbers.

His part in all this was mostly that of an interested spectator. The rocket was under the control of the techs at Biak, and his pirate vehicle was still just a dormant piece of payload inside a launch shroud. But he did have full information, so at least if something went wrong at the launch, he'd know right away. And anyway, it was exciting to be part of the control loop. He could almost imagine he was on top of that booster himself, just now breaking Mach 1 as he soared eastward along the equator.

The strap-ons burned out and separated, followed by the first stage. Everything nominal so far. David glanced at the clock and was startled to see that only three minutes had passed since launch. He knew it intellectually, but with the smart drugs coursing through his system, it had felt like hours.

The second stage reached maximum acceleration as it kicked the payload into a long ellipse stretching 350,000 kilometers toward the Moon.

"Pyros armed. Ten seconds to shroud separation. Four, three, two, fire pyrotechnics," said the calm-voiced controller, and then after a heart-stopping pause, he added, "Shroud separation confirmed."

As the unfiltered sunlight of space hit David's pirate vehicle, he began the startup sequence. "Direct link confirmed. Beginning system check . . ." The little checklist on his screen flicked all green as the satellite's cheap little onboard computer (which had about fifty times as much processing power as the whole Apollo program) ran through its diagnostics.

"System check okay," said David. "Ready for separation. Begin main engine start sequence."

"Separation confirmed," said the Indonesian controller,

whose job was now done. *"Al-ḥamdu lillāh,"* he added before his image turned into a silhouette and then vanished.

Biak handed off control, and everybody suddenly got a lot more attentive. In Tasbuget, on the other side of the world from David, Halfdan began working down a checklist of his own. "Fuel pressure check. Tank One at one hundred percent. Tank Two at ninety-eight percent. Battery at full charge. Engine diagnostic okay. Go for main engine."

"Roger," said David. "Begin thirty-second count for main engine start on my mark. . . . Mark."

A new timer window opened on the screen to David's right, and the numbers counted down to zero. "Engine start!" A thousand miles above him, pressurized monomethyl hydrazine and nitrogen tetroxide gushed into the engine reaction chamber and spontaneously exploded.

"Burn clock ten, nine, eight, seven, six, five, four, three, two, fuel valves shut, burn complete," said Halfdan. "The reaver sails the comet-road."

David's pirate satellite moved away from the spent booster. The rocket would eventually drop back down to Earth and burn up, but the satellite was now on course to the L_1 point.

The mission clock was at four hours and change when David could finally take a break. Every muscle was tense even though he'd been doing nothing more strenuous than sitting in an ergonomic chair at a conference table. He called room service for a party platter of empanadas, chicken wings, and celery sticks, then told the crew in Tasbuget he'd be off-line for a few hours.

While he ate, he checked his personal messages. Tifane had sent him a message at eleven o'clock local time, "Gnight luv u."

There was also a note from Anne Rogers. "Sorry I blew up like that. Buy me an expensive lunch and I'll forgive you. Will be in port until Tuesday."

Well, that sure as hell wouldn't work. On Tuesday, his mind would be up in orbit, steering the payload down to the capture. Oh, well, he decided. Crazy Boat Girl would have to go on without him.

. . .

AUGUST 24, 2031

Jack Bonnet watched the robots lift the cryo container full of liquid helium-3 onto the booster. The bots looked pretty comical in their baggy Moon suits. The whole idea of robots wearing spacesuits was pretty comical, until you saw what Moon dust did to any unprotected moving parts. The Moon had no wind to blow it away, no rain to rinse it, and the stuff was incredibly abrasive. Any system that you wanted to use for more than a week or so had to be carefully protected.

The dust also stuck to just about every surface, so the robots were as sooty as old-time coal miners, as was Jack himself. The only clean thing in his view was the cryo container itself, a big pure-white Ping-Pong ball twice as tall as a man. The robots held it by handles on the base and hefted it onto the booster stage. He didn't need to supervise them closely; they were optimized for this sort of work.

Jack and the other two men in the Babcock base weren't

there to do routine work. Their job was to cope with un-expected problems. Robots, even when controlled by the smartest supercomputer money could buy, were still lousy at problem-solving. They were quite good at problem-finding, though. They could get into trouble in ways no human ever imagined.

During the times when the robots weren't coming up with new problems for their human colleagues to solve, the three men could do a little science, as well. They had a laundry list of experiments that researchers on Earth wanted done. Astronauts had a long tradition of bitching about experiments, but in point of fact, they were a much more interesting way to spend downtime than playing games or watching videos.

The display projected on his helmet visor said they were on schedule for launch in twenty-two hours. All the launches took place during the Lunar night, when temperature regulation was a lot easier. The bots spent the long day sifting through regolith, cooking out the helium and other light elements. The gas they collected got sorted in the mass spectroscopy device, and then the helium went through a more precise extraction to separate the lighter He-3 atoms from the heavier and more numerous He-4.

Each night, the refinery had to process millions of kilos of dirt to cook out one payload's worth of usable helium-3. By now the transports were shuttling out ten kilometers or more to gather surface material. In another year or two, they'd have to pick up the whole facility and move to someplace with fresh dirt to process.

Opponents of fusion power liked to talk about how

helium-3 was a "nonrenewable resource," which was technically true, but the Moon could send a ton of it a month to Earth for the next two hundred thousand years. Presumably by then someone would have come up with a new source of supply.

The cryo container latched snugly on to the booster, and all the displays in Jack's helmet showed green. "Good job, guys," he said to the bots. They couldn't hear him, of course, and couldn't understand voice anyway. But it was impossible not to talk to them.

A reminder popped up under the clock display on his helmet faceplate. Time to head back to the habitat. It was a long walk, but he enjoyed the exercise. A dozen long bounds took him off the launch field, but then he had to hop along more slowly as he passed the fuel plant and the giant sintering machine that made the cryo vessels out of Moon dirt. It could make just about anything, given enough time, the right elements, and the right software.

Payload containers were easy. Rocket fuel was not. It all had to come up from Earth in the form of water. The crew drank the water, washed in it, and their waste processor broke it up into hydrogen and oxygen to fuel the boosters. Jack bunny-hopped past the fuel plant, under its big sunshade. Now that night had fallen, the plant was going full blast, and the radiators were glowing dull red as they threw off waste heat into space.

He reached the habitat air lock, but did not go through the hatch. The entry hatch was for emergencies only, and except for the monthly equipment test, it was never used. Instead he went around to the side, where three Moon suits stood leaning against the wall of the air lock like smokers taking a break outside.

Jack went to a small rectangular hatch in the wall, turned around, and backed up until he felt his bulky backpack bump against the rim. He bent his knees a little until he felt the pack slip into the hatchway, then pushed himself backwards until the edge of the hatch fit snugly against the rigid back of his suit. There were three latches on each side— big ones, with serious lever-arms to fasten them. One by one, he forced them shut, pinning himself securely to the wall with what everyone devoutly hoped was an airtight seal.

Once he was latched to the station, Jack reached over and hit the control plate for the hatch. Behind him he felt a bump as the hatch swung open and air filled the space around his backpack.

Now came the part that always made Jack's heart rate jump. He had to unfasten the backpack and let it swing back down inside the hatch so that he could climb out and go inside the hab. There were safeguards—the hatch wasn't supposed to open at all if the air lock was empty of air— but he couldn't keep from taking a deep breath before entering the four-digit code on his chest plate, which released the backpack latches.

He felt a series of clicks behind him, and then the back of his suit fell away. The air pressure inside the air lock pushed his arms and legs out. Jack wriggled and scrunched and finally got his head past the rim of the hatch. After that he could just grab the overhead bar and pull himself out.

"I'm hooome!" he called out to Harpal Singh and

Korekiyo Ueno, and got a couple of monosyllabic noises in response.

The habitat was a big tuna can made of aluminum and Kevlar. It was supposedly designed to hold six people, but even with only three it was crowded. The outer walls and the roof were lined with water tanks as radiation shielding, and outside it was covered with a meter of dirt. In the event of a big solar flare the crew could crowd into a lead-lined closet called the "storm shelter," but Jack was honestly not sure if he'd rather spend a day jammed into a box with Singh and Ueno or take his chances with the radiation.

"Vehicle's on the pad," said Singh. "Launch count at T minus twenty hours."

"It looked good," said Jack.

"The bots are hooking up the fuel lines now," said Singh. "Want some tea? Dinner's still cooking."

"Thanks." Jack gulped down the sweet milky tea, ignoring how it burned his throat as he swallowed. He checked the time. "I've got just enough time to take a leak and wash my face before my call. I'll have dinner when I'm done."

He got himself cleaned up and emptied out, then hurried to his bunk. Other than the toilet, the only real privacy inside the habitat was each astronaut's bunk. With the curtain tied shut, Jack was absolute master of two cubic meters of space.

One minute. The window on his tablet screen showed the Deep Space Network logo, and then switched to a view of Elizabeth Santiago in her unfurnished apartment down in Florida.

"Hi," he said.

Annoying three-second pause. "Hi," she answered.

The two of them spent a lot of time not saying things. Just looking at her face looking back at him was enough. They could send as much text back and forth as they wanted, but each astronaut had only twenty minutes of private high bandwidth open each day. Singh alternated talks with his wife, his parents, and his son in the Indian Navy. Ueno was unattached, and used his time to make live science broadcasts for an educational channel in Japan.

Jack spent his twenty minutes looking at Elizabeth. It made the Moon a much nicer place.

. . .

MISSION TIME 21:20

David slept a solid six hours and stayed in touch with Tasbuget all the next day as the satellite covered the distance to L_1. Ghavami gave him an update on the target payload. "The Moonbase is preparing to launch on schedule in twenty hours. We will be just in time to meet the payload."

"Well, if we miss it, there's always the next one," said David.

"No! It must be this one." Ghavami sounded unusually tense, even for him.

"How come?"

There was a pause, and then over the teleconference screen Ghavami gave him a reassuring smile. "Finances," he said. "Some of our backers are planning to take advantage of the market shifts our theft will cause. If we miss this capture, they will lose money."

"That's not very good operational security, you know. Cops look for stuff like that."

"It is all done through shell companies and cutouts. There is no way to trace it back to us."

"If you say so."

Checking out the satellite and troubleshooting some of the software bugs that somehow had survived all the pre-launch testing took up most of David's time that weekend, but he did make sure to contact Tifane a couple of times, just to reassure her that he wasn't lying around in bed with an entire girls' volleyball team from Vietnam or something. She didn't bring up the topic of babies, and neither did he.

He did think about it, though. His own family life had been minimal and mostly annoying. The thought of bringing a child into the world just to go through the same shit that he had seemed absurd. And yet . . . millions of people did it every day, even multiple times. They couldn't all be Catholics or Race Defender nuts.

David tried to picture himself as the head of a family, at some Norman Rockwell table lined with Schwartz progeny, with Tifane by his side, setting out a big platter of Thai roast duck or something. It didn't work. Tiff was nice, sexy as hell . . . but he couldn't imagine growing old with her. In fact, he was having a hard time even planning to move back into the condo once this mission was done.

. . .

AUGUST 25, 2031

Jack had wanted to watch the cargo launch in person, but the three of them were too busy actually controlling it from inside the habitat for him to get any surface time. So he compromised by sending one of the bots to a position just twenty meters away from the launchpad, and then kept a window open on his control screen showing the view from the bot's eyes.

The cargo carrier for Westinghouse payload number 38 was ready to go anytime they cared to press the button. The only time-critical part of the launch was making sure that the payload would hit the proper drop zone on Earth. This particular one was supposed to enter the Earth's upper atmosphere over the Indian Ocean and drop into the sea near Samoa.

The launch window was about half an hour. If they missed today's chance, it would have to wait twenty-five hours. Given the value of their cargo, the rule was always "when in doubt, wait."

But today the board was all green as the launch clock ticked down to T minus ten minutes and they started the final count. Ueno was in charge of guidance, Jack was monitoring the spacecraft itself, and Singh was on the link to the Westinghouse controllers in Cranberry Township. The actual launch control was a literal Big Red Button that some previous crew had cobbled together, and was plugged into Ueno's workstation.

The little rocket motor underneath Westinghouse 38 was pitiful by Terrestrial standards. On Earth, it wouldn't even be able to lift off the ground, just sit there making noise and smoke until the fuel was gone. But on the Moon, it was an interplanetary powerhouse.

It had to work only once, but everything had to work perfectly that one time. The design was deliberately kept as simple as possible—pumps and the power to run them added layers of complication, so the hydrogen and oxygen were pressure-fed. Cooling was entirely passive. Ultimately, the whole launch depended on two valves and one electric igniter. If they worked when they were supposed to, then in sixty hours, a fortune in helium-3 would drop out of the sky into the waters of the Pacific. If they didn't, then either Jack and the bots would have to fix the rocket by tomorrow—or they'd all get to watch a billion dollars explode. It had happened, a couple of times.

"T minus twenty," said Ueno, and put his finger lightly on the Big Red Button.

Fuel pressure was steadily rising as the liquid hydrogen and oxygen began to boil inside their tanks. There was no sunlight, but the Moon itself was still radiating heat from the long day, and the base itself made Babcock Crater a heat island. If they didn't launch today, Jack would have to bleed off the extra pressure, then top off the tanks again for the next launch opportunity.

"T minus twelve, eleven, ten . . . ," said Ueno. By the time he got to six, all three of them were chanting along at the top of their voices. ". . . THREE! TWO! ONE! IGNITION!"

Ueno pressed the Big Red Button. Two valves opened

just as they were supposed to. Pressurized hydrogen and oxygen flowed. An electrical igniter sparked. Westinghouse 38 left the Moon.

Launching from the Moon looked almost comical. There was none of the awe-inspiring rumble, no shock wave, no towering plume of exhaust, no agonizingly slow start. The bulbous cargo launcher leaped off the surface, scattering Moon dust and microscopic ice crystals as it went. The pale blue flame of the engine was barely visible against the blackness of space, and Jack's robot tracked the spacecraft with its cameras as it rose, curved away to the east, and eventually vanished beyond the crater rim.

There was no champagne for drinking a toast, but their supplies did include a few cans of ginger ale. The three of them raised their aggressively fizzing cups and drank a toast to their latest launch.

"May it have a speedy and uneventful voyage," said Singh, and they all drank to that.

. . .

When the mission clock read 23:54, the team in Tasbuget did a midcourse correction burn, and at 57:49, David personally did the first of two braking burns intended to pop the satellite into a semi-stable orbit at L_1. He used the pirate game interface for the second, as his sloop eased into a strait crowded with other sails. Some of them he recognized as pirate craft and flagged with the Jolly Roger. Others were simple science observers or comm relays, so he put the Swiss flag on them. Mostly harmless.

One satellite merited special attention. It was a propulsion test vehicle, American, which had attracted David's interest because Elizabeth Santiago was involved with the company developing it. She'd later dropped out of the project, so for the moment, David was reasonably sure it wasn't some secret Air Force pirate-hunter. Still, just to remind himself to keep an eye on it, he assigned it a frigate icon instead of a merchantman, and marked it with a Texas Navy flag.

By 58:50, David's satellite was in position. Now things began to move very quickly. David slapped on more drug patches to keep himself sharp. The target payload was only three hours away, lumbering up out of the Moon's gravity well. This one was moving a little faster than the last one he'd intercepted.

Ghavami fed him the latest intel. "They have reduced the helium mass by fifty kilograms, which gives the cargo module more fuel to maneuver."

"Cheap bastards. That's fifty mil we're not going to be able to spend."

"That also means your encounter velocity will be higher."

"I noticed that already. Unless they do some burns, that payload's going to pass through L_1 at about ten kilometers per hour. I can catch it, no problem."

"Oh, by the way—," said Ghavami. "There is a difficulty with the landing zone."

"I am so fucking tired of these fucking last-minute changes."

"It is nothing major. If you wish, you can hand off control after the capture and my team here can guide it down."

"Sure, whatever. Now, for the next few hours I'd like everyone to take a big steaming cup of shut the fuck up while I steal this thing."

. . .

AUGUST 26, 2031; 14:10 GMT

Elizabeth Santiago was finishing her second Bloody Mary of the morning when she got the call from Susan Kraus. "You might want to look at L_1. Something's going down right now."

Happily, Elizabeth's Air Force passwords and access to the MARIO working group were still active, so she could call up the ORBITCOM tracking display showing known objects in and around the L_1 point.

Westinghouse 38 was approaching the zone, on course for aerobraking and splashdown. But there was a suspicious character loitering among the satellites at L_1: a newly launched vehicle out of Indonesia, built in Pakistan and officially owned by a Namibian company with offices in Tunisia.

And there wasn't an Air Force bird closer than a quarter-million miles away. The SOTHIS vehicle was right there, but it was in quiet mode, and she didn't think anyone at Icarus wanted to risk it going pirate-hunting.

If she'd been more drunk or more sober, Elizabeth would have just said fuck it and gone back to feeling sorry for herself. As it was, she had just enough vodka in her to reach for her phone and dig through the records until she found David Schwartz's old number from the days when they'd been dating. It was probably long out of date, but she went ahead and hit the Call button.

To her surprise, the "I'm not available now" message was obviously David's voice, so at the tone, she tried to sound as menacing as she could. "We know who you are, we know where you are, and we know what you're trying to do. If Westinghouse 38 gets hijacked, you are going down hard."

When she clicked off, she realized how dumb that was. He'd know it was her. But at this point, prank calls were the only weapon at Elizabeth's disposal. The realization made her want another Bloody Mary.

She did send Jack another message, her third of the day. She tried to limit herself to just two, but this was actually kind of job-related. "Jack: Looks like your last payload's about to get jacked. Wish there was something I could do. Love you, E."

To her surprise, she got an answer back just a couple of minutes later. "Cost of doing business (shrug). 4 hr on surface today. Tired. Gorgeous view of half Earth above rim. Only 58 days left. Love, JB."

9

David's virtual pirate crew was working smoothly. As the helium payload approached, he boosted on an intercept course such that speed and position would match. Predictably, the enemy's ground controllers began evasive maneuvers, showing off a little with their lighter-than-usual load and extra fuel reserve.

David ignored them. The cargo had to strike Earth's atmosphere at a certain velocity and a certain time, so all their stunt-flying had to fit inside a very narrow range. They couldn't get away from him; all they could do was keep him from docking.

"Run out the guns," he said to himself, then over the link to Tasbuget, "Power up the VCR."

The VCR was the crowning masterpiece of the mission plan. The ultimate thumb in the Air Force's eye. It was not a vintage videocassette recorder. The initials stood for VIGIL CORE RIPOFF, and the device was a cheap, one-shot version of the Air Force electronic warfare system he'd narrowly avoided last time. It meant that his current probe didn't need to dock with the target, didn't need an arm, or oversized thrusters, or any of that heave-to-and-be-boarded crap.

All it required was a transmitter with signal power greater at a distance of a kilometer or so than the ground antennas could manage from a light-second away. With the inverse-square law working to his advantage, that meant David could drown out the legitimate command channel with a measly ten-watt transmitter. So all he had to do was keep within spitting distance of Westinghouse 38, and they could do all the orbital gymnastics they wanted to without inconveniencing him in the least. If it all worked according to plan. If not . . .

He activated the VCR and held his breath. Apparently one of the engineers at Lockheed Martin had gone with some Japanese colleagues on a sex tour to Bangkok, and revealed a surprisingly kinky interest in bondage games with underage Thai prostitutes. All consensual (sort of) and paid for—except that one of Colonel Ghavami's people had set up a camera in the hotel room.

The engineer had been given a choice: Hand over the encryption scheme and specs for the control system they put on the Westinghouse cargo module, or the video would go to his boss, the cops in Thailand, his local district attorney, and his wife. Ghavami's people had also warned him that they'd expect updates on any changes made before the payload launched.

David commanded the payload to change frequencies, then switched his own transmitter. A couple of seconds later, his traffic monitor bars spiked as the Westinghouse techs tried frantically to regain control of their vehicle.

"GOTCHA!" he yelled, then tapped the link to Tasbuget. "Okay, it's on the new frequency. I'm sending it the new encryption now."

Someone in Cranberry Township must have figured out what he was doing, because the Westinghouse signal power took a huge jump. Were they using the Arecibo antenna or something? Beings in other star systems along the beam would be thwacking the sides of their TV sets in a few centuries when the new command signals started drowning out their favorite soap operas.

But it didn't matter. They were using an encryption system that was thirty-five seconds out of date. The payload belonged to Captain Black now. On his virtual display, a pirate banner fluttered from the galleon's masthead.

"Okay, what's the new landing zone?" he asked.

To his surprise, Ghavami's image went live. "We are still working that out. Can you send the new encryption key to the guidance controller here? You can take a break."

"You *don't know* yet? What the fuck happened?"

"The people doing our recovery operation got raided by the Singaporean Navy. I am negotiating with a group in East Africa."

David called up his mission simulator and fiddled with parameters. "Okay, we can make an Indian Ocean drop, but it means an earlier deorbit burn. That means . . . sixty hours. I need to know by tomorrow."

"Don't worry," said Ghavami. "Now, send over the new key so you can get some rest."

"Yeah, sure." He emailed the new encryption, then sat back and sighed. The job had been almost disappointingly simple. It felt anticlimactic. You could automate it. Probably the corporate guys would come up with better data security, maybe some kind of call-and-response system to avoid games with the signal. And engineers less vulnerable to blackmail. But in the interim, piracy would be almost boring.

It was too bad he was working with crooks and spooks, thought David. He could patent his method and get a royalty every time someone stole a payload.

He felt like celebrating. Maybe invite Tiff over for a little space-pirate booty call?

No, he decided. Not if he was planning to break up with her. That wouldn't be right. In fact . . . he took a deep breath and made up his mind. He'd go tell her in person, right now. Tell her she could keep the condo, wish her luck in her new life, then grab his stuff and get the hell out of there.

The condo was ten minutes away on foot. Allow half an hour for good-byes and screaming, and another ten minutes to get back. He could spare an hour. It would work. There wasn't anything in the condo he couldn't stand to lose. David locked his business suite and began walking briskly uphill toward the condo complex.

It was just past eight in the morning locally, so Tortuga Pirate World™ was almost deserted. Down at the Pirate Adventure park, the families with kids were lining up for rides, and a few die-hard water-sports people were heading out to sea, but the bulk of the inhabitants were still in bed.

He unlocked the door with his keycard and went in. "Hello? Tifane? Are you here?"

No answer. Maybe she was giving a private dance lesson to some early rising retiree. Oh, well. It had been a good idea. He helped himself to some juice from the fridge, then wandered into the bedroom. Might as well grab some clean clothes while he was here.

She was dead. He knew that right away. She was lying on the bed facedown with her head hanging over the edge and her hair undone. Where her curls touched the floor, they were rooted in a pool of blood. David had never seen a dead person before, but her stillness and silence made it impossible to doubt.

He could see his pistol on the floor near her. Had she killed herself? He stepped closer. Now he could make out a neat hole in the back of her head. He knelt and looked at her face, then bolted for the bathroom but didn't make it.

After he finished vomiting, he cleaned his face, but his body kept trembling. He had to force himself to think. Tifane was dead. Someone had killed her. With his gun. Nothing was missing from the condo, so it wasn't a robbery. Someone had murdered Tifane. Why? Who?

The fog in his mind started to clear. It was him! Someone had come here looking for David Schwartz and found Tifane instead. And killed her.

Which meant he was being incredibly stupid staying in the condo even one more second. Trying not to panic, David ran to the door, then hesitated. Visions of a sniper watching the door through an elaborate gun sight flashed into his head. He could go out through the bedroom, drop down from the balcony to the patio . . . but that meant going past the body on the bed.

He opened the door and went out. Nobody shot him.

Where to go? The Tortuga gendarmes? "Hi, my girl-friend was just killed with a gun that probably has my prints and DNA all over it, but I didn't do it, because I was committing space piracy at the time. . . ."

Time for Plan GBM. Gingerbread Man. When he bought the condo in Tortuga Pirate World™, David had made plans for a quick getaway in case the cops came after him. Now he could see if the plan would work.

He had some essentials stashed in the ecological preserve area, outside the security surveillance envelope of the resort. Signing out a bike on his Doubloon card would give away his location, so he had to start running. He stripped off his shirt and tried to adopt the gait of a morning jogger, and took one of the springy-surfaced trails made of recycled tires toward the forest.

As he ran, he found himself noting all the cameras he passed. And those were just the ones he could see. He knew there were hidden cameras and mobile drones that could be tracking him.

Once in the forest, he was safe. No cameras (that he knew of), and his phone lived in a foil-lined pouch that kept it from blabbing its location to every wireless repeater in the vicinity. He made his way through the undergrowth to a distinctive cluster of ausubo trees where he'd stashed his getaway bag. According to the helpful sign on the trail, the ausubos would someday tower forty meters tall, but at the moment they were skinny saplings barely five meters high.

David dug with his hands in the dirt behind the trees until he got down about ten centimeters and found the heavy plastic garbage bag. There were three layers of plastic, and inside that was a metal suitcase. Despite his precautions, there were already rust spots on the shiny surface.

Inside, he had another couple of layers of plastic and a fistful of silica desiccant packs to protect the goods: a backpack holding a change of clothes, sunglasses, a hat, some hiking shoes, a decent fake South African passport, a credit card that matched the passport name, a virgin phone, an unused datapad, an encrypted keychain drive holding all his favorite files and software, and a bundle of Swiss francs, U.S. dollars, and rupees.

He ditched the shirt he'd been wearing, after using it to clean the dirt off his hands, put on new clothes and the shoes, stuffed everything else back into the backpack, and then reburied the empty briefcase and garbage bags. With the sunglasses and cap, he'd be difficult for face-recognition software to spot.

So much for the easy part. Now things got difficult. He had to get off the island of Tortuga and away from Haiti. As soon as someone found Tifane's body, the security staff would stop acting like ineffectual mall cops and turn into the Third World paramilitary mercenary force they actually were. The ferry to Port-de-Paix would certainly be watched, and not just by cameras.

Prospère. If anyone could get him off the island, it was Prospère. All David had to do was get across the security perimeter, use his virginal phone to call Prospère and cut a deal, and he'd be in the Dominican Republic by dinnertime.

At the same time he had buried the cache, David scouted out the security fence, and there were three places he could get out. Most of the drainage from the preserve land flowed into the resort's water features and irrigation tanks, but there were a couple of places where streams flowed out through the perimeter. They were culverted, of course, with heavy steel gratings to keep nonpaying guests from crawling in. But David had discovered that the gratings were secured on the outside of the culvert with a simple carabiner clip. An intruder couldn't reach the latch anyway, and it meant that forestry crews wouldn't need a keychain to deal with a blocked culvert or whatever. And who would ever want to escape from a luxury resort?

So David strolled casually but briskly toward the western edge of the Tortuga Pirate World™ tract, then worked his way north along the perimeter fence until he came to the nearest culvert.

Which was secured with a shiny brand-new padlock, the steel hasp as thick as David's finger.

"Fuck!" he said, and then he said it again about a dozen times.

Okay, time to think. The fence was designed to keep out desperately poor Haitians with muscles honed by harvesting sugar cane with machetes and nothing to lose by trying. Despite David's daily swim and twice-a-week aerobic dance session with Tiff, he was completely incapable of scaling it, even if there wasn't razor wire at the top and sensors that he really didn't want to trigger right now.

What about going *around* the fence? There was a security post on the beach where the perimeter met the ocean, so that resort denizens could take their seaside walks. Maybe he could con his way past the guard?

He had a couple of miles ahead of him to think about it. It was already getting hot. He wished he had put a water bottle in the cache.

It all depended on who the killer was, and what his motives were. If poor Tifane had been the victim of someone looking for David, then the murderer would presumably be trying to track him without attracting attention. There wouldn't be any hue and cry until someone discovered her body, which might not be for hours.

David suddenly thought about a body in a warm condo, and tropical insects, and flies . . . and then he forced himself not to think about it. Focus on survival, Captain Black.

Another thought came to him, and this time he did stop walking. What if the killer had been trying to *frame* him? The old "dead girl in your room" technique. The sort of thing some spook in a tropical-weight suit would arrange in order to get leverage over a notorious helium pirate who had managed to evade American and Indian law enforcement for years. That phone call from Elizabeth Santiago suddenly took on new significance. Did she *know* something? Had she been gloating, or trying to warn him, or both?

If that was the case, they'd already have alerted Tortuga security, and the Haitian authorities, and pretty much everyone else with a badge and a Taser in the Western Hemisphere. All the airports would be watched, with face-recognition cameras and DNA sniffers and credit tracking and probably some stuff that hadn't made it into the journals yet.

Faced with that kind of heat, Prospère would probably just shrug and offer him a drink while he called the cops himself.

He needed another way off the island. Something that didn't involve passing through any kind of security checkpoint, or using anything that would show up in a database to be sniffed out by the NSA. Something that wouldn't be watched by assassins or cops.

Tortuga was on an island. He needed a boat. And right then, he decided that the boat he needed was the *Carina*, registered Kingston, Oklahoma, which he fervently hoped was still in the marina.

David stayed in the forest as much as he could, until he reached a spot near the amusement park, then moved along with the families, trying to attach himself to groups as much as possible.

A vendor was selling character masks—cheap printed cardboard, not even the luxury of stamped plastic. David paid cash for a pirate mask and put it on, then went to the nearest vendor selling drinks, bought a bottle of beer, and walked unsteadily toward the harbor, waving the bottle at everyone he passed and yelling "Arr!" from time to time.

He kept the mask on while he hurried through the Tortuga Pirate Bazaar and the Tavern Court. He ducked into every bathroom he passed, taking off his shirt in the first one, removing his cap in the second, and finally putting everything back on and covering his shorts with a pair of sweatpants from his backpack in the third.

Still trying to walk like an amiable drunk, he passed the pricey seafood restaurant and Cap'n Kidd's Family Fare, which brought him to the marina. He squinted anxiously at the boats. There it was, a tubby-looking seven-meter cabin cruiser moored to a buoy, with a little orange rubber raft tied up astern. It hardly looked big enough to cross the harbor safely, let alone brave the ocean. Crazy Boat Girl was either crazier or more competent than he thought.

He found an unattended dinghy and paddled inexpertly out to the *Carina*. Cameras were almost certainly watching, and his ears were alert for the sound of an approaching siren.

"Hello!" he called out as he neared the boat. Was she even on board? "Ahoy!"

. . .

Anne Rogers sat in her cabin with her tablet on her lap, checking her credit balance. She was trying to decide if she could stay at Tortuga Pirate World™ any longer. The docking fees were steep. She'd need to economize by sleeping on her boat. No more spending money on rides, casinos, restaurants, or bars.

Of course, those were the only reason to stay in Tortuga in the first place. If she wasn't going to enjoy the attractions, she could save herself the docking fees as well by simply leaving. Head for Puerto Plata in the Dominican Republic, Punta Cana, and then Puerto Rico beyond. There were supposed to be some nice cheap places to stop off along the south coast of Puerto Rico, you didn't have to worry about the drinking water or ruinous currency exchange fees, and from there, she could go on to Vieques, and then start the long sweep through the Lesser Antilles to Grenada.

Assuming she could afford it, of course. Mr. Adorno's gift had seemed like infinite wealth back in Bay St. Louis, but the constant flow of docking fees, fuel, and food had drained away nearly half already. She doubted prices in the Lesser Antilles would be much better. At this rate, she'd be out of cash by Martinique.

"Ahoy!" Someone was calling from topside. Anne put down her tablet, pulled on a T-shirt over her bathing suit, and went up through the narrow companionway to the aft deck.

"Hello, who's there?" She recognized the guy from the club, sitting in a little dinghy, looking like he was about to tip over. He'd sent her an email afterwards. "Well, hey!" she called. "You owe me lunch. Come aboard—want something to drink? I've got Sprite and some beer. You like Prestige?"

"No, thanks." He looked worried, and he kept glancing back at the shore as she helped him tie his boat on and scramble aboard.

Once he was on the deck, he hemmed and hawed for a second, like a junior high school kid working up the courage to ask a girl out. "Um, listen, this is really important. I—" He hesitated again, then plunged ahead. "—I have to get out of here right now."

"You just got here," said Anne. He didn't look drunk or high, but he wasn't making much sense, either.

"No, I mean Tortuga. I've got to get away. You remember Tifane, the girl who came to the party with me the other night?"

"The skinny girl with the fake boobs?"

"Yeah—how'd you know they're fake?"

"Oh, please. Nobody with a build like hers has breasts like that."

"Well—she's dead. Someone killed her this morning, and I'm afraid the cops are going to pin it on me. I have to get out of here right now, and they'll be watching the ferry dock. I need your boat. I know it's a lot to ask, but—"

Her eyes widened. "She's dead? I'm so sorry! What happened?"

"I told you. Someone shot her. I think they're trying to frame me for it."

She didn't know if she should believe him or not. Shootings? Frame-ups? "Shot her? Really?"

"Yes, really. I have to get away before they find me."

She studied him. He didn't look like a murderer, but then she had never met a murderer. "Did you shoot her?" she asked.

The hatchway to the cabin was behind her, and the pistol was in the storage space under her bunk. She took a step back.

"No! Of course not!"

"Why run away, then? They'll find the guy who did it, and you'll be in the clear."

He looked uncomfortable again. "I can't let them arrest me. I'm—I'm involved in some illegal stuff. I stole a lot of money once, and if the cops figure out who I am, they'll put me in jail for a long time. That's why I can't stay."

"And you want me to take you off Tortuga?"

"Right. Please?"

It was crazy. She should be yelling for the cops right now. Tell him no, call the gendarmes, get him off her boat, and let the law sort it out.

"All right," she said. "Let's just go right now. I took on fuel when I got in. Do you need to pick anything up?"

"You'd better stay behind," he said.

"Forget it. You might steal my boat." There was no way Anne was giving up *Carina* to someone she barely knew.

"Don't be ridiculous," he said. "I'm running from the cops. You can't come with me."

"It's my boat," she said.

"Look, it's dangerous. You hardly know me. I might really be a murderer. You don't want to be out alone on a boat with me. It's crazy."

"If you really are a murderer, you can't have my boat," she told him. She was starting to enjoy this argument.

"I'm not a murderer!"

"Then I'm coming with you," she said triumphantly.

"Shit! I don't have time for this!" He looked genuinely unhappy.

Anne, however, was having the time of her life. This was the kind of adventure she'd hoped to have when she first turned her boat down the Red River. "Do you know how to sail a cabin cruiser?" she asked him.

"Sure I do!" he said, and then when Anne didn't say anything, "I can look it up. You've got a manual or something on board, right? I'm good at figuring things out in real time."

"I'm not giving my boat to someone who'll wreck it or get lost at sea. Now, where do you need to go?"

"That's . . . a damned good question."

. . .

McEwan didn't like voice messages. He either answered your call or ignored you. So after seven or eight rings, he said "Yes?" in the voice of someone trying to keep quiet in a noisy room. Elizabeth recognized the sounds of the Pit in the background, and for a Proustian moment could almost smell the air freshener.

"Westinghouse 38 just got jacked, right? There's a vehicle at L_1 you can use for an intercept. It's called SOTHIS, and—"

"They're still trying to regain control over the payload."

"You know that's impossible. Captain Black's probably loaded entirely new command encryption. That payload's gone; the only move left is to deny it to the enemy."

"You're proposing to destroy it? It's just a stolen helium cargo. No need to come in guns blazing."

For just an instant, Elizabeth wondered if he knew about the GyroJet launcher, but decided that he wouldn't be taking her call if he had. "Yes, destroy it. The SOTHIS vehicle can intercept and smash into it."

"No," he said. "Even if you can do a successful intercept, all it means is years of lawsuits trying to sort out who's responsible for the loss. I don't want to spend a lot of time getting grilled by lawyers just so you can—"

"Fine," she said. "Never mind. Sorry to bother you." She turned off her phone and pulled back her arm to throw it across the room, then set it gently on her bedside table.

It didn't matter. She tried to tell herself that and believe it. It really didn't matter. Not her mission. Not her job. If McEwan preferred to put on his dress uniform and go sit in front of a congressional committee to explain why the Air Force couldn't stop pirates from stealing a couple of billion dollars' worth of helium every few months, that was his choice. Not her problem.

. . .

MISSION TIME 64:46

Anne Rogers steered the *Carina* out past the harbor mole. The ocean swell made the deck buck and pitch under her feet. The days when a little chop made her seasick were long past. Now she could stand on the deck and thread a needle without even thinking about keeping her footing.

David wasn't nearly so good a sailor. They weren't half an hour under way when he was bolting for the gunwale and feeding the fish whatever he'd eaten for breakfast. Anne got out the Big Box of seasickness patches, slapped a couple onto his neck. Finding a spot that wasn't already occupied by drug patches was kind of difficult.

"What are these others?" she asked him.

"Oh—those are smart drugs," he said. "Neurotransmitter enhancers."

Five minutes after she gave him the patch, his seasickness seemed to ease. Or maybe he was just out of stuff to throw up.

"Westward ho!" Anne shouted over the noise of the motor, and turned the boat north, on a course to take them around the north side of Île de la Tortue and then west toward Cuba. Their destination was a set of GPS coordinates north of Bahía de Cárdenas on the north coast of Cuba.

"So who is this friend of yours?" she asked David.

"Barnacle Bill. His real name's Bill Benedict, but I call him Barnacle because it's his pirate name. Pirates all have to have pirate names so they don't catch us. He lives off the coast of Cuba. Did I show you the place? Do we have enough gas?" There must have been some kind of interaction between the seasick patches and his mysterious "smart drugs," because even the simplest question turned him into an incredible motormouth.

"Stop asking that," she said. "Yes, we've got enough diesel. If we go without stopping, it's only about thirty hours."

"We have to get there as soon as possible. From there, I can contact the colonel and figure out what's going on. The colonel's the guy who hired me. He's got a badass mustache. I'm pretty sure the mustache is real, but his name probably isn't."

"Since you're being so chatty," she said, "I want you to tell me the truth about who you're running away from."

"I don't know! Honestly, I don't know. I think it's the CIA, or maybe the Air Force or the Indians. Or the colonel—but if it's him, he probably won't tell me. He gave me the gun, so it's kind of hard to believe he wants me dead."

"Why are they after you?" she asked, trying to keep him on one subject at a time.

"I stole something. A spaceship. I stole a spaceship in space, right before I found Tifane. I wasn't in space myself, I did it from a hotel room. I think they call them business suites. But that's not important! The point is, someone killed her. If they were looking for me to kill me, then it could be the people I'm working for. Except that if they do that, everything I know will go to the cops. It's called a Dead Hand, like the Russian doomsday device. Did you ever watch *Dr. Strangelove*? Like that. But if they were trying to frame me, then it's probably the CIA or somebody. Trying to turn me so that they can catch the others. Frame me for killing Tiff and then blackmail me. But I didn't do it! Understand?"

"I think so," she said. "Who's this Barnacle Bill character?"

"I've worked with him before, a bunch of times. The last time I stole a spaceship, he was in charge of systems. He's an engineer, used to do bootleg software until I got him to help me steal spaceships. He's pretty good. I made him rich, so he owes me. I only call him Barnacle Bill because it's his pirate name. I already said that, didn't I? Anyway he lives off Cuba, so the CIA won't be able to get me there, not without starting a war or something. I can figure out what to do next when we get there. Shit, she's dead. Tifane. I can't stop thinking about her now."

"And after I take you to Bill, you'll pay me."

"Right, absolutely pay you. Ten thousand plus whatever the fuel costs. I can even give you some extra. Plenty of money. In two days, I can buy anything. Any fucking thing. I was going to break up with her, you know? Be a man about it for once, instead of waiting for her to dump me. I was going over there to tell her good-bye but she's dead. She didn't even do anything!"

"What happens in two days?" Anne asked. Listening to him was like trying to watch three movies at once. It was hard to keep from following David on one of his bizarre tangents.

"In three days, my ship comes in. Down. The spaceship I stole. In space. It comes down somewhere, probably off the Philippines or East Africa. The colonel will know. I'm going to be the owner of five percent of about two billion Swiss francs. That's a hundred million, all hard currency. I can buy you a fucking aircraft carrier! Captain Black is the supreme badass of space!"

Was he hallucinating? "Tell me more about Bill."

"I don't know much. I only met him face-to-face once, back in 2023. He has a beard. He doesn't know I know where he lives. I tracked him down by signal packet tracing when I was bored last year. He thinks he's so smart with his secret base, but I know everything because Captain Black is the supreme badass of space."

"Wait, he doesn't know you're coming? What do we do if he's not home?"

"Oh, that's what I'm hoping for. We'll be even safer if nobody knows we're there. We can hang out on his secret base and Darth Vader will never find us."

10

"That's where your friend lives?" Anne asked. *Carina* had reached the coordinates he'd given her, at least according to the GPS.

"Yep," said David, sounding almost proud.

Barnacle Bill's place was an oil platform anchored in a thousand fathoms of ocean, twenty kilometers off the Cuban coast. According to David, who either knew what he was talking about or was a master of improvised bullshit, it was a relic of the brief Cuban oil boom, seized by the Havana government after their Chinese partners vanished in the civil war. No one outside Cuba could buy the platform, because teams of lawyers representing different Chinese factions would try to seize it right back as soon as it left Cuban waters, and no one in Cuba had any use for it.

The platform was small, as oil platforms went—just a big floating steel can anchored to the seafloor by five cables of high-tech carbon fiber strong enough to hoist up a supertanker. It was designed to be fully automated, without a permanent crew. There was a well deck, an emergency shelter, and a helipad on top. Anne had sighted several just like it under construction in the shipyard at Pascagoula. The only difference was that this platform's helipad sported a garden and a pleasant-looking modular house with teak siding.

It appeared Barnacle Bill was in residence. A wicked-looking maroon cigarette boat was tied to a floating dock down at the waterline, and a faint scent of charcoal and cooking meat came on the breeze. The smell reminded Anne that she had missed lunch.

A more obvious sign came as soon as their boat approached within a hundred meters. "YOU ARE INTRUDING IN A PRIVATE AREA! LEAVE AT ONCE!" The sound level got louder and louder each time the message repeated in alternating English and Spanish, until it made Anne's teeth buzz. She could see the hexagonal shape of a sound blaster on the main deck of the platform, aimed right at them.

David spotted a man peeking over the edge of the main deck. He waved his arms frantically. "Bill! Bill Benedict! Hey! It's me, Captain Black!"

The deafening sound projector made it impossible for anyone to hear what he was saying, but the arm-waving and the obviously harmless look of the *Carina* apparently were enough. The noise stopped abruptly, and then a moment later a merely loud voice said "WHAT DO YOU WANT?"

"It's me, Captain Black the Space Pirate! I need help!"

Anne trained her binoculars on the man currently glowering at them over the edge. He looked about fifty, with a big gray beard that hung in a thick braid past his navel and no clothing she could see. "He doesn't look very happy to see you."

Barnacle Bill kept them waiting for nearly a minute before he called down through the sound projector. "OKAY, COME ABOARD."

Anne steered the *Carina* over to the floating dock, going very slowly and carefully. She had no idea what the profile of the platform was like below the waterline, and this "Barnacle Bill" character might have put in some obstacles. As the boat bumped the dock, she made David jump over to it and told him how to tie up to the cleats. When the boat was secured bow and stern, she cut the engine and followed him onto the platform.

They had to climb up a long ladder from the dock to the well deck. The rungs were wet from spray. The breeze, which had seemed pleasant enough on the deck of the *Carina*, now felt like it was trying to snatch Anne off the ladder and blow her out to sea.

The ladder took them up to the well deck, which looked as if it had never been used. It was now occupied by a big rack of batteries, four chest freezers, and an elaborate water-filtration system. An ornamental wrought-iron spiral staircase led up from there to the helipad.

The top of the platform was a big truncated triangle, the steel mesh surface of the helipad covered by teakwood slats. Most of the open space was taken up by planters made of old steel oil drums cut in half lengthwise. The deck was almost a jungle, with tomato plants, melons, beans, marijuana, sunflowers, and some vegetables Anne could only guess at, all growing lush in the Cuban sun. A hive of bees hummed at one end.

Bill Benedict himself was waiting at the top of the stairs. He was wearing a small apron with the slogan FINEST MEAT and held a pump shotgun pointing at the two of them.

"What the hell are you doing here? How did you find me?"

. . .

David half raised his hands and tried to look friendly. He'd been rehearsing this conversation in his mind for hours, and so far everything was according to the script. "Hey, it's cool. I tracked you down a while back, just hacking around, you know? Your sat phone sends position data every time you make a call. At first I thought you'd managed to spoof it when the GPS coordinates showed open ocean, but then I found some satellite images and spotted this thing."

"Why are you here? Who's she?"

"It's complicated. I'm running away from the cops—"

"Then you can get the fuck off my house right now!"

"Relax, relax! They can't follow me here. I told you, it's cool."

"Don't be too sure. They'll send a drone to put a missile up your ass no matter where you go, if they want you bad enough. I don't need that kind of trouble."

"This is a law enforcement situation. Cops, not the military. Somebody killed Tifane, back at Tortuga. The woman I was living with. I think someone's trying to frame me."

"Somebody? Who?"

"I don't know! It could be the Indians or the cowboys or even Ghavami's guys. It happened right around the time I stole Westinghouse 38. I need a place to hide out until I can figure out what's going on. Whoever it is might be after you, too."

Bill licked his lips. "Okay, you can hide out here for a *little* while. Two days. But if the cops come, that's it. I don't know you, you're just some guy who came to my platform—thank you, Officer, for taking away this dangerous criminal. Understand?"

"Absolutely. I need a network connection to find out what's happening."

Anne interrupted them. "Hi," she said. "I'm Anne Rogers. I brought him here on my boat. That chicken smells good."

"You want some? Sure," said Bill. He put the safety back on and uncocked his shotgun, then led the two of them over to the house. A Japanese-style hot tub stood by the door, with a black plastic tarp over the water.

"It's okay, ladies!" he called. "Come on out, now!"

Two young women—no, girls—peered out the door and then shyly approached. Both were naked and evenly tanned.

"This is Rasha, and this is Amira. They're my staff. This is a clothing-optional household," said Bill. He poked at the chicken on the grill, found a piece that met his standards, and served it up onto a stainless steel plate for Anne.

"Thanks," she said. Since nobody else was saying anything, she looked over at Amira. "Where are you from?"

"I am Egyptian," she said.

"They're Copts," Bill said. "I got 'em both out of a refugee camp in Cyprus. They were born there."

David couldn't quite figure out if this was an example of heartwarming charity or creepy underage sex-slavery. Before Anne could ask how Bill had managed to talk the refugee agency into giving him two teenage girls, David butted in. "Must get pretty rough out here during a hurricane."

Bill stamped on the deck. "The platform is rated up to a Cat Four—assuming the Brazilians who built it didn't cut any corners. And I've heard of platforms like this surviving a Cat Five with just minor damage. The house . . . who knows?" He shrugged. "I put that together myself. The worst storm we've had so far was Fernando, last August. That was a Cat One when it passed through here. The girls and I evacuated to Santa Marta, but everything was fine when we came back. Even a tropical storm is pretty scary to ride out, though."

"Where's Karen?" asked Anne.

David felt a rush of pure paranoia. Who was Karen? Did Anne and Bill *know* each other? Was this some kind of elaborate trap? It only cleared up when Bill answered "Passing over the Caymans right now. It's supposed to go up the Yucatán Channel into the Gulf and hit Alabama. Still just a tropical storm, but I'm keeping an eye on it."

"Do you want something to drink, miss?" Amira asked Anne.

"A Coke—no, wait. Just some ice water. I've been slugging down caffeine all night. Time to get some sleep."

"I'd like some, too," said David. "Listen, Bill—I really

need a network connection right now. I've been out of touch since Tuesday. My partners are going to be freaking out."

"Sure, I've got a spare tablet you can use. Here, have some chicken and I'll go dig it out."

David and Anne stood eating chicken while the two naked girls watched them.

"So," David said when he couldn't stand the silence any longer, "you two like it here?"

"It is better than the camp," said Amira.

"You could leave," said Anne. "You know that, right? He can't keep you here."

Rasha and Amira shook their heads together. "Mr. Bill sends money to our families as long as we stay with him."

Still unable to decide between heartwarming and creepy, David shut up and finished his chicken.

Bill returned with a tablet. "Here. You're logged in as Black, password 'cbtsp.'"

"Your network is password protected?" asked Anne. "Out here?"

"You never know who might be listening. I see drones fly by sometimes, and these waters are deep enough for submarines. Just the existence of a place like this offends statists."

David was too busy to comment. He gave his plate to Amira, found a plastic lawn chair in the shade of the house, wiped chicken grease off his fingers, and got to work typing one-handed while holding his Coke in the other.

Step 1: Find out who was after him. He checked the news from Haiti, searching the past forty hours for "Tortuga" "Resort" and "Shooting" in English, Creole, and Spanish. There it was: TORTUGA SHOOTER SOUGHT.

The article gave him a little hope. All the quotes were from Zhang Er, security director at Tortuga Pirate World™. His men were searching the entire island of Île de la Tor-tue for David Williams. No mention of Anne or her boat, no photos of David, no mention of his real name or the name on the passport in his pocket.

At the moment, it seemed that David was beyond the widening circle of pursuit, but that would probably change as soon as Tortuga Security passed the problem off to Hai-ti's national police and they contacted their pals in Miami. David detected the echo of some kind of jurisdictional piss-ing contest, since Zhang Er should have done that right away. The glorified mall cops at Tortuga weren't set up to investigate a homicide—but of course, they probably thought the same of the Haitian police.

The situation was ideal for an uptight Chinese security professional with badass martial arts skills to have wacky adventures with his laid-back but streetwise Rastafarian Haitian partner as they tracked down the elusive killer and learned to respect each other, but David didn't really want to be the target of a mismatched buddy-cop manhunt.

Of course, the absence of overt legal pursuit didn't mean nobody was after him. Whoever shot Tifane might be on his trail, although there weren't any boats in sight and it would take someone almost as smart as Captain Black the Space Pirate to figure out he'd be on Bill Benedict's secret floating island.

Step 2: Make contact with Ghavami. This was a bit more tricky. He still wasn't sure if his business partner was responsible for Tifane's death—but if the colonel wasn't involved, then he was David's best hope to stay out of jail and find out who had done it. David used an anonymous remailer to send a text message. "I am okay. Something happened at Tortuga and I had to get away. How's our cargo?"

A knock interrupted his work. It was Anne. "Give me my money now," she said.

"What?"

"Two hundred gallons of fuel, the seasick pills I gave you, a six-pack of sports drink you drank up without even asking, and thirty hours of my time. You said you could pay me, so pay me."

"Okay, sure. How much do you want?" He went to his bank account in the Caymans. "And where do you want me to send it?"

"Make it worth my while. Five thousand Swiss francs," she said, and gave him her online address. He transferred the money while she watched, and then handed her the tablet so she could check her own account herself.

"Great," she said. "First light, I'm out of here."

"You're going?"

"Of course I'm going. I'm spending tonight on my boat, and if your creepy naked friend puts one foot on board, I'm going to plug him six times with my daddy's pistol and throw him in the ocean. You can tell him I said so."

"He's not so bad. Plenty of people are nudists. Don't let the dwarf beard fool you. Bill's a good guy."

"Good guy? It's not the naked, it's the teenage sex slave

girls. I got Amira alone and asked her. He's fucking them both. She's fifteen."

"Don't be so judgmental. This isn't Oklahoma," he said. "And anyway, it's consensual."

She snorted. "Consensual, my ass. He's got them stuck on a platform miles from land, he's got their passports, they don't have any money, and their families are in some camp somewhere and depend on what he sends them. It's about as consensual as putting a gun to their heads. This guy's a rapist."

"Keep your voice down," he said. "Right now this is the only place I'm safe, so I'd appreciate it if you don't piss Bill off."

"Doesn't it *bother* you? Just a little?"

"Look, I'm not ready to judge, okay? I don't know the whole story. It's none of my business."

"I should have asked you for more money. Not ready to judge? *I'm* ready to fucking judge. Have fun with your pedo rapist friend. Maybe he'll let you borrow one of his little girls for the night."

He could hear her stomping on the metal stairs all the way down to the dock.

Step 3: The hell with Anne, anyway. No, that wasn't right. Step 3 was Check on the payload. There were a couple of public-access sites keeping tabs on everything in orbit. David looked up Westinghouse 38. It was still on course, still listed as "HIJACKED, Landing Site Unknown." Excellent, if not particularly surprising. When Captain Black the Space Pirate stole something, it stayed stolen.

Just to be sure, David went through a couple of cutouts

and tried to get access to the payload itself. Locked out. His passwords and codes were no longer valid. That was a nuisance he hadn't expected. It was only sensible, really. He'd vanished for thirty hours; Ghavami would be an idiot not to cut him out of the loop. David did have a couple of backdoors he had designed into the control setup, but he didn't want to use them yet. See what the colonel had to say first.

Step 4: What was Step 4? Sleep?

The little incoming-call window popped open on his desktop. Sure, why not? He accepted, and a video window appeared on the screen. It was Colonel Ghavami. "Where are you?" he asked without any preamble.

"I'm safe," said David. "I had to leave everything behind, but it's cool. Everything is encrypted, and the passwords are only in my head. If someone who doesn't type the way I do starts trying to use any of my computers, the memory gets secure-erased. How's the mission going?"

"It is going very well. Tell me where you are, and I can send someone to help you."

"Don't worry, I'm okay." David looked at the colonel's image in the little window, trying to read his expression. "Anything I should know?"

"What do you mean?" Ghavami looked offscreen for a moment, then back at the camera. "Tell me what happened. Why did you leave Haiti?"

"Someone shot my girlfriend." As he said it aloud, David realized he was crying. He'd been too busy running for his life before, and then too drugged to care. Now it was finally hitting him. Tifane was really dead. David didn't know how he was supposed to react, but he was crying.

Ghavami was saying something. "What?" asked David, mopping his eyes with the sleeve of his T-shirt. "Say that again."

"I said do you have any idea who killed her?"

"No, not yet." She was dead and it was his fault. But that wasn't the worst of it. The worst was that among the rush of emotions he felt, one of the feelings was relief. He hated himself for feeling that.

"I can help you," said Ghavami. "Obviously you are in danger. Let me send someone to guard you. And I have resources you lack. I can find out a great deal."

"Okay," said David. He wished he had one of his drug patches handy. Right now he needed to think very fast, but all he could think of was Tifane's hair glued to the floor with blood.

How much did he trust Ghavami? To ask the question was to answer it: not at all. At the very least, the colonel could change the terms of their deal and screw David out of his percentage. At worst—David had a vision of winding up like Bill's teenage naked girls, with no passport, no money, sitting in a bunker in Qizil Orda, stealing payloads for the colonel until he died of old age.

"Right now I'm safe. Can't say where because someone might be listening." They both knew that was a lie—if someone were listening, Ghavami's control center would be a smoldering pile of wreckage and David would be surrounded by Navy SEALs already. "I'll call you when I need to leave here. For now, you just keep an eye on our cargo.

I have to go." Before the colonel could reply, David closed the video window and disconnected from Barnacle Bill's wireless.

Now he knew what Step 4 was. Find out who killed Tifane. Get revenge for her. It wasn't much, and it was far too late, but it was all he could do for her.

. . .

It was pretty hard to investigate a murder from six hundred miles away, but he could start by checking the resort records. Had anyone checked in right before she died, and were they still there?

There were five thousand hotel rooms in Tortuga Pirate World™, not including the time-share condos. August was nowhere near peak season; that came after the tropical storm risk ended and the first flakes of snow started falling in Moscow and Chicago. Only half the rooms were occupied. David could rule out all the package tourists from China and Europe, and all the families with kids. Mom and Dad the CIA hit men taking the kids along would be another dandy action comedy idea, but it seemed a little unlikely in practice.

He spotted something. Very interesting: four men had checked out of their rooms less than half an hour after David hijacked the payload. All four had arrived on August 22, the day before the pirate vehicle launched. What were the odds their vacation would match his mission so exactly?

So who were these four? Their names were Gordana Nikolic, Lazar Vucic, Aleksandar Orlovic, and Mirko Draskovic, all listed as Paraguayan citizens. Well, maybe. Lots of immigrants in Paraguay; people there weren't all named

Juan Gómez or whatever. He did a little checking and found they'd come to Haiti together on a flight from Paris. That seemed like a rather roundabout way to travel. Perhaps they'd gone to visit the old country before stopping off in Tortuga on the way back to South America.

He told himself not to be an idiot. Were these the American agents Ghavami had warned him about before the launch? It was hard to believe it was just five days since that conversation.

Or were they Ghavami's people? Some of Vlad's crew? Of course, the CIA or whoever could hire Balkan goons, too. Or give corn-fed American assassins phony names. Living in a global society was annoying: you couldn't assume anything about people anymore.

David wasn't used to knowing less than other people. He hated that feeling. Captain Black the Space Pirate was supposed to be the all-seeing mastermind making fools of everyone else. He needed data.

"How's it going?" Bill asked him, sitting down beside David and looking at the screen. Having a naked dude sitting in personal contact with him made David nervous for no reason he cared to examine.

"I'm trying to find the people who shot Tifane. I think I've found them."

"Got any pictures?"

"No. Tortuga relies on physical security and old-fashioned bigotry. If you're white or Asian, you're a guest and can go anywhere. If you're black, you'd better be wearing a staff uniform. That's one of the reasons I stayed there—no pesky biometrics on file."

"Any idea who they are?"

"From the names, they sound like Balkan gangsters or mercenaries. Serbians or Croats or something, unless they're fakes. I don't know who hired them or why. Either my partners are trying to cut me out of my share, which is stupid because I've got a Dead Hand set up to spill everything I know to every cop on Earth, or the feds are trying to blackmail me."

Amira called from inside the house. "Mr. Bill, there is a call for you. I think it is important."

"Be right there," he called, then lowered his voice. "How long are you planning to stay here? I mean, all this talk about murder and shit is not something I want to hear. This is my little refuge from crap like that."

"Look, I'm sorry to drop out of the sky on you like this. I just need to figure out who's after me and where I'll be safe, then I'll get out of your life. Two days, tops."

"Mr. Bill!" Amira called again.

"Okay, okay!" He got up and headed for the door. "Two days," he said over his shoulder to David. "I'm holding you to that."

He dug deeper. All four of them had the same home address in Paraguay, which turned out to be the Crowne Plaza Asunción hotel. Their phone numbers were Haitel mobiles, suggesting that they'd bought prepaid phones at the airport in Port-au-Prince. They paid for everything with cash, which was remarkable these days, and intensely irritating to David because it cut off one way to learn more about them. The four of them had checked out of the hotel bright and early on the twenty-sixth, right about the time

David had started walking over to his condo. That made him shiver a bit despite the tropical sunshine.

Where had they gone afterwards? No way to tell without actually going back to Haiti and asking someone. Maybe Ghavami could handle that.

Then the signal bars on the wireless status display vanished and all his connections to the rest of the world froze up. "Bill?" he called out. "Your network just went down!"

"Sorry about that!" came a shout from somewhere else in the house. "It does that sometimes. Why don't you take a break and I'll fix it?"

David looked at the clock. It was close to 6 P.M., and he suddenly realized how tired he was. He'd slept a little on the boat, but not well, and one barbecued chicken thigh was all he'd eaten since . . . whenever he'd eaten last, which he couldn't remember. Time for a break. He'd have dinner, get a good night's sleep, and solve all his problems in the morning.

·   ·   ·

MISSION TIME 102:11

The clock glowing over her bunk read 3 A.M. when Anne opened her eyes. She lay for a moment listening, trying to figure out what had waked her. She could feel the ocean swell; it was getting choppy, but it didn't feel too bad yet. That tropical storm off to the west must have strengthened.

Then light washed through the little windows. Why was someone shining a spotlight on her boat? Had some

Cuban social service agency finally turned up to shut down Barnacle Bill's little island of teenage sex slaves?

She peeked out.

The boat nudging up to the dock was a big sleek cruiser twice as long as *Carina*. From the subsonic throb of the idling diesels, it sounded ridiculously overpowered.

As she watched, a couple of men jumped down to the floating dock and tied mooring lines. Two more followed, carrying guns. This was bad. Fast boats full of armed men arriving in the middle of the night were bad news no matter where you were.

Her father's revolver lived in a lockbox under her bunk. She took it out and loaded it in the dark. Her hands were shaking so much that it seemed to take forever to get six rounds into the cylinder. She stuck it in her back pocket, then went up the gangway to the pilothouse, crouching low.

She crept aft to the open deck and risked another look over the side. There were four men on the dock. A burly man with a big mustache gave the other three instructions. None of them were looking her way, so she untied the aft mooring line. Then she crawled over to the starboard side and climbed up onto the narrow strip (one could hardly call it a "deck") that ran between the boat's side and the bulge of the cabin roof in front of the cockpit.

With the cabin hiding her from the men on the dock, Anne crawled forward, struggling to keep her balance as the boat pitched more wildly in the choppy water. Once she fell heavily against the cabin, and the gun in her pocket made a loud thump. She held her breath and froze in place, listening for approaching footsteps, but there were none.

Another peek over the top of the cabin showed the men climbing up the ladder to the platform above. Were those four the only ones? She watched the other boat while her heart pounded about eight times, and then spotted the tiny red glow of a cigarette in the pilothouse.

Now for the difficult part. To reach the mooring line at the bow, she'd have to crawl across the open foredeck with nothing to hide her but the darkness. Fortunately there was no moon, so the only light was from the red warning lamps at the edge of the platform above.

Wait a sec, thought Anne. How come Babyfucker Bill's nifty sonic defense system hadn't gone off? Maybe he'd never turned it back on? Or was he *expecting* these guys?

Think about it later. She flattened herself on the foredeck and inched forward on her belly like a seal, hoping her dirty white tank top and canvas shorts would blend in with *Carina*'s paint job. She reached the cleat and tried to untie the mooring line one-handed, but now the rope was stretched taut and the knot was solid. Finally Anne fished in her pocket for her jackknife, opened it with her teeth, and sawed at the line until it parted.

With a last bump against the dock, *Carina* began to drift downwind, away from the other boat. Just then, the quiet sound of wind and water were interrupted by a gunshot from above, then a deeper boom, then a burst of automatic fire mixed with shouts.

Discarding caution, Anne yanked open the skylight

hatch down into the cabin and slithered in headfirst, leaving some skin from her elbows on the lip and bumping her head on the floor.

She scrambled back up to the pilot station and turned on the radio, hitting the red button for Channel 16. "Mayday Mayday Mayday!" she half-whispered half-shrieked into the handset. "This is *Carina, Carina, Carina*. Mayday *Carina*. My position is . . ." She looked at the GPS display. "Position twenty-three degrees forty-two minutes fifteen seconds north by . . . eighty one degrees thirty minutes three seconds west. The Nengyuan Guba Five oil platform. I require assistance. Pirates! People are attacking the platform. They're shooting. There's four people on the platform. Please help. Mayday, *Carina,* over?"

The speaker sounded incredibly loud. There were two voices responding, one loud and crackly, the other quieter but clearer. Both were demanding "Say again, *Carina*?"

A spotlight from the bigger boat flashed out, and then the windscreen shattered as a couple of shots echoed across the water. Safety glass cubes rained down around Anne. "Gunmen attacking the Nengyuan Guba Five platform! Please come!"

She turned the key and fired up *Carina*'s engine, then rammed the throttle all the way open and spun the wheel to get the hell away. Behind her she heard more shots and a *thunk* as a furrow appeared in the deck.

Anne looked back. The guy on the other boat was trying to untie and come after her. At least he wasn't shooting. Then she heard a scream and looked up in time as someone jumped from the edge of the platform. A second later she saw a splash.

The scream sounded like one of the girls. Anne spun the wheel the other way and got out her big flashlight. The sea was getting rough. Even the best swimmer would have trouble. All she could see was dark water and foam. There! A dark head emerged from the sea, then sank back. Anne kept the oval of light centered on it, and steered over. She kept the throttle wide open, then jammed the boat into reverse at the last possible moment. Belowdecks, the transmission gave an ominous shudder, but nothing sounded broken.

"Here!" She ran to the side and looked out. A wave lifted *Carina,* and for a moment she was afraid the boat was going to smash the girl in the water. Anne grabbed the life ring and scanned the water. There! "Catch!" she yelled, and threw the ring.

The girl in the water seemed to take forever to reach the ring. Anne heard the rumble of a boat engine and saw that the big cruiser was moving away from the floating dock.

As soon as she saw the girl grasp the ring, Anne hauled away on the rope, dragging the girl through the water until she was alongside. Without hesitating, Anne reached over and yanked her out of the water. She hadn't known she could do that. The two of them fell to the deck and Anne scrambled for the wheel. She opened up the throttle again and steered away from the platform. The big boat was turning toward her.

Which heading? Cuba was closer, but the thought of

navigating that reef-bound shore in rough weather at night was pretty terrifying. The Keys were north—and right at that moment, Anne Rogers wanted to be in U.S. waters more than anyplace else on Earth, preferably with the entire Navy and Coast Guard packed around her.

She switched off all the running lights and hoped for the best. Either the other boat would catch her or it wouldn't. Then she went aft to check on her passenger. It was Amira, and there was a pool of blood on the deck underneath her.

Anne saw a horrible ragged hole in the girl's left thigh. She ran for the first aid kit and tried to remember what she'd learned as a Girl Scout. Stop the bleeding. Was it arterial blood? By the light of the little flashlight, she couldn't tell. There was a tourniquet in the kit. Anne fumbled to get it around Amira's leg above the wound, then pulled it tight with all her strength.

What else? Shock. Get her warm. The girl's naked body looked small and pale. Anne toweled her off and wrapped her up in the shiny Mylar blanket from the kit, then dragged up her dense wool Hudson's Bay blanket and wrapped that around her for good measure. Pulse? She had a pulse. Anne couldn't tell if it was strong or weak. Should she give her a stimulant patch? There were only four in the kit. Save it in case the girl got worse.

She looked back. The bigger boat was still following. Was it gaining? Maybe. Anne felt in her back pocket for the revolver. Could she actually shoot at someone? The idea seemed ridiculous, even now.

"Help!"

Anne looked around, panicking. That wasn't Amira. It was a man's voice. It sounded like it was coming from the bow. She stared hard into the darkness, looking for anyone crouching on the foredeck. Nothing there. But she heard the voice again, and this time, she realized it was coming from over the side of the boat.

She leaned over the side and saw a pale, wet figure clinging to the low rail at the bow. Anne went through the cabin to the foredeck hatch again and climbed up, then flicked on the little flashlight from the medical kit.

David Schwartz was hanging over the edge of her boat. His fists gripped the mooring cleat desperately, and his head was just above the edge of the deck. The rest of him was dangling into the bow wave as the boat sped through the heavy chop. "Help!" he yelled at her over the noise of the engine.

She could shoot him, Anne thought. She could take out the revolver and shoot him right there. He was the one who'd gotten her mixed up in all this with creepy midocean pedophiles and boats full of gunmen. His face was slack from the effort of hanging on, and he winced every time the boat bounced on a wave. She wouldn't even have to shoot him, Anne realized. He'd drop off into the water soon enough.

"Fucker!" she yelled at him, and crawled forward. Getting him aboard was much more difficult than rescuing Amira. He weighed twice as much, and there wasn't any place to brace herself on the wet foredeck. Finally Anne managed to hold the edge of the foredeck hatch with her left hand and extend her right for him to grab. She pulled as hard as she could while he scrambled with his feet, and then he managed to get himself up on the deck and collapse. Anne half dragged him down through the hatch into the cabin.

"What the *fuck* happened back there?" she screamed at him once they were inside. "Amira's been shot!"

"They killed Rasha and Bill," he croaked. "I hid in the hot tub."

"Who are *they*?"

"Looking for me," he said. "Guys I was working for. Vlad Draganovic." He was starting to shiver, so she sacrificed her last towel to get him dried off.

She went aft to check on Amira. The girl was still unconscious. Her pulse was rapid but steady, and the hole in her leg wasn't bleeding so much. Anne didn't know how much blood the girl had left in the ocean.

"Mayday Mayday Mayday!" she called into the radio again. "*Carina!* I'm being followed by a boat full of armed men. There's a girl on board who's been shot. I need help right now!"

"Roger that, *Carina*," said a voice in the professionally calm tone of emergency responders everywhere. "Maintain your present course. Cutter *Key Biscayne* is en route."

She looked at the GPS. Sixty-two miles to Key West. It would take more than an hour to meet the cutter. The boat behind her was still gaining.

"Hurry!" she said. "They're getting closer!"

"Roger. Can you identify the other vessel?"

"It's a big yacht, about twenty-five meters, gold and brown. I think it's a Ferretti."

"Can you make out—?" Anne couldn't hear the rest of

the transmission as a burst of bullets shattered what was left of the windscreen and tore away the radar unit on the roof.

"David!" she screamed down the companionway to the cabin. "Get up here and help me!"

He came up a moment later, still pale but no longer shivering. Anne ducked as more bullets raked the boat, but David just stood there dumbly.

"Get Amira down to the cabin!" she told him, and then when he just stared down at her, she punched him in the leg. "Do it!"

He moved like someone underwater, but he did get his arms under the injured girl and move her past the shattered glass on the deck to the cabin door.

Still sixty miles. The other boat was closing in now, only a hundred yards or so behind the *Carina*. The man piloting it was apparently alone, as he took a moment to adjust the boat's course, then fired off another burst from his big black gun. The rounds punched holes in the deck and the canopy, and as the sound of the engine changed, Anne suddenly felt sick. Something was hit; every few seconds, the engine sputtered. Fuel line, maybe.

Carina slowed and the bigger boat loomed astern. In desperation, Anne pulled out the revolver and braced her arms on the gunwale, trying to draw a bead on the man dimly lit by the control displays in the yacht's pilothouse. If she hit anything, she couldn't see it, but maybe the muzzle flash was enough to warn him off, because the yacht veered off, then cut sharply toward *Carina*, slamming into her port side just behind the pilothouse.

The little boat's stern dipped and the bow rose into the air. Seawater washed over Anne as she clung to the wheel. For a moment, she was sure the yacht was going to break her in half, but with a scrape and a shudder, *Carina* bobbed free and her bow slapped down into the water. The other yacht slid past and Anne hit the deck as the gunman emptied his magazine at her.

The silence when the shooting stopped was eerie—and then Anne realized why. *Carina*'s engine had stopped. Her boat was dead in the water. She scrambled for the controls. Set throttle, turn ignition. Nothing. She tried again, still nothing.

The other boat slowed and circled around to starboard. Anne pulled open the engine compartment cover, hoping that the damage was something obvious and simple. She got a faceful of smoke and diesel fumes, but couldn't see what was wrong.

Over the starboard side, she could see the other boat bearing down again, its engines throttling up to a roar like an angry dinosaur. "David!" she yelled. "Get Amira up here and put a vest on her! Now!"

There were three rounds left in her revolver. Anne fired all three at the onrushing boat, but it didn't turn or slow.

"David!"

"I can't get her through the door!" He was trying to push the limp girl through the companionway. Anne grabbed her shoulders and pulled. Amira didn't look good. She took the spare vest and started trying to buckle it onto Amira, but the blankets were tangled and wet.

"Too late," said David, looking past her. Anne glanced

over her shoulder at the oncoming yacht. It was only fifty yards now, closing the distance every second. She turned back to David. "I'm really sorry," he said.

"Jump overboard," she told him. "I'll hang on to Amira."

The yacht was only thirty yards off now. Suddenly its entire pilothouse seemed to puff apart like a dandelion blossom, scattering glass and fiberglass in all directions. A second later the sound reached her, an incredibly loud zipper noise coming from overhead. She looked around wildly, and then a winged shape passed over her boat low enough for her to see the red Coast Guard stripe on the white fuselage. It banked for a turn, and she could see the blind bulbous head of a drone. She waved anyway.

The big yacht, still running at full speed but with no one at the wheel, rumbled past *Carina* with a couple of feet to spare and disappeared into the darkness. Anne sat down heavily on the deck. David was still trying to get a vest onto Amira.

"I'm going to bill you for this," she said, gesturing around at the broken glass and bullet holes. "I'm going to bill you for all of it."

11

The man who sometimes called himself Colonel Ghavami watched the display on the big screen in his Dubai hotel room, routed through a couple of anonymous cutouts from the mission control room in Tasbuget. It showed the stolen payload dropping toward Earth.

He divided his attention between that and the laptop screen in front of him, which currently displayed the price of helium-3 futures. That price was dropping more or less in synch with the payload. A whole cargo of stolen helium hitting the market at a steep fell-off-the-truck discount would drive the price down worldwide, at least for a little while.

The big powers should thank him for that, Ghavami thought, and smiled.

He tapped at the keyboard and occasionally touched the screen to click a button. The colonel (he was actually a full general, but using his real rank when dealing with expendable assets might make it too easy for hostile forces to figure out who he was) was buying helium. Over the past year, he had set up twenty fake companies, fattened their bank accounts, even done some desultory trading to create plausible histories.

Now the fake companies were acquiring all the helium-3 anyone was willing to sell. He was taking current stocks, futures, everything. Ghavami's shell companies already controlled about a tenth of a percent of the world's helium supply—about nine kilograms—and he was doling out his last few million dollars, looking for bargains.

Timing was essential. Buy too soon, and he wouldn't make as much money. Wait, and the whole deal might fall apart. The big unknown right now was Captain Black. If he fell into the hands of the American authorities, it would introduce a lot of uncertainty into Ghavami's plans.

It might still work, even if Captain Black told them everything. That arrogant little Jew didn't know as much as he believed he did about this project. But a clever person armed with what Captain Black knew and without Schwartz's arrogance could potentially figure out the scheme in time to stop it.

If that happened, Ghavami would lose most of the money he had just invested. He would also be on the short list for a fatal accident or an "insurgent" bombing arranged by his superiors—not to mention having to worry about getting vaporized by an Indian or American drone every time he ventured outdoors.

But those were all fairly abstract worries. Things were going well. The payload was on course, and the man who called himself Vladimir Draganovic was in the Caribbean to make sure Captain Black didn't get the chance to tell anyone what he knew. Vlad was good at that.

Ghavami placed his last order and logged out of the secure brokerage. The price would continue to drop for another ten hours or so. Then things were going to start changing very rapidly.

■ ■ ■

AUGUST 28, 2031; 06:08 EDT—MISSION TIME 105:35

David had been afraid that his helicopter ride from the Coast Guard cutter would end at some kind of maximum-security military base where he'd be waterboarded and given the "cattle prod to the nuts" treatment. But the chopper touched down at Lower Keys Medical Center, and everyone was much more interested in Amira's bullet wound than in slapping David Schwartz around.

They dried David off, dosed him with antinausea meds to counteract the effects of a helicopter ride through the fringe of a tropical storm, gave him hot tea with lots of sugar, put bandages on some scrapes and cuts he hadn't even noticed, wrapped him in a blue cotton blanket, and parked him in a waiting room near the ICU while Amira went into surgery. His body knew exactly what to do now that he was warm, dry, and not in immediate danger: he slept.

Anne found him there when the cutter finally docked, still sound asleep.

"Wake up. I told them what happened," she said.

"Everything?"

"Just the facts I witnessed. We were visiting your friend, these guys showed up, gunfire, we got away. I didn't see what happened up on the platform and I don't know how much you told me is the truth anyway."

"The doctor said Amira *is* going to make it. The bullet clipped her femoral artery, but she said you got the tourniquet on her in time. You saved her life. Mine, too."

"They want your statement."

"I'd better make tracks, then. Don't want to wind up getting shipped off to some secret camp somewhere."

"Oh, please," she said with real irritation. "Just stop it, okay? I'm tired of you making up all this fight-the-power crap so you can justify stealing from people. You almost got us all killed. If we'd just sailed right into Key West in the first place and talked to the police, none of this would have happened."

He didn't argue. Much the same thought had been running through his own mind since he saw Vlad put a bullet in Barnacle Bill's forehead. Still, he didn't want to go to jail if he could help it.

"Look, I need to go do something. Amira's still in the ICU and won't wake up for hours."

"Something? What's something?"

"If you must know, right now all I own in the world is a pair of damp shorts, a wet fake passport, a dead phone, and a Doubloon card that won't work anywhere outside Tortuga. I need money, clothes, and coffee, and I need to strike down my enemies with furious vengeance."

"I'll be here. Amira needs to see someone familiar when she wakes up. She doesn't even have any clothes."

His first stop was the closest nurse station. "Hey, is there someplace I can send an email? I want to let my family know I'm okay."

The nurse, whose lanyard ID said he was named Gene Bart, looked sympathetic. "Here, I'll log you in as a guest." He passed David a tablet with LKMC EMERGENCY ROOM DO NOT REMOVE written on the case in marker.

"Thanks." David routed a message through a couple of remailers to trigger his Dead Hand archive. Teach Ghavami to fuck with *him*, he thought.

When that was done, he asked Gene Bart if there was a bank nearby.

"There's an ATM in the main lobby," he said.

"No, I need a real bank. I need to get some U.S. currency."

"You'll have to go downtown for that. Duval Street."

Eventually David talked Gene into swapping five dollars U.S. for a soggy Swiss ten-franc note, then walked out into the warm morning air. He rode a bus downtown and waited until the IberiaBank office opened. In any other town, a shirtless, barefoot man trying to arrange a large electronic funds transfer might have seemed a little odd, but this was Key West. Just ahead of him, a woman in a smashing little black party dress and four-inch heels who was almost certainly a tranny deposited eight thousand dollars in cash, so David felt right at home.

Twenty minutes later, he left the bank with a shiny new debit card and a brochure about financial planning, which he dropped in the first wastebasket he passed. The shops were just opening, so he bought sandals and an extra-large T-shirt with Ernest Hemingway's picture on it, then spent half an hour in an electronics store buying a new phone. The dip in the Gulf had ruined his old phone but not the memory, so he was back in business at the old number. He bought a new tablet and no longer felt naked and helpless.

The smell of roasting beans led him to a decent-looking coffee shop in an old metal-roofed house. He walked the cute dreadlocked teenage barista through the process of making him a Thai iced coffee, then took a seat in the front yard at a cast-iron table under the banana trees out front.

"Hello, David," said a gravelly, Balkan-accented voice. Vladimir Draganovic dropped heavily into the seat across the table from him. He was wearing a Disney shirt and mirror shades, but the magnificent mustache was unmistakable.

*　*　*

Elizabeth kept her alarm set for six, even though she had absolutely nothing to do all day. That wasn't entirely true—she had a call to Jack scheduled at three in the afternoon, but the other twenty-three hours were all her own. She forced herself to keep on a proper daily routine. Wake up at six, morning ride, breakfast, and shower by seven . . . and then the routine kind of broke down because after that, she really had nothing but daytime television or websurfing until lunch. The knowledge that she had half a fifth of rum in the cabinet kept rising to the top of her consciousness, and that was disturbing.

Her selection of civilian clothes was way too small. There

were only so many combinations of three ratty tank tops and two pairs of jeans. Her sundress was too nice to wear if she was just going to hang around the apartment. She put on the least ratty tank top and checked her mail.

The top message made her pulse race more than biking to Buck Lake and back had done. CAPTAIN BLACK'S REVENGE was the header.

Dear cops, grunts, spooks, geeks, and corporate drones:

Ahoy! Captain Black the Space Pirate here. Some scurvy rat has tried to screw me over. I'm going to screw him right back. The first two attachments to this document provide a complete outline of our current mission. The other two tell everything I know about the helium hijacking industry. And since I practically invented helium hijacking, that's a lot. Arr! Have fun reading it. Keep in mind that Westinghouse payload 38 is due to hit the landing zone in only 14 hours. If you get a move on, you may get it back. And maybe roll up the whole distribution network. Tell them I said hi and am fucking their mothers. Good luck, me hearties!

She checked the message details, but of course, it came through an anonymous remailer. If this really was from David Schwartz, probably a couple of anonymous remailers. Elizabeth opened a phone window and called McEwan.

He picked up after ten seconds, which was impressive, considering it was still five in the morning in Colorado Springs. "Santiago?"

"Check your mail. Captain Black just did a giant infodump about his piracy operation. I think someone must have double-crossed him."

"You're sure it's him?"

"Read the message. No one else on Earth would blow the whistle on a major criminal conspiracy in cheesy pirate talk."

"Is it solid?"

"I can't say for sure. I suppose the whole thing could be a huge disinformation op. He's just smart and weird enough to try that. But . . . why bother? They've still got the payload, right?"

"Sadly, yes." There was a pause while McEwan skimmed the file. "There's a lot here. The intel people will love it."

"What about the drop zone?"

"I'll pass that along to the Philippine Navy. They're covering that sector." He tapped at his keyboard as he spoke. "You still think it's this Schwartz character?"

"Absolutely."

"Because if he's burning his bridges like this, he might be ready to cut a deal, come in out of the cold. Can you get in touch with him?"

"I can try. I have a phone number that might still reach him. What can I offer him?"

"Don't make any promises. I'll find an FBI guy who can negotiate. They're good at that kind of thing. Just get Schwartz talking, if it's really him. Tell him we're ready to talk."

"Yes, sir. I'll do what I can." It was only after the call ended that she remembered he wasn't her commanding officer anymore.

. . .

David could feel himself entering a kind of adrenaline trance. His heart was thumping like someone was pounding the inside of his rib cage with a hammer. Could he get away? Get to the cops?

Vlad raised his left hand. "Don't move. I have pistol under the table."

"So what? Shoot me anywhere below the chest, they can fix that shit nowadays. We're right across from the town hall on a busy street. No way you're getting away."

Vlad smiled at that. "First shot keeps you from running. Second between the eyes. And American police do not frighten me."

"Okay, go ahead, then!" said David, surprising himself a little. "If you're going to kill me, stop dicking around."

The gay couple sitting at the other table three yards away stopped their conversation to look over at David and Vlad.

Vlad must have noticed them, because he gave a hearty laugh. "Okay, you get the part! Fabulous!" he said loudly. He leaned forward and spoke more quietly. "I won't shoot if you keep quiet. Just need to talk."

"Why the fuck didn't you just talk on the platform?"

"Things got out of control. Naked man had gun and would not listen."

"I saw you shoot a teenage girl!"

"Wasn't me. Istvan did that. She was screaming, and Istvan panicked. Very unprofessional. Where were you?"

Keep him talking, David thought. Surely some Key West cops would come in for morning coffee. Or Coast Guard.

Somebody. "I was in the hot tub, if you must know. When I saw you guys come up the stairs, I just ducked underwater and pulled the cover shut. There was enough air between the water and the cover to breathe. I saw everything through a little gap at the edge."

"Clever," said Vlad.

"Once you guys started searching the house, I made a run for the rail and dove right in the ocean."

"Your boat pilot is very skilled man."

"My boat pilot is a crazy chick from Oklahoma who saved my ass and the other little Coptic girl. You guys got *dominated* by a woman. Humiliated yet?"

Vlad said nothing. David remembered that there was still a pistol under the table pointed at him.

Time to change the subject. "Well, never mind that. How'd you wind up here?"

"We took the naked man's boat. This was logical place for you to go. Just looked at all coffee places until I found you."

It was a little disappointing to be so predictable, thought David. "Okay, you've found me. What do you want to talk about?"

"What have you told the American police? FBI and Air Force?"

David looked around again while he tried to keep his face still. *Vlad didn't know.* Ghavami hadn't noticed his little infodump, or Vlad hadn't checked in with the boss since docking. The big scary guy had fucked up badly on the oil platform, and was trying to fix things before getting in touch with Ghavami.

Which explained why he hadn't just shot David in the groin upon sitting down, or between the eyes. Vlad was still trying to capture him, or at least keep him hiding until the payload was down. Vlad still thought he was worth more alive than dead. *That* would last until about one second after Ghavami could get him on the phone.

The barista girl came over to collect David's empty coffee glass. "Something for your friend?"

"Nothing, thank you," said Vlad, giving her a big smile. "Anything else for you?"

This was his best chance, thought David. Tell her to call 911, maybe kick the table over onto Vlad, run screaming into the street, hope it didn't become a bloodbath.

Just then he heard the shrill ringing of a phone. David stared at Vlad—was this the call from Ghavami? Vlad stared back at him, impassive.

The phone rang a second time, and then a third. Every muscle in David's body was tense.

"Aren't you going to answer that?" asked the barista.

David looked up to see her staring at him, and realized it was *his* phone, the new one. He hadn't changed the ring to one of his custom ones yet. He felt himself blush from a mix of embarrassment and relief. "Right, thanks. Um, nothing for me."

He flashed Vlad an apologetic glance and took out the phone. The display showed a familiar number. Elizabeth Santiago. "Hello?" he said, trying not to sound eager.

"David? Did you send out a mass mailing this morning?"

"Yes, that's right, sweetie." If Vlad figured out what they were talking about, David wouldn't live to finish the call.

He could hear her derisive snort. "Sweetie" was not something people called Elizabeth Santiago. "Tell me honestly: Is that for real? Or is this just another Captain Black mind screw?"

"I wouldn't lie to you, honey," he said. "My phone fell in the ocean and I couldn't call."

"What are you talking about?"

"Baby, you know you're the only one for me. I'm not with Tifane anymore."

"Look, David, I didn't call to flirt. That phase of our lives is over and done. My superior asked me to get in touch with you. We're willing to work out a deal. We can offer you protection in exchange for information. Are you interested?"

"That sounds really good, sugar tits. But listen, I'm right in the middle of a meeting now. Some business thing. Can I call you back?"

"Sure," she said with an uncertain tone. "Are you all right, David?"

"No, no," he said with a chuckle. "Not at all. Anyway, I can't talk now, sweet cheeks. Let's get together just as soon as possible, okay? I'm looking forward to it." He made a kissing sound, tapped the Mute control, but didn't end the call, and clipped the phone to the neck of his oversized T-shirt.

"Sorry about that, Vlad," he said. "One of my babes. Which reminds me: Why did you shoot Tifane? She never did anything to you." He tried to keep the anger out of his voice.

When Vlad looked puzzled, it only made David angrier.

"You know, Tifane? The woman in my condo on Tortuga? Dark hair, great legs, bullet hole in the back of her head?"

"Another accident," said Vlad.

"Oh, well. I guess that makes it all right. See, when I walked into my condo and found Tifane *dead*, I guess I kind of overreacted, you know? Flew off the handle. I got all worried—I thought someone might be trying to *kill* me, or set me up. You know, frame me, get the Tortuga cops to arrest me, keep me tied up there. Arrange for me to get shanked in jail. Crazy, *crazy* stuff like that. That's why I ran. But now that I know it was an *accident*, all is forgiven. Anyone can make a mistake, right?"

"I regret what happened," said Vlad. "Now. I have an offer for you."

"Let me guess: If I keep quiet about the operation, Colonel Ghavami will pay me in full and you won't pull the trigger on the gun in your pocket? That's an offer I can't really refuse." He hoped desperately that Elizabeth was hearing all this. But even if she could hear everything, what good would it do?

"You agree?" asked Vlad. "Come with me. We keep you safe in luxury hotel. Just the way you like."

"Do we have to go right this instant? I'm kind of enjoying hanging out in scenic downtown Key West, absorbing the local atmosphere, taking in the sights. The oldest house in town is just across the street from this coffeehouse, did you know that? We could go take the tour."

Vlad's face was impassive behind the mirror shades. "Go now. I have car waiting."

"Okay, fine, I'll leave here with you. Which hotel are

we going to? It had better be one with a day spa. I've got a hankering for a massage."

"Very nice hotel. You will like it. Now, come on."

"Sure, sure. Let me settle my coffee shop tab. Miss?" He waved to get her attention through the door. "Can you come out here? What do I owe you?"

"You're fine," she said with a cheery wave. "You all have a nice day, you hear?"

"Come on," said Vlad.

"I'm coming, I'm coming. Don't be in such a rush, Vlad." David spent as much time as he possibly could shutting down his new tablet, finishing the last dregs of his coffee, blowing his nose into the napkin, trying to lob the crumpled napkin into the wastebasket, and finally scooting his cast-iron chair back from the table as slowly as he could manage.

Vlad simply sat there, his face unreadable, until David was actually on his feet. Only then did he take his hand out of his pants pocket and get up. Even without his hand on a gun, his massive presence made David feel like a skinny, undersized middle-schooler again.

They stepped out onto the sidewalk just as a bike cop came coasting up. He was wearing skintight cycling shorts and looked like a male stripper in a police costume. "I'm looking for a Mr. David Schwartz?" he said.

"That's me," said David. Vlad put his hand in his pocket again.

"Mr. Schwartz, are you—?"

"He's got a gun!" David yelled, dodging into the street to get a parked car between him and Vlad.

Maybe his shout did some good; maybe it distracted the officer. Vlad's hand came out of his pocket holding an automatic as the cop reached back to unsnap his holster. David watched in horror as Vlad stuck his gun right in the policeman's face and then the entire left side of the cop's head flew apart in a spray of blood and bone.

Amazingly, the officer got his own gun out and managed to pull the trigger even as the impact spun him toward David. Vlad swore as a new hole appeared in his Donald Duck shirt. He fired twice more at the falling policeman and turned to aim at David.

The shot smashed the car window as David dropped below the door. He bolted across the street and heard a car's brakes screech. The barista in the coffee shop was screaming. David dodged behind a parked car on the opposite side of the street as Vlad fired at him again. He actually heard that bullet go past him.

Another car skidded to a stop in front of the coffeehouse, and Vlad tumbled into the backseat. The other passenger in the back of the car emptied a pistol into the car David was hiding behind as the driver accelerated off down the block. He could hear what sounded like a hundred sirens screaming toward him.

. . .

His momentary sense of relief evaporated when David thought of Anne and Amira at the hospital. If Vlad and his crew were in Key West to finish the job, they might want to get rid of any other witnesses to their murder spree on Bill's floating house.

Of course, Vlad wouldn't know whom to look for if David hadn't bragged about his Crazy Boat Girl. Way to fuck things up, Captain Black!

He pulled out his phone and started to run. "Gotta make another call," he panted in case Elizabeth was still listening. He ducked into an art gallery to search for the hospital number, then spent what felt like hours getting the voice menu to connect him with Amira's room in the ICU.

"Anne?"

"David. You bothered to call. I didn't expect to hear from you ever again."

"How is she?"

"They patched up her leg and are pushing so much fluid into her, I'm afraid she might dissolve. The doctor said she lost about half her total blood volume."

"But they still think she's going to be okay?"

"The doctor says so."

"Good. Listen, I ran into the guys with guns again, here in Key West. I'm afraid they might go to the hospital to get rid of you two. I'm on my way right now, but I want you to get some security. Explain what's going on to the doc and don't take no for an answer. Vlad shot a cop right in front of me, and he's got three guys with him."

He looked up and down the street before sprinting out of the art gallery, heading for the tower of the Holiday Inn. By the time he got to the entrance, he was panting and drenched in sweat, but there was a taxi. He more or less dived into the backseat and told the driver to get him to the hospital.

David tried to remember what Vlad's car had looked like. Some kind of SUV or minivan. Gray or light blue—or maybe silver? It had all happened so fast. Every car on the road looked like it might hold a band of gunmen. David kept himself down out of sight in the backseat of the cab. The driver, thank God, was a black guy. David didn't know much about Balkan gangster/mercenary outfits, but he was pretty sure they weren't big on diversity hiring.

The cab jerked to a stop in front of the hospital, and David swiped his new debit card through the reader, then bolted. There was no sign of beefed-up security, no locked doors. He hustled up to the information terminal and found Amira's room number. Nobody stopped him from getting into the elevator. He was torn between anger and panic as the elevator doors closed. The place should be crawling with cops, he thought—and then he remembered that most of Key West's police were probably at the coffee shop downtown.

The doors opened on the third floor, and David felt an actual physical sense of relief as he saw two alert-looking police officers standing in the corridor. Safe. Anne and Amira were safe. He was safe.

Then they tackled him. The larger of the two shoved him face-first against the wall and grabbed his arms while the other hung back with a hand on the butt of his gun. "You're under arrest," said the one holding him as the handcuffs locked shut on his wrists.

"Okay," he said. "That's okay."

. . .

Elizabeth followed Detective Edward Okome through a couple of security doors to the interrogation room in Key West police headquarters. It was windowless, with a table bolted to the floor and very bright lighting.

"Mr. Schwartz," said Okome, "this is Elizabeth Santiago. She wants to ask you a few questions. This is entirely informal, and of course, you have the right to remain silent or have an attorney present."

David looked up at her. He looked extremely tired, and about twenty years older than when she'd seen him last. "No, I don't need a lawyer. Right now, jail looks like my best option. Hi, Elizabeth."

Elizabeth sat down across from him. Okome took a seat off to her right, where he had a clear view of both of them. She put her phone down on the table, in recording mode.

"I got the Captain Black download," she said. "Did you send that out?"

"Yes," he said, and he sat up a little straighter and his face got a little of its old cockiness back. "I'm Captain Black the Space Pirate. Accept no substitutes. And everything I sent out is pure golden truth."

"Why are you doing this? Over the years, you've done a fantastic job of staying hidden. Now you're telling everyone everything. What happened?"

"What happened is my fucking partner Colonel Ghavami sent his fucking goon Vlad—that's Vladimir Draganovic—to fucking kill me! And he killed Tifane Lamartine in Tortuga. And Bill Benedict and Rasha in Cuba, and he shot Amira and a cop right on the street in front of me! He's a fucking death machine, and you need to call out the National Guard or somebody right now!"

"Why is he trying to kill you?"

"I don't *know*! It doesn't make any sense! I mean, if Ghavami's trying to screw me out of my share, he's spending almost as much money as he's going to save. Plus nobody in their right mind will ever work for him again. It's fucking insane. It's *stupid*!"

Now she was sure he was telling the truth. David was an amoral, selfish, manipulative bastard, but he absolutely hated stupidity. When people were rational, he could move them around like chessmen. Irrational, stupid people didn't do what he expected them to, and that annoyed him.

"Okay," she said. "ORBITCOM tried to regain control of Westinghouse 38, but it didn't work, even using the encryption keys you put in your download."

"Yeah, they probably changed the codes. I've got a backdoor I didn't mention to Ghavami. Wanna hear it?"

"Of course," she said.

"There's a second command channel. Transmit on seven gigahertz using standard AES encryption. The encryption key is the first seven digits of pi times e in binary. That should give you root access, and you can lock out the other channel."

"I'll pass that along," she said.

"You won't be doing it yourself?" He looked startled, and then looked at her blouse, finally taking in the absence of any insignia. "Are you still in the Air Force?"

"I resigned a couple of weeks ago."

"Deniable civilian black-ops contractor?"

She had to smile at that. People always wanted to believe the government had legions of secret agents, warehouses full of supertech weapons, and universal surveillance. If they knew their defense was in the hands of a bunch of ordinary people like themselves, it would terrify them.

"No, I'm just a volunteer. My old boss asked me to help out, and I'm between jobs at the moment."

He looked disappointed. "What's going to happen to me?"

"I'm not a lawyer, David." She gave the detective a questioning look.

"He's in custody right now because he was on the scene when Officer Woods got shot. We're trying to determine if he's an accessory," said Detective Okome.

"How's he doing? The cop, I mean. Woods. Is he going to make it?" asked David.

The detective considered for a moment before answering. "He's not going to die. The bullet missed his brain. Still waiting to hear if they can save the eye. He's going to need a lot of surgery to rebuild his face. New teeth, new jaw, probably an artificial ear."

"He saved my life," said David. "I'm glad he's going to be all right."

"Help us catch the person who did it, then," said Okome.

"I've told you everything I know! The guy who shot him is called Vladimir Draganovic. Big guy with a big mustache. He came in on a boat sometime this morning. Ask Anne, she'll confirm everything."

"We've already gotten a statement from Miss Rogers."

"I need to get in touch with General McEwan and pass along this information," said Elizabeth. "I think I'm done here. Thank you for letting me talk to him, Detective."

. . .

Halfdan sat in an uncomfortable Soviet-made office chair in the control center at Tasbuget. The place was old, with brown moisture streaks down the concrete walls and linoleum peeling up off the floor. Colonel Ghavami's people had replaced the ancient fluorescent fixtures with tiny LEDs, which hung in the big empty rectangles in the ceiling like captive stars.

Halfdan's body sat in the chair. He was dressed for war, in a utility kilt, a necklace of replica lion claws, and a homemade *hachimaki* headband bearing the kanji for "Spirit Warrior" and the black sun-wheel of the Thule Society.

His mind was in a very different place. Halfdan had little use for the world of physical reality. He didn't like it and it didn't seem to like him either. So he avoided it as much as possible. The interface glasses bolted to the bridge of his nose overlaid the mundane world with a much more interesting reality.

In Halfdan's world, most men were represented by sniveling pale Elves. Enemies were fearsome wolf-headed fighters, and his handful of friends were idealized warriors. Women had to embody the Triple Goddess archetype, which meant they were either pale blond Maidens imported from a teen porn archive, redheaded Mothers imported from a "mature" porn archive, or Crones rendered as cartoonish witches. The damp concrete around him was replaced by an *Arabian Nights* fantasy skin, and the various display screens were magic mirrors held by Nubian slave girls with glowing eyes.

Halfdan touched one mirror and plunged through it to the deck of the reaver. Captain Black's interface choices lacked excitement, so Halfdan had replaced them. When he commanded the captured payload, he stood on the deck of a dragon-headed longship in deep space, manned by a crew of shirtless Vikings with oiled muscles.

The ship was dropping down over the night side of the Earth, and he could see the lights of cities on the Amazon below. Tiny red daggers marked the location of known military assets with possible low-orbit reach. Happily, there were none under the payload's faintly glowing path across the South Atlantic.

A translucent tentacle reached out from the globe below, groping for the ship, but it was unable to grip the hull, and Halfdan's reaver slipped past. He grinned. Captain Black had tried to hide a poisonous maggot in the heart of his code, but Halfdan had found it and slain it.

He touched the big kettledrum that stood beside him on the deck of the longship, and a goat-masked drummer appeared with sticks raised. Halfdan began the countdown to the burn. The ship was diving deep, dropping ever closer to the black curve of the Earth below, and he wouldn't put the rowers to work until just before it reached perigee at three hundred kilometers.

Ghavami had promised Halfdan that once the mission was complete, he could end the frustrating operational secrecy and tell the world who trod the deck of the longship.

Captain Black the Space Pirate was an important path-finder, but now the Galaxy belonged to Halfdan the Space Reaver.

. . .

Elizabeth fired up her tablet and opened a phone window to McEwan. "He seems to be cooperating. I've got a possible backdoor command channel we can try. Ready?"

"Shoot."

She relayed David's information. McEwan did a little hunting and pecking as he sent it on to the crew down in the Pit. "We'll see if this is any good. What's your take?"

"He seems pretty sincere. He's also scared to death. I think he's telling the truth: His partners in crime have turned on him and he wants protection. When's the FBI going to show up?"

"Agent Yu said he'll be down there tomorrow to take Schwartz back to Atlanta."

"I think that will make David very happy. He's more scared than he's letting on."

"Here," said McEwan. "I'm adding you to the mission observers list. You'll be able to see the tracking and listen to the command traffic."

A new window appeared on her tablet, with a tiny version of the familiar big board display in the Pit. There was Westinghouse 38, already below geosynch and falling faster each second.

Elizabeth listened as the crew in the Pit tried the backdoor command frequency David had given her.

"No response from Whiskey Three Eight on seven gigs with the key provided," said McEwan over her phone link. "You think your source is feeding us bogus intel?"

"He seemed pretty sincere. The backdoor may not be as secret as he thought. He does tend to underestimate other people."

"Oh, well. It was worth a shot. Thanks, Elizabeth. Would you mind staying in Key West until Agent Yu gets there? I might have more questions for Schwartz, and you're the best person to ask them."

"Sure."

Elizabeth wanted to get up and talk Detective Okome into letting her into David's holding cell so she could kick him in the balls, but she suppressed the impulse. McEwan hadn't disconnected her from the command loop, so she kept quiet and listened.

"Philippine recovery force is en route," said the Navy liaison. "Aircraft are launching now."

Over the next hour, Elizabeth watched the little red triangle representing the stolen payload creep closer and closer to the big globe in the center of the screen. The time to perigee display ticked down as she watched.

"It's missed the reentry window," said Tracking as the clock passed five minutes to perigee.

"They may be going for a different drop zone," said McEwan. "Watch out for a correction burn."

"There!" said Tracking right as the payload skimmed low over Africa. "Burning! Wait—it's not—it's accelerating, not slowing down."

"What?" said half a dozen voices all at once.

"Confirmed," said the Tracking officer in a calmer voice. "Velocity's increasing by fifteen . . . twenty . . . thirty meters per second. Burn's done."

"So what's the new drop zone?" McEwan asked.

Everybody saw it at the same time. "Free return!" said Tracking. "It's heading back to the Moon."

There were sounds of relief over the command loop. "I guess they decided if they can't have it, nobody can," someone said.

Elizabeth had a dreadful idea. She activated her phone window to McEwan.

"You saw it? The bastards decided to go hard-land it back on the Moon."

"General, what's the impact zone on the Moon?"

"Eh? Hang on. Looks like . . ." He paused and then said, "Oh, *darn*."

Her worst fear come true. "Babcock," she said.

"Looks like it. I'm impressed at their precision."

"That's no accident," said Elizabeth. "It all fits. That's why Captain Black's partners were trying to kill him. That's why the recovery force couldn't locate the pirates on the water. There aren't any pirates. We thought this was another payload theft mission, but it never was. They've weaponized it." She did some quick calculations. "Four tons will hit the Moon at Lunar escape velocity—that's as much energy as five tons of TNT!"

"No air to carry the shock wave," said McEwan. "They'd have to hit the bull's-eye."

"If we can think of that, so can they. I bet they've saved

some propellant for terminal guidance. The only question is whether they're going after the habitat at the base or the refinery."

McEwan didn't bother to answer. She could hear him on the command loop. "Are there any ships that can hit that payload with a missile? Engage at will!"

The Navy liaison relayed the orders, and everybody watched in silence as the red triangle passed over the Indian Ocean, now gaining altitude as it swung back toward the Moon.

"INS *Chennai* has a firing solution. They're launching. Missile away!" said the Navy guy.

On the other side of the world, in a hazy tropical morning, alarms sounded over the decks of a trim gray ship cutting through blue water near the Nicobar Islands. Crewmen scrambled to shelter as a hatch on the foredeck popped open and a pillar of fire shot forth.

The missile blasted skyward, cracking the sound barrier just a few hundred meters up and continuing to accelerate. The first-stage booster dropped away and the second took over, lofting it miles higher. The third stage fired, pushing the warhead beyond the atmosphere. The target was above and ahead, moving fast. . . .

The chatter over the comm from the Pit went silent as everyone watched the display. Elizabeth clenched her fists and bent as close to her tablet as she could. The red triangle continued to track eastward past Singapore . . . Borneo . . .

"Shit," said someone.

"*Chennai* confirms no impact."

Over the western Pacific, the missile reached the top of

its arc, hung there for an instant, and then began to tumble helplessly back toward the ocean below. The payload continued to rise. Ahead of it, the thin crescent of the Moon shone against the dark of space.

. . .

David sat in the holding cell in the Key West police station, staring at the television with a growing sense of despair. The story of the failed shoot-down was all over the news, and watching it was pure torture for him. All this time, he'd thought he was the smart one, but Ghavami had been playing him. Now it all made sense: The plan was never to steal the payload. It was a military operation aimed at the helium-mining base at Babcock Crater. But the trail ended with Captain Black the Space Pirate, now better known as David Schwartz the Complete Fucking Idiot.

Who was behind it all? Colonel Ghavami. And who was Colonel Ghavami? Almost certainly some guy with a different name. David didn't know. He could guess at Ghavami's nationality—Turkish? Iranian? Uzbek?—but there was no proof. Everything he thought he knew could easily be false. The guy could be from Queens.

And if Vlad Draganovic had been able to kill him, then the trail would be colder still. The only reason Vlad hadn't killed him back on Tortuga was to keep him from dumping his information until it was too late to stop the payload. Ghavami had spun him that story about CIA hit squads and he'd swallowed it like a teenage groupie in a rock star's dressing room.

And now? Now the best possible outcome was federal prison in the U.S. for a very long time. That was assuming he could stay out of Vlad's sights long enough to reach the prison gate.

"Schwartz! You've got a visitor. Your lawyer," said the deputy in charge of the jail.

"I don't have a lawyer," he said.

"Au contraire," said the deputy, leading him back to the conference room.

Anne and a balding man with a gray beard were waiting. "This is Mr. Flint. I got him to represent you."

"Call me Josh," said Flint as he shook David's hand. "Ms. Rogers told me about your detention here. I can file a motion to have you released tonight, tomorrow at the latest. At present, there's no charges against you. It's unconscionable to keep you here."

"Uh, I'm not sure that's a good idea. There's still a guy out there trying to kill me. I'm safe here."

"We can request police protection for you."

"How's Amira?" David asked Anne. "Is she going to be all right?"

"Yes. Josh is trying to get her asylum until we can find her parents."

"That's great. Um . . . thank you," said David. "You didn't have to do this."

She shrugged. "Maybe. I hired Josh to help with Amira. You're just a side project."

"Insert witty comeback here. I'm too tired to think." He turned to the lawyer again. "Listen, Mr. Flint—Josh— thanks for doing this, but it's close to midnight already, and

I'm about to pass out. I can stay in jail till breakfast. I've slept in worse places."

"As you like. In the meantime, let me advise you not to say anything more to the police or anyone else unless I'm present. Miss Rogers says you want to help, and that's good, but you don't have to give up your legal protections to do so. No matter what anyone tells you."

"Thanks. I'll keep my mouth shut."

The two of them went out, and as they passed through the security door David got a glimpse of the waiting room beyond. Elizabeth Santiago was still there, curled up in one of the plastic chairs. The tablet in her lap lit up her face with shifting blue and green. As the door swung shut, he could see her watching Anne, and her expression was almost predatory.

12

Jack Bonnet's image on Elizabeth's tablet was clear as long as he sat still, but whenever he moved, it de-rezzed into a crude mosaic.

"It all depends on how good their terminal guidance is," he said. "Either they hit us or they don't. Not much we can do about it either way."

"Can't you evacuate the base?"

(Annoying two-second pause.)

"Where to?" he replied. "The ferry can't get here in time, and the closest habitat with a pressurized rover is Daedalus, more than a hundred hours away. There's seventy-four hours left before impact, and our suits can keep us alive for only twenty hours, tops. There's just no way."

"I can't believe there's no emergency backup," said Elizabeth.

(Annoying two-second pause.)

"There's no backup because the designers didn't think of anything that could destroy the habitat which wouldn't kill the crew right away. I think it was a mistake for Mission

Control to tell us about this at all. We can't do anything, and we probably won't get any work done the next three days. Be better to find out when it hits. Save us a lot of stress and bother."

"You're coming back. Understand? You are coming back here when your tour is up. You are not going to die on the Moon."

(Annoying two-second pause.)

"Is that an order?" His face went all abstract, and then the image settled down to a broad grin.

"No, it's a promise. I am not going to let that payload reach the Moon. Understand?" She looked up in time to see David's lawyer and the young woman whose boat he had commandeered coming out of the security door. "It's late here. I'll talk to you in the morning."

(Annoying two-second pause.)

"I'm not going anywhere," he said, and cut the link.

She looked at the clock, hesitated, and then called her ex-superior officer. McEwan was still up, but in the phone window, she could see what looked like a bedroom behind him. "What?"

"We've got to intercept that payload. If there's—"

"No," he said. "You've been a big help, Elizabeth, but you're done. I'm not interested in hearing suggestions about things I've already considered. We don't have any assets in place, neither do the Russians, and the Chinese are too busy trying to pin the blame for this on each other. All we can do now is wait and hope for the best. Maybe pray, if you think that'll do any good. Now, I've been up since you woke me twenty-two hours ago, and I am going to sleep now. I recommend you do the same. Good night, Ms. Santiago." He switched off before she could get a word in, and when she called back, McEwan was off the grid.

She watched them move David to the county jail in an armored van, flanked by two guards in tac vests carrying M4 carbines. A taciturn Key West police officer ferried her to her motel, and she collapsed into bed. But sleep wouldn't come. She stared at the trapezoid of orange light on the ceiling cast by the security lamps in the parking lot, going over the situation in her mind again and again, trying to find an angle McEwan might have missed.

She was on the verge of getting up and finding an all-night liquor store for some rum to help her get to sleep when an idea came to her. There was a chance to stop the payload, practically under her nose. Elizabeth looked at her watch. Three A.M. Best to wait a couple of hours. She rolled on her side and this time drifted off easily.

. . .

"You shouldn't have told her there was no hope," said Singh when Jack finished talking to Elizabeth.

"You shouldn't have listened."

"You were speaking loudly and the privacy curtains are thin. It is sometimes a kindness to lie to a woman."

"I can't do that."

"I expect you will learn the trick, if you marry her."

Jack smiled, a little sadly. "Not much chance of that now."

"I cannot believe you are giving up! Ueno isn't. I'm not. We have talked the Daedalus people into sending their pressurized rover. We just need to find a way to meet them."

"But the math doesn't work!" said Jack. "The rover can't go any faster or carry more load. The more oxygen we take, the slower we go and the sooner we stop. By the time the Daedalus rover finds us, we'll be dead."

"Think of a way. The three of us are intelligent men. We can come up with something."

Jack took out his tablet and stared at the numbers again. Babcock Station had just one rover. Fully charged, it could go about fifty kilometers. The rescue vehicle coming from Daedalus could plod along at five kilometers per hour. Even if they left right away—and he doubted the crew at Daedalus could start for another hour or more—there was still a gap. The Babcock rover would run out of juice and stop, and the crew in their suits would run out of oxygen before the rescue vehicle could reach them.

If only their rover could cover more distance, or go faster! Reducing the mass of the rover might stretch things by a little, but the vehicle was already stripped to the bone.

Okay, he thought, think outside of the box, Bonnet. If you can't drive to safety, can you travel some other way? Load up on a booster and fly? The thought of trying to control one of the cargo boosters while sitting on top of it in a Moon suit made a pretty terrifying picture. Maybe with a few thousand hours of practice, he could manage it. Unfortunately, he had less than three days.

Perhaps they could jury-rig one of the rocket motors to the rover and blast across the Lunar landscape at hundreds of kilometers per hour! He chuckled aloud. The first boulder in their path would end that trip in seconds.

And then Jack's face went blank and he stared off at nothing as he thought his way out of the box.

"Harpal!" He got up so quickly, he bounced in the low gravity, then ricocheted through the habitat to where Singh was trying to come up with ways to stretch their life-support capacity. "I had a thought: staging. Use one of the big dirt hauler bots to tow the rover and carry extra oxygen. We travel as far as the hauler can go—"

"—Then start from there in the rover with a full battery and fresh tanks," said Singh. "Yes, I see! But will it work?"

The two of them bent over Jack's tablet. After a bit of tinkering with the spreadsheet, Singh looked up. "Three people is still too much. But one can make it."

"Which one?"

Singh frowned. "There are arguments for all of us. You would have a better chance of keeping the rover going. Ueno is smallest and will make the oxygen last longer."

Korekiyo sat down on the other side of Singh from Jack. "What are we talking about?"

"There might be a way for one person to meet the Daedalus rover," said Singh. "I think it should be you or Jack."

"You have a wife and kids," Jack reminded him.

"My son is a man now, and my daughter is engaged to be married. My wife will not be alone. The two of you both have your lives ahead of you."

"Stop trying to be noble."

"Stop it yourself! Do you think I want to die? I am just trying to be logical."

"I say we leave it to chance," said Ueno. "That way the survivor won't spend the rest of his life feeling guilty."

"Okay," said Jack, and felt horribly selfish for saying it.

"I agree," said Singh, who looked relieved.

"Cards or dice?" said Ueno.

"Dice," said Jack decisively. He had no desire to argue about high versus low cards, suit values, whether aces counted as ones or thirteens, and the question of the Joker.

"Wait," said Singh.

"We agreed—," Jack began.

"Yes, but not yet. We will get everything ready, then roll the die to decide who goes."

"Why?" asked Ueno.

"This way all three of us will have an incentive to work as hard as possible," said Singh.

Before getting to work, they stopped to eat, and without any conscious decision-making, it turned into a farewell feast. Ueno made a salad of the last fresh tomato and some lettuce from the garden, Jack fried up six servings of fish filets and made lime sauce for tacos, and Singh revealed a secret stash of Cadbury Dairy Milk bars for dessert.

After that, they slipped into their suits and got to work. The rover was a slightly updated version of the classic Apollo design, so there wasn't much to strip off. The passenger seat went, and the toolbox. They kept the inertial navigator and the radio, but yanked the backups.

"The trouble with stripping down space hardware is that it's all stripped down already," said Ueno. "All we're doing is cutting down the safety margins."

The robot dirt hauler was an anorexic-looking dump truck on wide metal-mesh wheels, with little to strip away. As with all the other bots, it wore baggy protection over all moving parts. The three of them loaded the bucket section with the rover and some extra oxygen.

"Time to stop," said Singh at last. "At this point, the more we remove, the less chance of the passenger surviving the trip."

They decided to sleep and have breakfast before picking which man would go. Working on the surface had left them all exhausted, so they spoke little before bedding down.

. . .

05:01 GMT—TIME TO IMPACT 67:49

Mike Levy answered her call the third time she tried him. In the video window, he was puffy and rumpled. "Hello? Elizabeth? Do you know what time it is here?"

"It's five. I've been waiting to call you. I've got an idea how we can save Jack. The SOTHIS vehicle's still at L_1, right?"

"No," he said.

"You moved it?"

"No, it's still at L_1. I meant no to whatever you're going to suggest."

"Jack's going to die in less than sixty-eight hours when that payload hits the base at Babcock!"

"Look, the Air Force and NASA and I don't know

who-all else have people working on this, Elizabeth. If they need my vehicle, I'll give it gladly."

"Then why are you waiting? Why not do it yourself? I can get a plane up there and we can work out how to intercept that payload."

"Here's how it works, Elizabeth: That payload's been hijacked. Anything happens to it, blame the hijackers. We take action against it, all of a sudden the insurers and the owners can blame us. They'll sue us—they'd be remiss if they didn't. Icarus can't even win a suit. We're on the edge of bankruptcy right now. On top of that, all my potential customers are trying to solve this problem. If I go blundering into the middle of everything, Icarus can kiss any future business good-bye."

"What about Jack?"

"I said no. I want to help Jack—hell, he's my best friend in the world except for Yumiko. You know that."

"We can save his life, Mike!"

"I can't trust you, Elizabeth. You lied to me, and now you want me to do something crazy and illegal. I don't want to endanger everything I've worked for—everything Jack's worked for—because you had some wild idea."

"A helium payload at Lunar escape velocity will hit like five tons of TNT. If it hits the habitat or the power plant, they're just dead."

"Elizabeth, I know all that. But I can't help you. Can not. Look—the Air Force has good people working on this. The best. You know them. They'll figure something out. Jack will get home without us trying anything crazy."

"That's it, then?"

"That's it. Go back to bed and get some sleep. You're under a lot of stress. We all are." His image went black.

Elizabeth got up and paced around the room a couple of times. She wanted to throw a chair through the window. She wanted to scream. She wanted a drink. But none of those things would slow down or divert the helium payload heading back to the Moon. *That* was the problem she needed to solve.

Identify the problem. Identify the tools available. Apply the tools to the problem. What tools did she have? Not many. Her hands, her brain, a modest savings account, some furniture in storage. A car parked at an airport up near Titusville. A pistol. Some family members in South Texas who knew an awful lot about citrus growing but not much about space warfare. A boyfriend on the Moon.

And Captain Black the Space Pirate, sitting in a jail cell less than a kilometer away.

She stood still in the middle of the room, thinking. After five minutes, she nodded to herself, took a deep breath, and began getting dressed.

. . .

At 6 A.M., Elizabeth picked up a rental car at the Key West airport, drove over to the Naval Air Station and bought a couple of disposable phones at the PX, then found a grocery open early where she could get the other items on her list.

Then she took up a position in the parking lot of the Monroe County jail. It didn't look like a jail. It looked like a small shopping center, a big windowless box with palm trees around it. She sat in a visitor spot with a good view of the entrance and used her personal phone to call Special Agent Yu every fifteen minutes. He finally answered at half past eight.

"This is Dominic Yu."

"Hi, Agent Yu. Elizabeth Santiago. I sent you the data dump from our space pirate. I hope this isn't too early to call you."

"No, no."

"Good. Do you have David Schwartz in custody yet?" She knew he didn't, but it was the sort of thing she would ask if she wasn't sitting in front of the jail, watching the door.

"I'm just going to pick him up now."

"Okay. I have a couple more questions I need to ask him about that stolen payload. It's still on track to hit the Babcock habitat. Can I meet you and talk with him before you go back to Atlanta?"

"I don't see why not."

"Great. Where do you want to meet?"

"He's at Monroe County Detention. Know where that is?"

"I can find it," she said, watching the building as she spoke.

"I should be there in ten."

"See you there," she said. She put on her Air Force cap and made sure all her insignia were in their proper places. At this point, she wasn't breaking any laws, but if she represented herself as a serving officer, that would change. Well, a lot of things were going to change.

She had set up a little display on her phone, with two sets of numbers counting down. The first one read TIME TO IMPACT and was Jack's remaining life span if nothing happened. It currently stood at 64:23. Below that was TIME TO INTERCEPT, which marked when the payload would pass through the L_1 point. It read 49:23. That was how much time she had to change the top number.

▪ ▪ ▪

The three men at Babcock Station slept late and ate an indulgent meal of scrambled eggs and tea for breakfast. When all of them were done and the dishes cleared away, Ueno dug into his personal gear bin and then placed a single die in the center of the table.

"The lowly twelve-sider. The tall pimply girl of the dice set. Even the four-sider gets more action. I will roll it, using a cup. On a result of one to four, I'll ride the rover. On a five through eight, it's Jack. And on a nine through twelve, it's you, Harpal. Does that sound fair?"

Singh nodded.

Ueno dropped the die into one of the aluminum drinking cups and covered it with his hand. He gave it several vigorous shakes, then launched the die into the air. It hit the table, bounced slowly a few times, and rolled to a stop against the raised edge in front of Singh. The top of the die clearly showed a twelve.

"Congratulations," said Jack, with complete sincerity.

"After all our work yesterday, I think I might be safer with a payload crashing on my head than trying to cross a hundred kilometers in the rover," said Singh.

"There's always the chance you won't have to go anywhere," said Jack.

"Do you really think they can intercept the payload before it hits?"

"I know Elizabeth said she would try. She has a lot in common with this payload coming at us."

. . .

Special Agent Dominic Yu didn't want to be in Key West. He didn't like places like Key West. Oh, it was nice enough, but Dominic was a city kid from San Francisco. The only time he'd ever enjoyed being on a boat was in Venice, and the island he liked best was Manhattan.

Key West did have one thing in its favor: It was compact. Almost like a proper city. None of Atlanta's over-the-horizon sprawl. He got his car at the airport, stopped at a Waffle House for breakfast, and was at the county jail five minutes after paying the bill.

No sign of Captain Santiago. Well, he wasn't going to wait around for her. He'd booked seats for himself and Schwartz on a plane leaving in two hours. He wasn't going to miss it just because the Air Force couldn't get up before noon.

Agent Yu walked into Monroe County Detention Center and began the tedious but necessary process of getting a suspect signed over. He was pleased to see they had a retina scanner to make sure he was really who he claimed. Too many places still relied on printed credentials, even though anyone with a laser printer and a laminating machine could fake any ID in about half an hour.

He had to do a little glad-handing. The Monroe County sheriff—a fireplug of a woman with a perpetual grin—made sure to stop in and say hello. Occasions like that made Dominic grateful to old J. Edgar, who'd given his agents such a reputation for being aloof and superior that a naturally shy man like Dominic could just keep quiet, smile a little, and everyone just chalked it up to Bureau culture.

A deputy brought Schwartz out. He looked older than the photos in his file, and was very subdued. Good. Dominic wasn't in the mood for a chatty suspect, or a whiny one. Fortunately for everyone, this kid was cooperative and nonviolent. All Dominic had to do was escort him to Atlanta, get him housed, and then strip-mine his brain for everything he knew about the underground flows of money and helium.

Schwartz spoke only as they headed out. "Can I bring my tablet? I just bought it."

"The one they confiscated? I've got that. Could be a while before the forensic data people are done with it. Your attorney can put in an official request."

"It feels weird not having a connection."

"We can probably arrange some kind of supervised access for you," said Yu. "But we're going to be on a plane for the next couple of hours anyway, and the Bureau won't pay extra for in-flight wireless."

"Jesus. Do you have to bring your own toilet paper to work, too?"

They had just reached Dominic's rental car when he saw Captain Santiago hurrying over. "Agent Yu! I was afraid I missed you!"

"You still need to talk to him?"

"Yes. I'm really sorry about this, but we're all working around the clock to stop the payload. It's going to hit the base at Babcock Crater in—" She glanced at her phone "—about sixty-three hours. There's no way for the crew there to survive unless we stop it." She was looking right at Schwartz when she said that, and she wasn't hiding her anger very well.

"I told you everything," said Schwartz. "That file dump had my complete design specs in it, the mission plan, everything."

"I know," she said. "But we don't have time to sift through everything. First of all: terminal guidance. Do you know how well they can aim the payload?"

"I wasn't in the loop for that part of the plan. I thought we were just, you know, stealing it to sell."

"Do you remember what kind of maneuvering reserve the payload had when you stole it?"

Schwartz squinted up at the sky—a good sign, according to Yu's interrogation training—then slowly said, "About . . . twenty percent on the cold gas thrusters, and thirty seconds of burn time on the main engine."

"Okay, so we can work out how much they used in the perigee burn. Give us a target oval. Did you upload a guidance package?"

"I did—it's in the file. Simple deorbit burn. The drop zone kept changing, so it was a simple on-command package."

Dominic kept glancing at his own watch, estimating how much time it would take to drop off the rental car, get to the terminal, get through security, and get on the plane. He hated running through airports, and the TSA uniforms sometimes made a real production number out of checking out Bureau credentials. But Santiago just kept going on and on! It was like some kind of space engineering seminar out here in the parking lot.

"Sorry to interrupt," he said at last. "We have a plane to catch."

"But I still have a bunch of things to ask!" she said. "Hey—can I ride along? I can get a cab at the airport."

"I suppose so," he said. Standing here arguing about it would just use more time.

He put Schwartz into the backseat, and was just about to get behind the wheel when he felt something pressing against his back, just below the shoulder blade on the left.

"I'll drive," she said.

. . .

Vladimir Draganovic found a pay phone and called the county jail. It was crazy, but in America, you could just phone people even when the police had them.

"I'm sorry, sir," said the duty sergeant at the jail. "That individual is no longer at this facility."

"Where is he?"

"He's currently being transferred to federal custody."

"You said FBI?"

"That's correct, sir."

Vlad hung up at once. The American FBI had offices in every state capital. What was the capital of Florida? Miami? Orlando? One of those places. If Schwartz was on his way there, he'd be in a car speeding north and there was no way to find him.

But: Vlad also knew that the FBI's helium-piracy investigation was run out of the Atlanta office, by an agent with a Chinese name. Yu. Atlanta was too far to drive. They would have to fly. Vlad got back in the van and told Lavrenti to head for the airport.

He felt naked going into the terminal without his gun, but fifty different kinds of insanity would break out if he walked in the door with a concealed weapon. At the airline counter, he put on his best cheerful smile and asked about his good friends David Schwartz and Donald Yu.

"I'm showing a Dominic Yu and a David Schwartz booked on the eleven-forty flight."

"Have they checked in yet?"

"No."

One chance left. Vlad hurried back out to the van. He had Lavrenti circle around and pull up at the corner where Faraldo Circle met Highway 1. Schwartz and the FBI man would have to pass through there to reach the terminal or the rental-car lots, and Vlad and his crew would riddle their car with bullets when they did. It was crude, but it might work. He'd present Ghavami with a messy success instead of a failure.

But as the time ticked down, he got more and more nervous. Where the fuck were they?

Finally, at eleven forty-five, he phoned the airline desk at the airport to make sure the plane had left. "I want to check on a passenger. His name is David Schwartz. Did he make the flight?"

"Nope," said the airline agent. "Looks like your friend missed his plane."

Schwartz wasn't at the jail, and he wasn't on the plane to Atlanta. Which meant . . . Vladimir Draganovic felt a surge of professional respect for David Schwartz. He had somehow escaped from FBI custody in broad daylight! Maybe he wasn't such a little shit after all.

How to find him? Especially with the whole FBI and everybody else searching?

"Take us to the hospital," he told Lavrenti.

. . .

"You don't want to do this, Captain Santiago," Agent Yu said evenly. "Put that away, and we can talk things over."

"You're damned right I don't want to do this! I also don't *want* to watch Jack Bonnet get smashed by a helium payload, or listen to him dying slowly waiting for a rescue crawler that won't get to him in time. I am officially saying fuck the rules right now, Agent Yu. Now, get in the car and put your hands on the dashboard. David," she added, "reach inside his jacket and get his weapon and his phone. Don't get between us."

"I don't want to be part of this. You're kidnapping him!"

"Agent Yu, I want you to observe that I am threatening Mr. Schwartz with force right now and he is an unwilling participant. David, get his fucking gun or I'll shoot you."

"Elizabeth, you know you don't want to use that gun," said Yu, in the annoying calm voice agents were trained to use in potentially violent situations.

"I need David—I don't need you, and I've already crossed the line. At this point, the question is just how long I'm going to spend in jail. I got kicked out of the Air Force for being too aggressive, I'm probably an alcoholic, I haven't had sex for two months, and right now I'm emotionally distraught and under a great deal of stress and my period's about to start. *Don't test me!*"

He lapsed into silence. She started the car and pulled out of the lot, drove past the botanical gardens, and turned left onto Highway 1. They got past the Naval Air Station and Shark Key; then it was a fast two-hour run northeast through the islands to the mainland. The road was slick from intermittent rain showers, but Elizabeth went as fast as she dared, slowing down to the speed limit only when the causeway crossed one of the inhabited islands. Robot cameras were probably racking up an impressive number of speeding tickets, which would show up on Yu's FBI credit card, but that no longer concerned Elizabeth very much.

When they reached the Florida mainland, the view outside changed from water to swamp and the signs started calling it the Dixie Highway instead of the Overseas Highway. Elizabeth began to look for a place to pull off. The access road for the Glades Canal looked like a good spot. There were no cars at the boat launch where the highway passed over the canal, so she stopped there. All around them was a vast flat marsh dotted with pine trees and shrub-sized live oaks.

"You get out here, Mr. Yu," she said, unlocking the doors.

"Here?" He looked alarmed. This was a good place to hide a body.

"I'm letting you go. I figure I can get up into the Miami suburbs and find another vehicle before you can check in and get the police looking for us. And then I'm going to force David at gunpoint to regain control of that payload and hard-land it someplace far away from Babcock Crater. I'm sorry about all this. I know this will be a career-killer for you. Good luck."

"Elizabeth, there are other ways to—"

"Shut up and get out!"

She waited until he left the car, then burned rubber getting out of there. "David, do you know how to steal a car?"

"Are you kidding me? I started with cars and worked my way up to spaceships."

"Then get to work. I don't want them tracking us."

It took Special Agent Dominic Yu fifteen minutes to flag down a passing car and borrow the driver's phone to report in. It took another fifteen minutes for one of Yu's fellow agents in Atlanta to contact the rental agency and ask them to trace the car. By then, David had already been at work under the dashboard with Elizabeth's multitool so the car's internal locator didn't respond to the tracer ping. Meanwhile, the Bureau talked to the Florida Department of Law Enforcement, and the FDLE talked to county and city police.

The search for the car began an hour after Elizabeth left Yu at the canal access road. It ended seventy-two minutes later when a police drone buzzing five hundred feet over

Homestead Air Reserve Base spotted the car's QR code sticker in a parking lot.

After that display of efficiency, things got slower. Drones couldn't go door-to-door at the base, asking people if their cars were missing. It took the base police nearly two more hours to establish that Elizabeth and David had taken a white minivan belonging to a civilian contractor who worked on-base.

．．．

"There," said David, pointing to the parking lot of a supermarket off Old Dixie Highway. "Pull around back, by the loading docks. I see some cars there."

"We can't keep stealing cars," said Elizabeth.

"Actually we can—but I'm not going to. This one is fine and has plenty of cup holders. I just want their license plates. Stop behind those two and get out like you're on the phone."

While Elizabeth leaned against the driver-side door with her phone pressed to her ear, David slipped out the big side door of the minivan and duck-walked around to the rear of the van. With the multitool, he took the plates off their stolen vehicle, then attached them to a beat-up old Toyota.

Elizabeth was almost bouncing up and down from frustration as David then put the Toyota's plates onto a brand-new Tata, and finally installed the Tata license plate on the white minivan. As soon as she heard the side door slide shut, she was back behind the wheel and mashing the accelerator. "We don't have infinite time! What was the point of all that?"

David looked smug. "As soon as the cops figure out which car we've stolen, every police department in South Florida's going to put all their drones in the air, looking for our license plate number."

"I understand that. What I don't understand is why you had to switch plates *twice*."

"Think it through. They find our plate number. About ten minutes later, the cops descend on that car's location. Some guns may get pointed, some poor supermarket employee gets slammed against a wall and handcuffed, but eventually they'll figure out that he's not us. When that happens, they'll search for *his* plates—"

"And find that other poor guy."

"Exactly. We gain at least an hour this way."

"You really have done this before."

"Remember how I used to brag to you about how much money I was making stealing cars? I wasn't bullshitting. The only reason I went into stealing spaceships is because it's way cooler."

. . .

"There's not really much point in tracking them," said Agent Yu to the Florida Department of Law Enforcement lieutenant coordinating the search. "I know where they're going anyway. Santiago's bound to be headed for Icarus Propulsion in Titusville. She wants to stop the helium payload, and that company's got everything she needs. Get the cops there to stake out the offices and wait."

By 4 P.M. on August 29, 2031, there were two Titusville

police cars waiting at the Icarus Propulsion Systems headquarters, and Agent Yu was humming north on I-95 in an electric sedan from the Bureau's Miami motor pool.

At about that time, Elizabeth was using a brand-new pair of bolt-cutters to open the door to Mel Koenig's home-built observatory in Kenansville, Florida, eighty miles away.

The observatory smelled musty inside, and there was a buzzing wasp nest up at the top of the dome. The air inside was incredibly hot—just opening the door was like standing behind a jet powering up. The telescope wasn't what Elizabeth had expected—it was squat and massive, like a cement mixer, thoroughly swathed in layers of plastic tarps.

That didn't interest her. What she wanted was the control station for his satellite dish array. The electronics were obviously Jack's work—obsessively neat, standard connectors, everything labeled and color-coded, backup lines included. The control device was an ancient Dell desktop with about as much processing power as a grade-schooler's Hello Kitty phone.

"What a piece of junk!" said David.

"Are you quoting?"

"Of course I am. This will do. I can slave it to my tablet. How much power can we push through this crazy thing?"

"Mel Koenig said he wanted to be able to get the first word in with aliens if he ever detected them, so . . ." She peered at the fuse box and followed a conduit to a plastic-shrouded box on the floor. "Looks like he's got an old C-band radar transmitter. The baud rate will be decent. Power level . . . Can you work with ten kilowatts?"

"Output or effective?"

"Output."

"*Oh* yes. We're going to open every garage door in Florida when we start that sucker up."

"So I can add the FCC regulations to the long list of laws I'm breaking. This is getting to be addictive," said Elizabeth.

"We're breaking them together," said David. "I'm as screwed as you are."

"You just stole a helium payload and a car. I held an FBI agent at gunpoint and kidnapped a federal prisoner."

"Are you trying to be a bigger badass than Captain Black the Space Pirate? It can't be done. I'll tell everyone you were my minion. All the best villains have minions."

They spent a few minutes working in silence, powering up the servos that steered the array of old satellite dish antennas and figuring out how to control it through David's tablet.

"I was afraid you wouldn't help," said Elizabeth. "I thought I might have to keep you at gunpoint the whole time."

He finished installing some software before answering. "A week ago, maybe so. I didn't know Vlad was going to start killing people. I didn't know they were going to weaponize the payload. It was all just fun, you know? Robbing big companies like Robin Hood. Captain Black the laughing rogue. But these guys . . . yeesh."

"You mentioned a woman in Tortuga. Were you close?"

"We should have been," he said. "Tiff actually loved me. Can you believe it? She even waited for me when I vanished off to Pakistan for three months. I was getting ready to dump her when she died. Because I'm a fucking idiot." A couple of tears mingled with the sweat running down his cheek.

"I'm sorry," said Elizabeth, wondering what else she could say.

He mopped his face. "So, this guy on the Moon—"

"Jack."

"You must like him a lot to blow up your life like this."

"That's right."

There was another long silence while he ran a check on the new software package. From outside they could hear the clicking of the chain drives as the antennas moved in unison.

"Do you think we could have made it work?" he asked her.

"You mean us?" She looked up at the wasp nest above them before answering. "No, I don't think so."

"Me neither," he said.

. . .

They worked until past midnight, ate some granola bars and Slim Jims for dinner, then slept in the car, which Elizabeth had shrouded in a big blue tarp to shield it from the eyes of hunting drones. David curled up on the rear seat, and Elizabeth cranked the driver's seat back all the way. It was about the least comfortable night David ever spent, and in the morning, his knees ached and he felt sticky all over. Elizabeth slept like a stone until her watch alarm woke her. She ran through a basic set of stretches and warm-up exercises while David went behind the observatory to take a dump.

"Can I use my phone?" David asked her when he was done cleaning himself with Handi Wipes.

"Not if it can lead someone here."

"I can fix that," he said. "I'll use a network connection through one of my offshore sites."

She actually smiled at that. "You know, for years I've been frustrated by how good your security is. Now it's actually helping me. Were you always so paranoid?"

"Yep. I don't like people knowing stuff about me. It's not like I've got some tragic Freudian childhood. Just wired this way."

"What kind of childhood did you have? If you don't want to talk about it, I understand."

"I can't talk about it, because if I did, we'd both pass out from boredom." He tapped his phone and listened; then his grin faded.

*   *   *

Anne Rogers sat very still in a chair, breathing through her nose. She would have liked to get out of the chair, but the rope around her body and ankles kept her from moving. She would have liked to see, or talk to someone, but the duct tape over her eyes and mouth made that impossible.

She could hear the television. The men who had invaded her hotel room were watching cartoons. She could smell the take-out fried chicken they were eating for breakfast, and wished they would offer her some.

She wished they weren't going to kill her.

A couple of them exchanged words in a language she didn't know. The television went mute. Someone approached her. He smelled like rubbing alcohol. He bent close to her ear. "I am taking the tape off your mouth now. Don't scream."

She nodded, and he peeled one strip of tape off her face.

"I have to pee," she whispered.

"Later," he said. "First I want you to talk to your boyfriend."

"He's not my boyfriend."

He punched the side of her head so hard, her ears rang. "Shut up. Talk to Schwartz. Tell him we have you, and you die if he doesn't come here."

He pressed her phone against her cheek. "It's ringing," she whispered.

Then she heard a click, and David's voice. "I can't talk right now. Leave me a message and I'll call you back."

"David, this is Anne. They came to my room and they're going to kill me unless you come back here."

The man took the phone from her face. "You know who this is. I am not playing. Come here by dawn or she dies."

When she heard a strip of tape being peeled off the roll, Anne spoke quickly. "Please let me use the bathroom! Please, I won't try to get away!"

He taped her mouth again, then spoke to the others. Someone laughed. The sound of the television came back on.

TIME TO IMPACT 43:10

13

When they untied her and took off the blindfold, Anne didn't know whether to be relieved or terrified. The man with the biggest mustache held up a military-style combat knife. "If you scream, I cut your throat. Understand?"

She nodded.

"Good. Stand up."

Her joints were stiff after hours of sitting immobile. She got to her feet and swayed a little.

"Bathroom," he said.

Anne didn't need to be told twice. She hurried over to the little bathroom. The man with the knife who smelled like rubbing alcohol followed her and stood in the doorway, holding the door open with his whole body. The knife in his hand looked very sharp.

"Can I—?" she began, but he shook his head.

"Just piss," he said.

Well, she decided, if they were going to rape her, they'd have done it already. Anne tugged off her shorts and sat on the toilet. Having a man watching her made it hard to start, but she closed her eyes, bore down, and was rewarded with a thin stream of relief.

It seemed to go on for hours. Whenever she thought she was done, she discovered that there was still plenty left in her bladder. When at last she was really empty, she opened her eyes. The big man was still watching her, and the slight leer on his face made her hold her knees tightly together.

"Schwartz. The Jew. Are you lovers?" he asked her.

"No!" she said—and then stopped herself. These were the men who'd tried to kill them all at the platform. David said they were looking for him. But wasn't he in jail? The guy with the knife seemed to think otherwise.

"I don't like him," she explained quickly. "But he's got some kind of crazy stalker crush on me. He kept trying to hit on me all the way from Tortuga. That's why I was sleeping on my boat—I didn't want him trying to climb into my bunk."

The man with the knife looked at her wordlessly, and she felt herself blush.

"Can I get up now?"

He nodded, but didn't turn his head a millimeter. Blushing even more, Anne stood and tried to pull her shorts up while keeping her legs pressed together. When they were finally fastened and zipped, she tried to look him in the eye again.

"Please don't tie me up again," she said. "I won't try to get away, I promise." What floor were they on? she wondered. If she hurled herself against the window, would it give way? How far could she fall and survive? Two floors? Three?

"Turn around," he said, and raised the knife.

"Don't hurt me," she said, fighting panic.

When she heard the sound of duct tape peeling off the roll, she felt a surge of relief. Maybe he wasn't going to kill her. The first strip went over her eyes, and then he wrapped more around her wrists, pinning her arms behind her back. She could walk, but that was all.

"You better be right about Schwartz," he told her. "If I get him, you go free, alive. Understand?"

"Yes," she said, and then he covered up her mouth with more tape.

. . .

Vlad Draganovic sat in one of the armchairs in his hotel suite, trying to decide if he should go ahead with the plan, or just kill the woman now and get the hell out of Key West. It had been nearly an hour, and Schwartz hadn't called back. The little shit might be too far away for Vlad to catch him and kill him, and as the hours ticked down to impact, it became less important to get rid of him. Sure, he might be able to identify Vlad or Ghavami, but so what? He didn't know anyone's real name.

The mission was already a success. Ghavami had shown the Americans and Indians that mining the Moon didn't make them immune to Earthly concerns. That was the whole goal. Their base would become a new minor crater, and there would be quiet champagne toasts in a number of national capitals. In the afterglow of victory, one or two screwups would be forgiven. Vlad's job was done.

Except . . . it wasn't. He really wanted to see the look

on that little shit Schwartz's face as he put a couple of bullets into his gut. The little asshole had fucked with him twice, and Vlad wanted to make sure the third time it would be Captain Black the Space Pirate getting fucked.

Besides, he had to think of his reputation: a hard man who takes risks and gets the job done is a badass; a hard man who screws up and abandons the job is a non-badass. Being a badass paid better.

His phone buzzed in his pocket. The number was unfamiliar. He hit the Mute button on the TV remote and shushed his men, then put it to his ear.

"Hello? This is Captain Black. Let me talk to Anne."

"Hello, David. Good job, escaping prison. How did you do it?"

"Let me talk to her, please."

"Come to meet with me, and I will give her to you," said Vlad. "Safe and sound."

"I need to know she's alive. Put her on."

Vlad didn't answer right away. Let that cocky little bastard sweat. Finally he got up and went over to the woman tied to the chair. He peeled off the tape on her mouth. "It is Schwartz. Say hello to him."

"David!" she shouted. "David, they came to my room and tied me up. Don't—!"

Vlad got his free hand over her mouth and motioned for one of the others to come tape her up again.

"You heard her. She is alive," he said into the phone. "Come to meet me, and I will let her go, still alive." And then I shoot you both, he thought but did not say.

"Okay, I—" There was a scuffling sound at Schwartz's end.

"Give me that!" said a woman's voice. She sounded angry. "Hello, who is this?"

"Who are you?" he asked. "Tell Schwartz if he tries anything, I kill her instantly."

"David's not in charge here, I am. I'm Captain Elizabeth Santiago, and I kidnapped David from the FBI. Don't fuck with me."

"You kidnapped him? Is this a joke? You think this is time for joking?" He picked up the combat knife from the table. "I can cut her throat right now!"

"Go ahead," she said. "I don't even know who she is. I never met her and I certainly don't care about her. If you want Schwartz, you have to persuade me to give him to you. Why should I let him go?"

In the background Vlad could hear Schwartz yelling something at the woman. He sounded very upset.

Vlad put the phone down and tried to think. Captain Santiago? The name was familiar. She was with the American Air Force. If Schwartz was working with her, that could be bad. But why did she say she had kidnapped him? American interservice conflicts never reached the gunplay stage. Fish for more information.

"All right, listen to me," he said. "I have the woman Anne Rogers. I can kill her anytime, you understand?"

"Tell me why I should care," she replied.

"Because—" He groped for words. "—it's your job! You are a soldier, yes? You defend your country. She is an

American citizen, so you must protect her. I am a dangerous man. Maybe I torture her before killing her. You don't want that."

"I have other problems."

"It is common human decency! What is wrong with you?" he shouted into the phone.

"Okay, okay. I'll grant for the moment that I don't want her to die if it can be helped. What do you want?"

"Schwartz."

"And you'll give me this Rogers woman in exchange?"

"Yes. Unharmed."

"Yes, yes. All that," she said impatiently. "Now sweeten the pot," she said.

"What?" Vlad was not in control of the conversation, and it made him feel very odd.

"I'm in a lot of trouble already for kidnapping Schwartz. If I give him to you, I don't have any cards to play. I'll need money."

"Wait," said Vlad. "You want *me* to give *you* money?"

"That's right. If you're hooked up with the helium, I assume you've got a budget. You've got plenty of money. Say, ten thousand Swiss? In cash?"

"You want me to pay you ten thousand francs for Schwartz?" He glanced at his men, who were sitting on the bed staring at him with absolutely shocked expressions. It took a lot to shock them, but this Santiago woman had managed it.

"Yes. And you give me Miss Rogers. That sounds about right, don't you think?" said the voice on the phone.

She must be insane, he thought. That explained everything. Fine—promise her anything, just get her and Schwartz into pistol range. "Yes," he said. "I will give you ten thousand francs in cash and the Rogers woman. You give me Schwartz."

"Great!" she said. "Where do you want to make the swap?"

"Where are you now?" Tell me where to find you, he thought.

"Up by Orlando," she said. Sensibly vague; she might be crazy, but she obviously wasn't stupid.

"Drive south," said Vlad. "Call again when you reach Miami."

"Okay. Oh, David says he wants to talk to Anne when we call you back. Keep her safe or the deal's off. And don't forget the money!"

Vlad cut off without responding. The conversation was getting far too weird for him.

*　*　*

"Are you fucking crazy?" David yelled at Elizabeth when she turned off the phone. The sound of his voice frightened some of the crows that had been roosting on the dish antennas, and they flew off with a great deal of noise.

"What do you mean?" she asked him when the cawing died down.

"All that crap about letting Anne die! What if he went ahead and did it?"

"Then I wouldn't have to worry about her," said Elizabeth. Her face was entirely calm and serious.

For a moment, David could only goggle at her. "You

know why it never would have worked out between us? Because you are fucking insane!"

"Right now, quite possibly. Now, let's get back to work. We've got just a few hours to take over SOTHIS before the payload gets to L_1."

"What about Anne?"

She looked at her watch. "It's, what, three hours from here to Miami? I'll call him back this afternoon." She set the alarm to remind her.

"We'd better get going." He started to pull the tarp off the minivan.

"No," she said. "We're not going anywhere. If we go to exchange you for her, it's guaranteed to be an ambush."

"How do you know that? He could keep his word."

"Don't be stupid. That's why I asked for money. He agreed right away, no haggling. He has no intention of keeping his word. All he wants is to get us close enough to kill us. That doesn't help us at all. So we're staying here and stopping that payload."

"Okay, how about this: You stay here, I'll go." His mouth was dry as he said it. He wasn't sure he could actually do it.

"No," she said. "I need you for the mission. You know how to steal spacecraft and you were able to beat me in space combat."

"Give me the keys, Elizabeth."

"I said no."

He looked at her, sizing her up. They weighed about the same. She did an hour of exercise every morning, but he'd been swimming a lot in Tortuga and had built-in testosterone. She'd undoubtedly had some kind of self-defense training, while he'd spent his whole life avoiding physical fights. And she had the gun.

Was he willing to die for Anne? Take a bullet just to see if Elizabeth would really pull the trigger? He realized that just thinking about the question answered it. Elizabeth believed he would be dead either way. She wouldn't hesitate.

"Can't we call the cops?"

"And tell them what? We don't know where Vlad is. 'Somewhere in South Florida' doesn't narrow it down in any useful way, and they'd have absolutely no reason to believe us. If he's smart, she isn't in the same place that he is anyway."

"Okay," he said. "You win. She's going to die and it'll be your fault. How's it feel?"

"I can live with it!" she said. Then her voice softened a little. "She's not going to die. That's not part of the plan. Now, come on back inside. We've got a lot of work to do."

. . .

AUGUST 31, 2031; 12:57:41 EDT—TIME TO IMPACT 23:00:12

At the offices of Icarus Propulsion Systems, Mike Levy sat in a swivel chair that creaked dangerously every time he shifted his weight. He was reading Alexei Leonov's autobiography while keeping half an eye on the mission director workstation for the SOTHIS spacecraft. Even though the vehicle was just station-keeping at L_1 someone had to be ready for emergencies. With Jack gone on the Moon and the rest of the company on unpaid leave, Mike and Yumiko had been working double shifts. They got a break at night when an intern from Embry–Riddle came in to sit in the MD chair and play some orc-fighting game.

He was just reading about the first spacewalk ever when a flickering in the corner of his eye caught his attention. SOTHIS was going active. The screen showed all the data traffic coming from the spacecraft, but he couldn't see any commands being sent up. In effect, he could see one side of the conversation. The vehicle was reporting on its systems status and command access.

Somebody was talking to his spaceship. No: someone was trying to *take over* his spaceship. Mike put down the book, cracked his knuckles, and started to type commands. Lock out the bastard.

Wait a sec—frequency shift? He hit Enter on the blocking command just an instant too late, and had to waste valuable time shifting to the new band. This son of a bitch was good, but SOTHIS was Mike's baby. He quickly got rid of all the alternate command frequencies in the memory; to change the channel, the would-be hijacker would have to upload the frequency, and Mike would see it.

Password login? That bastard! Well, two could play at that game. Mike erased all passwords but his own. Login now, asshole.

Crap! The intruder was using the same password from the file! Mike couldn't get rid of him without locking himself out as well. With his free hand, Mike pulled his phone out and called Yumiko. "Sweetie? I need you to get down here pronto. Someone's trying to steal SOTHIS."

"Who?"

"I don't know. Maybe the same son of a bitch who's aimed a couple of tons of helium at Jack."

"I'll be right there."

Now it was a straight fight between Mike and the mystery hacker, and it came down to who could come up with new strategies and which one of them could type faster. Neither one could see what the other was sending, only the replies SOTHIS was sending back. Which meant that each was trying to guess what the other was doing. It was like a fencing match in the dark.

Mike didn't do fencing, but back in college, he had swung a foam-covered wooden broadsword in SCA battles. In those matches, he'd overcome a number of people with superb technique by just hitting over and over again until one of them simply wore out.

Shut her down (shutdown mode blocked). Override the block (shutdown checklist deleted). Load new encryption key (signal encryption disabled). Shift to auto mode—that worked for a moment as SOTHIS switched to the instructions for dealing with a loss of command. During the pause, Mike loaded a backup shutdown procedure and the shutdown instruction. Sure enough, the clever bastard was able to kick SOTHIS out of auto mode, which meant that she started right into executing Mike's shutdown command. Ha!

Shutdown interrupted. Now the other guy was loading

his own encryption keys. Mike disabled it this time and emptied the onboard encryption memory. They'd have to work in plaintext for now. Both of them were trying to fight off the other without crippling SOTHIS, which limited what they could do—Mike couldn't permanently destroy the spacecraft's ability to communicate, and the mystery hacker couldn't prevent it from receiving new commands.

Okay, this dude was good at software. What about hardware? Mike sent a command to rotate the spacecraft. The returning data stream turned to gibberish and then nothing as SOTHIS lost its signal lock. That gave him a window of about sixty seconds to prepare before the high-gain antenna was pointing at Earth again. He typed furiously and kept a finger resting lightly on the Enter key, waiting for the signal to reacquire.

There! The little signal-strength bar graph jumped, and he slammed his finger down so hard, he was afraid of breaking the keyboard. A new command string shot up to L_1, telling SOTHIS to run a diagnostic series. That would keep the spacecraft's pea brain busy.

What was the other guy doing? Sending something, but what?

Son of a bitch! He'd changed the diagnostic! SOTHIS began turning its receiver on and off, so that Mike couldn't tell when it was listening. He typed a short script and hit Enter—now his system was sending the same command over and over until . . . There! He'd interrupted the on–off cycle. Now to tie up SOTHIS by filling the memory buffer with the same request, over and over. Keep hitting until the other guy wore out.

He heard Yumiko's footsteps approaching from behind him. "I think I've got the bastard on the ropes!" he called out without taking his gaze from the screen.

Suddenly his wife jumped into his lap, grabbed his head, and started kissing him. Mike leaned back, and the chair failed entirely under their combined weight. He tumbled back onto the cheap rubber floor mat with Yumiko on top of him.

"Jesus, Yumi! I've got to—!"

"Shut up," she said, kissing him again. "Elizabeth Santiago called while I was riding over. She's stealing SOTHIS to stop that helium payload."

"I told her—" he got out before she could kiss him again. "Yumi, stop it!"

She clung to him like a starfish as he got to a sitting position. "Mike, you're outvoted. I bet Jack would want to let her use it, and I do, too. The board has decided: We're lending our vehicle to Captain Santiago."

"This is serious, Yumi. Get off me."

"I'm serious, too. Let it go, love. Let her take it."

He got to his feet with her still hanging on him, but a look at the screen told him it was too late. The feed from SOTHIS was simply gone. The space pirate had taken control and shut him out.

"Damn it!" He balled up his fists.

Yumiko let go of him and dropped to her feet. "Don't be mad. This is the right thing to do."

Mike looked down at her. "I ought to give you a spanking for doing that," he said. He picked up the broken chair and tossed it into the corner, a lot harder than he needed to.

"It's the right thing," she said. "Proof of concept, remember? SOTHIS already did what we built it to do. We've got our engine performance data. The thermal engine works. If Santiago can use it to stop that payload, she can have it. And since she stole it, nobody can sue us. It's not our problem."

"Crap. You're right, but crap anyway. I guess I better call up ORBITCOM and let 'em know some unknown person stole our bird."

"Let me buy you breakfast first," she said, taking his arm. "Waffles?"

"Hell with that," he said. "We just threw away a fifty-million-dollar spaceship. I want . . . blini. And champagne. Come on. I know a place up in St. Augustine."

. . .

TIME TO IMPACT 18:53:30

Elizabeth used her own phone to call the kidnappers at 4 P.M., sitting in the broiling minivan parked outside the observatory. David stood at the open side door, his eyes wide with alarm as it rang and rang. When she heard Vlad's voice say "Hello?" she nodded and David let out a huge sigh.

"Okay, we're just north of Miami now," she said. We're at—" She squinted at the map display on her tablet. "The Burger King on 167th Street. Where do you want us to meet you?"

"Go to Homestead, to Homestead General Aviation Airport," Vlad said. "Call again when you get there."

"That's a heck of a long way from here. It'll take us a couple of hours in this traffic."

"If you delay too long, she goes in the canal."

"Let me talk to her first. I'm not taking David anywhere near there until I know she's alive."

"Hold on."

A moment later, Elizabeth heard Anne. "I'm in a car somewhere. I can't see anything."

"Are you okay?"

"I'm really thirsty."

"Just hold on," said Elizabeth. "Just a couple of hours more."

Vlad's voice again. "She is alive. Now come here."

"Tell me where, again?"

"On the west side of the canal, less than a kilometer west of Homestead General Aviation Airport on 217th Avenue. You have two hours. Don't try anything. We can see for a mile in every direction from here."

"Okay. I'm driving a white minivan. See you in about two hours. And don't try anything or you won't get David."

Elizabeth turned off the phone and put it back in her shirt pocket.

David looked horrified. "How can you tell her everything's going to be okay? We're two hundred miles away! Those bastards will kill her. Call the cops, at least."

"Hello, Homestead Police, I'm a stranger you probably think is a dangerous fugitive. Here's my cock-and-bull story about a kidnapping. Go drive up to a bunch of armed men with a hostage who'll kill her as soon as they see you."

"They might at least send a car to check it out!"

"Then the bad guys kill Anne, plus maybe we get a couple of policemen shot, too. Not an improvement." She looked at his anguished face. "Okay, David, there is one chance for her. It's not a sure thing, but it is a chance, and calling the cops will only mess it up. Now, we've got our own job to do and the clock is ticking."

"Okay, what is this chance?"

"I just called him on my own phone."

. . .

Special Agent Dominic Yu took off the headphones. "Did you get a location?"

"Not precisely," said the wiretap technician. Her ID badge said SONI, SABITA M. "I know what antenna cell they're in, but the phone GPS was disabled. According to AT&T, they're just east of Kenansville."

"That's here in Florida? What's there? Anything?"

"A lot of lakes and cow pastures, mostly. What should I be looking for?" She called up a photo map and zoomed in on the center of the peninsula.

"Santiago and Schwartz have taken control of the SOTHIS vehicle. We don't know why. They need some way to communicate with it. We know they aren't using any of the commercial antenna farms or the NASA network— and Schwartz is apparently no longer cooperating with whoever's controlling Westinghouse 38, so it's likely he doesn't have access to overseas antenna sites."

"I'm sorry," said Ms. Soni after a pause, "I don't see any relevance."

"Look for something that could hide a large antenna. Something that could communicate with a spacecraft half-way to the Moon." He stretched and got up. The FBI office in Miami was a low-rise building right next to a busy highway interchange. The view from the window was nothing but concrete and unhealthy-looking live oaks. Yu wished they were downtown. Someplace he could go out for a walk. He had spent far too much time lately driving up and down the Florida peninsula.

She clicked around the map for a while, and then said "Huh. How about this?"

He looked over her shoulder. There was a white domed building in the center of the screen, and right next to it was a field of nineteen three-meter dish antennas arranged in a hexagon.

"What's that?"

She did some typing. "Private property, owned by a Mr. Melville Koenig of Palm Bay. Here's a news story about him. *Osceola News-Gazette:* 'Watch the Skies! Mel Koenig Hopes to Find Aliens Before NASA.'"

Yu just rolled his eyes as he tapped his phone. "Captain Huizenga? We've got a lead on two of our perps. They're in Kenansville. Ms. Soni is sending you the address now. I need you to contact the local police and get a couple of cars there. I know Santiago's armed, so tell them to use caution and wear their vests. But try to talk first, no tactical entry."

He switched off and looked at Sabita for a moment. She had straight dark hair, good cheekbones, and an aristocratic nose. "How tall are you?"

"Me? Uh, five ten without heels."

"Good. Get a vest and come with me."

. . .

Halfdan the Space Viking watched the intruder approaching his longship as it dived toward the Moon. His interface represented SOTHIS as an armored demon with the Air Force symbol on its outstretched bat wings. The avatar wasn't all that different from the actual spacecraft—SOTHIS itself had those big solar wings that flexed and turned like something alive.

The big question in Halfdan's mind was how much propellant that bat-winged interloper was carrying. His own longship had a little maneuvering reserve, but he had to conserve every gram for terminal guidance. His target circle was still fifty meters across, and he'd need to tighten it up as the payload fell toward the Babcock habitat.

A window opened in space, and Colonel Ghavami spoke to him, with a hotel room visible behind him. "We have confirmed that Schwartz is controlling the SOTHIS machine now. The Americans are trying to find him. For now, do nothing."

"If Captain Black offers battle, Halfdan will fight."

"Don't waste resources! Their police may find him before he can do anything."

"Halfdan will not raise his sword. But if Captain Black maneuvers, Halfdan will evade."

"Please do not do anything foolish. We are very close to success."

"Halfdan is bold, not foolhardy. He is not a berserker. Trust Halfdan."

"At this moment, I have no choice," said the colonel, and he sounded a little bitter about it.

Halfdan closed the window and told his interface to block incoming calls from Ghavami. Of course it would come to a battle. A glorious battle. Captain Black would try to stop him, and Halfdan would win the fight. He was deep in archetype territory here: the young hero confronting his mentor, now in the service of the enemy. Victory was certain.

TIME TO IMPACT 16:20:02

14

In the observatory, Elizabeth flapped her sweat-soaked shirt and wished for the tenth time that she was someplace cooler. Back in the old days, when you screwed up, the Air Force assigned you to Thule or Nunavut. For a moment she imagined tundra and ice outside, but that didn't keep the sweat from dripping into her eyes. The two of them were going through bottled water like a rocket burning kerosene.

She watched the Air Force tracking display—luckily McEwan still hadn't revoked her access. "Whiskey Three Eight is two kilometers away from SOTHIS and closing. Relative velocity is five meters per second."

"How much delta-v have we got on board?" asked David.

"Five hundred meters per second in the main tank, maybe another two if we use the cold gas thrusters."

"Right. Now, if you don't mind, I need you to stop talking and let me work, okay?"

David had his face right against the laptop screen. His groovy pirate interface was part of Ghavami's system, so for now he was working with simple orbital graphics and numbers. Fifteen hundred meters away now, almost at minimum distance. He started the burn clock.

Fifty thousand miles overhead, SOTHIS's two petal-shaped wings curved and flexed, pouring a hundred kilowatts of raw sunlight onto the black ball of the engine chamber. As the display on David's screen counted down to zero, the black surface of the engine turned cherry red, then dimmed slightly as the fuel flowed in. When the little box labeled BURN began flashing red on David's screen, a plume of superheated gas shot from the engine and SOTHIS began accelerating toward the payload.

In two seconds, he had matched speeds with the payload, so that the two of them were falling together toward the Moon, just under a mile apart. The easy part was done. Now he had to catch it and nudge it off course before both spacecraft smashed down into Babcock Crater.

"Uh-oh," said Elizabeth. "Fuel pressure's changing. We've got . . . Shit! We're almost dry. Eighty meters per second left."

"You just said we had five hundred!"

"Must've had a bum sensor. As soon as you opened the valve, the pressure reading went nuts. Now it says . . . seventy-five."

"Which figure is correct? Five hundred or seventy-five?"

Elizabeth tapped her keyboard. "Flow rate matches the lower pressure. Probably lost it all to boil-off while SOTHIS was sitting idle."

"Oh-kay." David leaned back and cracked his knuckles, then hunched over the keyboard again. "Now we find out how much of a reserve they've got on that payload."

Even without his custom interface, Captain Black the Space Pirate could imagine the situation up at L_1. The captured treasure ship (which he pictured flying the Jolly Roger and manned by mustachioed Barbary corsairs) was fourteen hundred meters away.

His own vehicle was closing slowly now, at about one meter per second. The faster he approached, the less reserve he'd have for capture maneuvers and shoving the heavy payload off course.

But of course, the longer he waited, the more time he gave Halfdan and the rest of Ghavami's underpaid mooks in Central Asia to notice him and do something about it. He goosed SOTHIS up to an approach velocity of ten meters per second. Two minutes until contact. Time to grapple and board!

. . .

Anne Rogers could feel wind in her hair and sunshine on her skin. She was sitting on grass, and the seat of her jeans soaked up moisture from the wet soil. Somewhere nearby, she could hear helicopters and airplane motors. She could not smell the ocean, just the muddy scent of a canal. The car trip had lasted long enough for her captors to watch an entire French action movie, with a long stretch of silence afterwards. From what little she remembered about Florida geography, that put them somewhere on the mainland, maybe in the Miami suburbs.

They still hadn't raped her. She thought that was a good sign. And the fact that she was sitting here on the grass—

wherever "here" was—meant that they hadn't killed her. Maybe they weren't going to kill her.

Maybe they were digging a grave.

One of her captors said something that sounded like a warning. A hand grabbed her upper arm and hauled her to her feet. "Come on," said the man. "Car coming. They are here. Do what I say and you live, understand?"

He peeled the tape off her eyes and mouth, none too gently. The sudden glare of South Florida sunlight blinded her. Through watering eyes, she could see that she was standing on a shell road beside a canal covered with duck-weed. Two cars were parked at the side of the road, and her four kidnappers were standing around with guns in their hands. On the far side of the canal, she could see orange groves, with a little airport beyond them. As she watched, a helicopter buzzed low over the airport, then circled around over the swamp behind her. A white minivan with tinted windows was approaching on the shell road.

The boss man with the mustache looked at her. "When I tell you, walk toward the van. Understand?"

She nodded. He didn't need a gun or a band of armed men to make people obey him.

The van stopped about thirty meters away, and for a few seconds nothing happened. Then the driver's door opened and a tall woman got out. She was wearing a blue uniform and big mirrored sunglasses. "Let me see her!" she yelled.

The man holding Anne pulled her into the middle of the road, keeping the muzzle of his pistol pressed against the side of her head. The man with the big mustache stood on the other side of her, his own gun down at his side. "Here she is!" he shouted back. "Where is Schwartz?"

The woman went to the side of the minivan and slid the door open. For a moment she just stood there, apparently talking to someone inside.

"Come on!" the boss yelled. Nothing happened.

He said something she couldn't understand, and the man holding her clicked the safety on his gun.

. . .

TIME TO IMPACT 15:44:20

At one minute to contact, the payload began to maneuver. A quick burn of the steering thrusters, giving it a little side vector. David matched it. Forty seconds. At thirty, the payload dodged again, and David corrected again, closing in steadily.

Whoever was piloting the payload must have had nerves of steel, because he waited until SOTHIS was only a hundred meters off before ducking aside like a matador avoiding a charging bull. David swore silently as SOTHIS shot past the payload, missing by a good ten meters.

The payload was transmitting something, en clair. A voice message. David clicked on audio.

"Halfdan salutes you as one warrior to another. The circle is now complete. When you left, Halfdan was but the learner. Now Halfdan is the master."

"Only a master of plagiarism, you dumb fuck," said David aloud.

"What?" Elizabeth asked.

"Nothing."

A thought struck David. Maybe Halfdan didn't know what was really going on. He set up a transmission relay, also en clair, and spoke into the computer in front of him. "Halfdan! You know people are going to die if this hits Babcock, right? The three astronauts there can't get to safety. Do you want to be a murderer?"

Might do some good, he thought. He used the gyros to rotate his vehicle and got ready for another burn. Just before he started the motor, he got back a voice message.

"Halfdan will give them the greatest gift a man can give another man: a warrior's death."

"So much for negotiation," said David, and hit the burn control. He ran the main engine until his vector pointed right back at the payload. Fifty-three meters per second of propellant left.

Halfdan didn't do any evasion this time as SOTHIS approached, but David suspected he was just playing chicken. The bastard had to conserve his own propellant. David kept his fingers on the cold-gas thruster controls. At twenty meters, the payload scooted left, and David tried to match it. But though he opened the valves wide open, his spacecraft barely changed vector at all. SOTHIS passed a few meters by the target without contact.

"What the hell? Where did my steering thrusters go?"

"Nitrogen pressure's gone. I think we must have had some boil-off there, too." Elizabeth's voice was pure professional calm now.

"Tell your old boss he should get a refund from whoever sold him those pressure sensors. Because they suck balls."

As he spoke, David hit the brakes right away, trying to keep the distance close. With some of his precious main-tank fuel, he brought SOTHIS to a stop about forty meters from Westinghouse 38 as the two of them fell toward the Moon. His opponent just sat there. Somehow David knew he was smirking.

Time to get creative. Signal delay at that distance was about one second—which meant two seconds for a signal to get down to Earth and a response to come back up, plus human reaction time on the ground. How fast could Half-dan react? Call it at least three seconds. If David could get inside that loop, he'd be able to clobber the payload, maybe rupture the pressure vessel and let a couple of tons of boiling helium blow the flimsy aluminum shell safely off course.

Trouble was, with the anemic drive power Elizabeth and her corporate overlords had given SOTHIS, it would take at least nine seconds to cross those forty meters. David had to work the vehicle to within about six meters in order to have a sporting chance. And he had to do it without letting Halfdan figure out what he was doing. All with only—he checked the fuel figures—forty-three meters per second of delta-v left in the tank. Maybe less.

He tried a low-speed burn, at five meters per second. Sneak up on Halfdan. The payload just sat there as David approached, but then four seconds before impact, it ducked aside. David braked to a stop fifty meters out, but deliber-ately overdid it a little, so that SOTHIS was drifting back toward the payload at walking speed.

According to his stolen Westinghouse specs document,

the payload didn't have any onboard sensors to speak of, just simple cameras for steering by the stars. These guys were probably tracking SOTHIS with ground-based radar, or maybe optical telescopes. Maybe they wouldn't notice his slow approach until it was too late. And how much juice did this bastard still have?

Enough for another burn, evidently, as it began moving away from him when he was twenty meters off.

Close enough! David opened up the throttle. With only a little fuel left, SOTHIS was lighter and more nimble than ever. The vehicle covered those twenty meters in six seconds. Was that quick enough?

"Bastard!" David said aloud as the payload scooted aside, the solar wings of SOTHIS missing by inches. He immediately swung the engine around and reversed thrust.

"We're losing propellant again," said Elizabeth.

"I really don't need to hear that," said David. "How fast?"

"Slow but constant. You're losing about one meter of delta-v every minute or so."

Enough for two more tries. Using the gyros, he lined up SOTHIS for another run.

Halfdan couldn't brake or accelerate—that would throw him too far off target, and there wasn't any point to moving toward or away from SOTHIS. That left one axis of movement. The payload could duck either left or right.

Which meant David had to outguess Halfdan. He ran the motor up to full power again, accelerating toward the payload, then commanded his bird to jink . . . left.

Two seconds later, he learned he had guessed wrong.

Halfdan had gone right. The son of a bitch must have been looking over his old mission logs. Was he getting too predictable?

He halted SOTHIS twenty-five meters out. He had enough fuel for one attack run left. If he missed, then some guys on the Moon he'd never met would probably die. Babcock Station would join the list of names like "World Trade Center" or "Notre Dame." The names people always hesitated before saying.

Why should he care? Elizabeth *probably* wouldn't blow a hole in him if her boyfriend got squished. He'd done his best, helped her steal SOTHIS, danced around with the payload, but the other guy had just managed to . . . beat him.

Nobody beats Captain Black the Space Pirate. Especially not that pretentious jerk Halfdan. "Is there any way we can get more power out of this motor? Can we hack the mirrors to get more heat?"

"Nope. Can't increase the energy, and if you concentrate the heat on a smaller spot, you just burn a hole in the engine."

David looked off at the bare cinder block wall for a moment, then started typing madly.

"What are you—?"

"Quiet. The captain is working."

. . .

"Show me Schwartz now or she dies!" Vlad yelled.

"Just a second!" called the woman from where she stood

by the open door in the side of the minivan. "He's freaking out over here."

Anne could feel the man holding her tense up. She looked sidelong at the gun, which was pointing directly at her temple. Was his finger on the trigger getting redder?

The sound of the helicopter motor grew louder. It was coming right at them now, swooping low over the swamp from the west, a military chopper like a big black insect. One of the men yelled.

Something warm spattered the side of Anne's face. The sound of a rifle shot echoed across the swamp from the direction of the orange grove, followed by others. She turned in time to see the man who had been holding the gun to her head topple to the ground. Most of his own head was simply gone. A second kidnapper slumped against the fender of the car, looking down at a bloody hole in his chest.

Vlad shouted something and ran for the shelter of the parked cars.

Anne ran forward, toward the minivan and away from the car her captors were hiding behind. It was hard to run because her wrists were still taped together. Up ahead, men in battle gear with wicked-looking guns piled out of the open door of the van, and the sound of rotors deafened her as the helicopter passed just a few yards overhead. It slowed to hover over the canal and rotated to swing the cockpit toward the gunfight.

Anne stumbled on the gravel and fell, scraping the hell out of her chin on the sharp oyster shells. Right next to her face, the ground exploded in a puff of dust and shell fragments. She struggled to get to her feet again and keep running.

"Anne Rogers! Stay down!" the woman crouching next to the minivan yelled. Off to her right, Anne heard the ripping noise she'd heard out at sea north of Cuba, as the helicopter's guns tore through the parked cars.

After the noise, the sudden silence startled her. She raised her head and looked around, just in time to get clobbered as one of the armored men from the minivan flung himself on top of her. "Sorry," he muttered. "Stay down."

Two more armored figures ran past them and Anne could see them warily approaching the cars, weapons ready. They dragged one man out of the second car and handcuffed him. A second man in the grass by the canal raised his hands. His shirt was bloody. Someone called for a medic.

The soldier got off her and helped Anne to her feet. In his combat gear, he loomed over her like a giant from a fantasy game. He produced a combat knife and cut the tape binding her wrists. She noticed that his hands were trembling. "There's an ambulance on its way, ma'am," he said. "Are you all right? Were you hit?"

"I'm okay, I think," she said. She peeled the remains of the tape off her wrists and then with a shock realized her shirt was covered in blood. Had she been shot?

She felt herself with her hands. There was blood everywhere, but the only place she hurt was the cut on her chin. And then she realized the blood wasn't hers. It must have come from the man who'd been holding her. Which meant the little hard bits were pieces of his skull, and the white blobs were his brain. Some of his brain was stuck to her face.

Anne dropped to her knees and threw up on the shell road. She felt tears in her eyes, and didn't hold them back. The soldier knelt next to her and patted her shoulder awkwardly. "It's okay, ma'am. You're going to be all right. We got 'em. You're safe now."

A dozen cars and SUVs skidded to a stop behind the minivan now, full of uniformed police, paramedics, and men in suits. The soldier helped Anne up and found a packet of Kleenex to wipe her face and hands clean.

"Are you Anne Rogers?" A small man in a suit came running up to her. The ID clipped to his lapel said YU, DOMINIC FRANCIS. "Do you know where Santiago and Schwartz are?"

"Isn't *that* Captain Santiago?" She pointed at the tall woman by the minivan.

"No, no," said Yu, and chuckled. "Let me introduce you. Sabita!" He led Anne over to the other woman. "Anne Rogers, this is Specialist Sabita Soni, from the Miami FBI office."

"I'm so glad you're all right," said Ms. Soni.

"How did you find me?" asked Anne.

"Phone intercept," said Yu. "I got a monitor order for Schwartz and Santiago. His phones were all impossible to trace, but she started making calls with no security at all. We could listen to everything. When these guys started talking about exchanging you for Schwartz, I decided we had to make a move. If you ever decide to take a hostage, Miss Rogers, don't do it when you're five miles away from the country's main special-ops base. The Navy lent us a whole squad of SEAL snipers."

"Where is David, then?"

"We think he and Santiago are hiding out up in Kenansville, near Orlando. There's a bunch of local police on their way there now."

The implications finally sank in. "That Santiago woman said everything would be fine! She was going to let them *kill* me!"

"I guess she and Schwartz are busy. They stole another spacecraft just half an hour ago. We're still trying to locate them."

Just then one of the other FBI agents came running up, carrying a ziplock bag with Anne's phone in it. The phone was ringing.

. . .

TIME TO IMPACT 15:08:43

Elizabeth heard the cars approaching the observatory while David was still typing commands. "Oh, fuck," she said. "They're here."

"Give me five more minutes," he said.

"Seriously?"

"Seriously. Five minutes, maybe less."

"I can do that."

She went to the door. It was a good tough fireproof steel door, probably salvage from a motel or something. The padlock on the outside was useless since she had cut it herself with bolt-cutters. Elizabeth dragged all the furniture that wasn't supporting David's space mission over to the door to make an impromptu barricade.

The police were taking their time. She imagined them approaching the observatory warily, half-crouching, guns drawn and pointing at the grass. They'd circle wide at first, to get a view of the door, then rush up. One would shelter against the wall, covering the entrance, while the other crept forward to try the door.

Right on schedule, the knob jiggled and the door opened a half-centimeter before it hit Mel Koenig's beer fridge. The officer pushed, but the fridge was backed up by a steel equipment cabinet and a crate of spare washing-machine motors.

The officer pounded on the door and shouted. "Osceola County Sheriff! Open up!"

"Show me a warrant!" Elizabeth yelled. She didn't know if that would work, but they said it a lot on cop shows.

"Put down your weapon and come out!" Evidently it didn't work.

"My weapon's in the car outside!" she shouted back. "Nobody in here is armed."

On a sudden inspiration, she took out her phone and hit the speed dial.

"This is your last warning!" the cop yelled.

"Just wait five minutes and we'll surrender! We are not armed!"

The phone rang and rang, and she was about to throw it across the room when she heard a voice at the other end.

"Hello?" It was a woman. A good sign.

"Is this Anne? Are you okay? I need to talk to an FBI agent." The door bumped the fridge again, harder this time. "Wait!" she called out.

"You selfish bitch!" said Anne on the phone. "Guess what? I'm not dead! Like you care! I hope they catch you and put you in jail until you rot!"

"I really need to talk to Agent Yu *right now*," said Elizabeth. The Osceola County deputies had evidently decided not to wait. The whole mass of furniture she'd piled in front of the door shifted a couple of centimeters, then stopped as the edge of the cabinet caught on a crack in the concrete slab floor.

"Is this Ms. Santiago?" said a new voice on the phone. It was Agent Yu.

"Hi. Can you tell the Osceola County sheriff deputies to stop trying to break in? We just need a few more minutes."

"Elizabeth, it's time to give up. Put down your weapon and surrender. You can't do anything."

"We can stop that payload!"

Yu seemed to take forever to answer. "I don't think that's possible," he said. "Schwartz could be lying to you about what he's doing."

"I know what he's doing! I made him do it! We're trying to knock the helium payload off course so it won't destroy the Babcock base! Just five more minutes, please?"

The deputies had decided to use mechanical advantage. She could see the edge of a crowbar appear between the door and the frame, followed by grunts from outside. The cabinet began to squeak and crumple, then finally with a loud screech it pivoted upward as the beer fridge slid under it and the door slammed open.

. . .

David ignored the commotion around him. His body was in the sweltering chaos of the observatory, but his mind was up at the L_1 point surrounded by silent space and cold stars. In place of his custom interface, his own mind was turning the numbers on the screen into a picture. The payload was almost close enough to touch, but he didn't have enough fuel to reach it.

He searched through the onboard software to find the subroutines controlling the solar-thermal propulsion system. It was elegant work, with lots and lots of helpful comments inserted. Very different from his own slapdash last-minute hacking.

There! The focal-point parameters. He checked the radar and the spacecraft attitude, mentally calculating the new coordinates and hoping everybody was using the same units.

Behind him there was a loud crash, then shouts of "Down! On the floor!" He ignored them.

Ten thousand miles above the Moon, two spacecraft fell together, twenty-five meters apart. One was a bulbous gumdrop, massive and compact, returning home to its launch site after a five-day absence. The other was a delicate moth with huge silver wings, soaring higher than it had ever flown.

The moth's wings swiveled to face the Sun, and flexed into hollow curves. Part of the moth's body glowed red, and it began to move toward the gumdrop. As it had done several times before, the gumdrop fired small rockets and moved out of the way of the approaching moth.

As the moth passed, her wings pivoted and flexed again. The red glow faded from her engine ball—and a dazzling white spot appeared on the skin of the gumdrop. Fiberglass insulation boiled away into space, exposing the aluminum skin of the helium tank beneath.

The Viking sitting on the steppe far away must have noticed a temperature sensor, for the gumdrop fired its thrusters desperately. But the moth just flexed her wings to keep the bright spot centered. And then both were enveloped in a cloud of aluminum droplets and bits of insulation as the tank finally ruptured. A great plume of boiling helium shot from the side of the payload.

"Yes!" yelled David, and then the room whirled as a hand grabbed the back of his neck and expertly steered him into a hard landing on the floor. A deputy who felt as big as a small truck pressed a knee into the small of his back and yelled at him not to move.

"Nobody beats Captain Black the Space Pirate!" said David.

"Great—now, shut the fuck up," said the deputy.

■ ■ ■

TIME TO IMPACT 00:01:00

Jack Bonnet and Korekiyo Ueno sat at the little aluminum table in the middle of their habitat on the Moon. It was dark outside. Even though their six-room cabin had no windows and all the lights were on, the two of them could still *feel* the darkness. It made one wish for a fireplace.

Jack's tablet lay faceup on the table, with big numbers counting down until impact. They had long since run out of things to say. At 00:00:30, Ueno raised his cup of instant cocoa. Jack nodded, and they drank their cocoa.

At 00:00:00, both tensed. After a second, Jack exhaled loudly and the pair of them began to laugh.

Ueno tapped his earphone. "Houston, Babcock Base here. Everything's fine. Nothing has hit us."

"Roger that. Tracking shows impact seven kilometers northwest of your position. We'd like you to check your seismic data at impact."

"Roger, Houston. As soon as you can give us a grid number, we can schedule an EVA to the site. I think all of us want to see how big a hole it made."

Jack was on a separate channel. "Harpal? Do you read? You can come back now. Nobody's dying today."

. . .

Amid the chaos of the command center, Halfdan sat motionless. The other techs were blanking disk drives with big ceramic magnets, tossing papers and memory storage devices into an oil drum full of yellow flames, and grabbing whatever they could stuff in their pockets before leaving.

The image of the longship's deck had vanished, and his normal overlay was shut down, so Halfdan could only see the bare concrete floor, darkened displays, and overturned chairs that surrounded him in physical reality. It was all very depressing. The last of the hired technicians hurried out the door, but still Halfdan sat in his uncomfortable chair.

How could it have gone wrong? Captain Black had beaten him! That wasn't how Halfdan's story was supposed to end.

He stood, took a deep breath, and coughed. The smoke from the burning papers was getting thick. Despite it all, Halfdan smiled. His story was supposed to end in triumph, yet he had just been beaten. Logically, then, this wasn't the end of the story. Yes, it had been too easy. A proper triumph came only after hardship and setbacks. Halfdan *needed* a defeat now, to make him stronger. It was time for him to seek a new mentor, master new weapons, and come back for a final victory.

Ignoring the smoke, Halfdan walked calmly out of the control center. He turned on his interface glasses again, and once more the dull mundanity around him was replaced by the world of Halfdan's dreams. He had no idea how he was going to get out of Kazakhstan, but something would turn up. The Saga of Halfdan was not yet done.

*   *   *

MESSING ABOUT IN MY BOAT

February 2, 2032
Location: 24° 33′ 42″ N by 81° 48′ 47″ W

It took a lot longer than I thought, but *Carina*'s in the water again at last, and I'm setting my course for Bimini a second time.

Thanks to everyone who donated money to support the voyage of *Carina*. I've definitely got enough to reach Trinidad this time. Maybe even Brazil!

Special thanks to Carol, Fred, and Junior at Jackson Boatbuilding, who've done amazing work making sure *Carina*'s properly seaworthy. You can read all about the new modifications <u>here</u> and <u>here</u>.

Extra-special thanks to Joshua Flint, super-attorney and *Carina*'s newly commissioned first mate. He's on board for the trip to Bimini, and he says he's going to fly back to Key West from there. He doesn't know that Captain Anne Rogers isn't going to let him jump ship. I'm going to carry him off to Charlotte Amalie! (Josh: Don't read that last sentence.)

. . .

The man who no longer called himself Colonel Ghavami woke in the middle of the night and lay still, listening. The house was fortified, he had half a dozen guards, and he was pretty sure the Americans didn't know where he was.

He heard footsteps outside—not running footsteps of commandos assaulting the compound, or stealthy footsteps of an assassin. Just someone walking into the outer room. One of his people, then. He relaxed and composed himself again for sleep.

The door of the room swung open. Ghavami could see one of his guards silhouetted against the light beyond. "What is it?" he called.

When the man didn't answer, Ghavami reached for the

pistol he kept under the pillow. His guard put four shots into Ghavami before he could pull it out.

His last thought, as the guard approached to put a final shot through his head, was to hope it was his own side that had ordered his death. The alternative was too humiliating.

. . .

MARCH 5, 2032, 20:17 EST

Everyone agreed that the bride's family did a great job with the wedding reception. At the suggestion of the groom, they rented the planetarium at Eastern Florida State College for the evening and engaged a taqueria in Titusville to handle the catering. Even the bride's grandmother admitted that the food was acceptable. The music was bluegrass, performed by a quartet that included the first human to set foot on an asteroid. Mike Levy provided ten cases of champagne.

The bride was catching up on news from some cousins she hadn't seen in decades when she spotted someone out of the corner of her eye who shouldn't have been there. She let her cousin finish talking about his new real estate venture, then excused herself and crossed the room. Her quarry was pretending to study an autographed photo of Sally Ride on the wall.

"How did you get here?" she asked.

"I drove. Don't worry—I got permission. They know where I am." He gestured at a heavy yellow ankle band just visible below his pants cuff. "Where's yours?"

"Don't have one."

"You broke more laws than I did!"

"Agent Yu didn't press charges about the kidnapping, which was awfully nice of him. I pleaded guilty to everything else. I took a dishonorable discharge, lost my pension, and I can't own any firearms or hold a federal job ever again. They gave me a suspended sentence plus mandatory counseling for anger management and alcohol abuse." She held up her champagne flute. "Lime seltzer. Oh, and I can't associate with known felons, so maybe you shouldn't be here. How'd you get in, anyway?"

"I forged an invitation. I wanted to wish your husband good luck."

"Wait a bit. He's telling my niece how they go to the bathroom on the Moon. Have you heard from Anne?"

"Not directly. She was pretty serious about the whole 'never want to see you again as long as I live' thing. Dominic says she's hooked up with that lawyer from Key West and they're seriously trying to sail that boat around the world."

"'Dominic'? You're getting awfully chummy with the feds, Captain Black."

"I might as well. I spend about ten hours a day working alongside him and a couple dozen other mooks from the Bureau, the SEC, and a bunch of other alphabets. I'll be doing it for the next ten years. Community service instead of jail. It's great: I get to take my revenge on Ghavami's bunch, and Uncle Sam picks up the tab."

"I'm glad you're enjoying your sentence."

"What about you? If you can't work for the government,

you can't stay with Icarus. Not if they want any NASA business."

"You haven't heard? Wait a bit," she said.

The next time the band took a break, Mike Levy grabbed the microphone and called for quiet. "I've got an announcement—some of you probably know it already. When the newlyweds come back from Cozumel, they won't be working at Icarus Propulsion Systems anymore. We're starting a new venture! Phoenix Space Security Solutions! We're going to provide orbital and deep space protection to any clients worried about space piracy and sabotage. Let's have a big hand for Jack and Elizabeth, the chief designer and chief pilot of Phoenix Space Security Solutions: the Space Privateers!"